MY WIFE
JODIE

V. A. Rudys

BLINKENLIGHT

First paperback edition published May 2021

Book design by Ignas Zurumskas
Cover Photography by Patrick Coleman

ISBN 978-1-8383911-0-2 (paperback)
ISBN 978-1-8383911-3-3 (ebook)

www.mywifejodie.com

Author's note

I have been battling dyslexia my entire life. The thought of me writing a book was always met with laughter by my friends and family. I don't blame them, I laughed too. But the day comes that, even if the path ahead seems much more difficult than to others, you have to stand up and do it anyway. Because it has nothing to do with others. It is your own battle. A battle which I won.

To Justina,

PROLOGUE

Jodie

A snowflake landed silently on Anneli's nose, mixing with a tear. She lay where she had fallen, staring down the mountain at the impossible stretch of slope beneath us.

'You have to keep trying - it's the only way you will get better.' I brushed the snow from her tiny, child-sized helmet and took her hand to help her up. 'Uncle Ethan and your dad will catch up with us, but let's make a head start, shall we?'

Slowly we moved down the mountain, manoeuvring cautiously around the corners. Anneli balanced herself well and learned quickly from her mistakes, her movement becoming more fluid with each turn. I lifted my eyes to look at the view, the morning sun lighting up the whole valley. It was a perfect day.

Suddenly, Anneli fell again, sliding down the slope with her gear scattered around her. I turned quickly and intercepted a wayward ski as it made a bid for a free life in the valley. Anneli turned around to face me and burst out laughing as she spat the snow out of her mouth.

'I'm doing it, Aunt Jodie!'

'You are, honey!' I lifted her small body, placing her upright, reattached a ski and brushed off some of the snow. 'Let's try again!' I said. She nodded with determination.

Now she seemed to have even more confidence, her hands no longer awkward, and her hips sweeping from side to side in sync with her skis. We were approaching the intersection with the red track, and I shouted to Anneli to watch out for skiers coming fast from above us.

An excited male voice shouted from behind, and as I turned to look up the mountain I saw Ethan flying by. He was so good at this, no fear at all. I was proud to have married this man.

Moments later, Anneli cheered for her father who was trying to catch up with Ethan, trying to compete with his best friend. But none of us - even Theo - were close to Ethan's level.

After they had passed, Anneli and I continued our slow descent. Fifteen minutes later, with plenty of stops, we finally reached the bottom of the slope. I saw a group of people blocking the path. I directed Anneli to the side of the slope, and I saw Theo standing, alone and still on the edge of the crowd.

'Look, it's daddy!' Anneli shouted happily, but something wasn't quite right with the scene. Theo had taken off his skis, his helmet and his goggles. He was just standing there, staring at nothing I could see, until he noticed us approach.

We slowed to a stop, and he staggered towards us, fighting through the snow in his clumsy ski boots. I was a couple of meters away from him and I could see his face was red, his eyes full of tears.

'Jodie, it's Ethan. He... he fell.' Theo's entire body was shaking.

I was staring at the crowd now, and I could just make out Ethan's legs in their bright ski pants. They were twisted horribly, and completely still.

'People are... they said, he's...' Theo didn't finish his sentence. Then Anneli screamed, and I closed my eyes.

PART I

CHAPTER 1

Ethan

SATURDAY 20 AUGUST 2016

I held Jodie's new canvas in front of me, balanced on top of the stepladder with one hand on the wall. The scene was a snowy forest, a dead leopard, and a splatter of blood. I was spreadeagled like spiderman, halfway up the wall of our apartment, hanging the painting right in the centre of the hall.

I lunged again for the hook, and the ladder wobbled. Jodie appeared from nowhere and put her foot on the bottom rung.

'Careful, old man.' she said, tilting her head slightly. Her blonde hair tumbled over her shoulders and down her back.

'I'm always careful, babes!' I chuckled as she rolled her eyes. I looked back up at the canvas I was holding up against the wall. 'I'm not going to lie - this painting is a bit disturbing.'

'It's just life. Life doesn't last,' she said.

Hanging her painting, I stepped down from the ladder. 'Well, maybe next time you should paint a BDSM dungeon... or a rapist in the act.'

She shook her head. 'You're disgusting.'

I let the subject drop. 'So, twenty more paintings and you might be able to open your gallery?'

'One day,' she smiled, admiring her latest piece, and then she came closer to me and wrapped her arms around my waist. Her forehead gently touched my clean-shaven face and I kissed her hair, inhaling her sweet perfume.

'Well, this one's a beauty, *babes.*'

She untangled her arms and slapped my bottom - hard.

'How about I make a nice anniversary lunch for us today? Something naughty?' I grinned at her.

'...lasagne?' She raised an eyebrow.

'Yes!' I picked Jodie up by the waist, and we spun together like they do in cheesy romantic comedies, her hair flying behind her.

After I had cleaned up, I followed Jodie into the bright and spacious living room that stretched right through our apartment. At one end, we had a miraculously tidy kitchen with marble worktops and, on the other, a dining room with windows looking out over Tower Bridge, Jodie's new detective thriller lying discarded on a corner sofa. She was such a fast, prolific reader, sometimes finishing five books in a week.

Jodie reminded me of my mother, who was also

a bookworm - but after my father died of an insidious immune disorder, she had no time to read. Money had always been tight, growing up, and I craved independence and a life in London.

Today, in the dining room of our apartment, in a small frame amongst a jumble of holiday photos, hung a lottery ticket. The faintly printed numbers were still visible today: 9, 12, 13, 15, 21, and 33.

Jodie had bought it for me on my birthday, as a joke - but on the 12th of July, 2003, those numbers won me the National Lottery's jackpot of four and a half million pounds.

I assumed I would never need to work again, but after investing most of my money in Kodak a few years later, I lost almost everything. My degree landed me an entry-level job as a law clerk at a firm in Liverpool Street. From that, I built a career as a high-profile defence lawyer in the city, defending the rich and famous from their misdemeanors.

***

My phone rang, the screen blinking impatiently on the dining room table. It read 'Other Boyfriend.' I looked at Jodie, who was struggling to hide a smile. She gave me a cheeky wink as I answered.

'Hello, Ethan speaking.'

'Well, that's a very formal way to pick up your phone.' I recognised Theo's voice instantly.

'Hey, sorry! What's up.' I turned back to Jodie, who was now giggling silently, eyes fixed on her book. She had this thing where she would rename contacts on my phone to something ridiculous. Once, she'd renamed my mother's contact to The Psychic. Another time she had changed it to Angelina Jolie. It was pretty funny.

'Free for some quick Saturday shopping?

'I'm free, though I promised Jodie a lasagna for lunch.' I could hear a loud, electrical buzzing through the phone. 'Theo?'

'Excellent, I'm just putting the finishing touches on my internet-connected microwave; it is so cool—'

Theo is the world's biggest geek, and if I didn't stop him, he'd go on for 15 minutes about his new toy.

I interrupted - 'Theo, how about you tell me everything when we meet? Outside Tesco in half an hour?' I imagined him rolling his eyes. He knew what I was doing, that I wasn't interested in his tech.

'Fine … don't be late,' he said in mock outrage, hanging up his phone, making me smile. I adjusted the name of the contact back to Theo as Jodie started to speak, still holding her book.

'How is your boyfriend doing?' I turned to see her cheeky smile.

'He's fine …' I replied, smiling and slowly approaching her. 'How are you doing, you naughty girl?' I jumped on her lap, growling like a dog and knocking the book out of her hand with my head; she burst out laughing.

I looked up at Jodie's beautiful diamond-shaped face, how her perfectly smooth skin glowed in the sunlight. Her cool hands stroked my forehead, pushing my hair back. She liked playing with it. I traced a line from the top of Jodie's shoulder down her arm, slowly, barely touching her. She smiled, probably thinking I was trying to tickle her. Her hand moved up to my ear. She opened her fingers, cupping my ear, and massaging it. I closed my eyes, the furrows in my forehead slowly relaxing. Then softly, as if plucking a grape with my mouth, I touched Jodie's lips with mine. For a moment, we shared the same breath. Her nose lightly brushed my skin as it moved up my face. As soon as I could no longer feel it, I opened my eyes, and Jodie's smile greeted me.

'I like you,' she said.

'I like you too... *babes.*'

Her smile widened. 'I got you a little something...'

'Jodie! We said no anniversary presents this year!'

Jodie dropped down onto her knee and opened a shoebox that was tucked under the couch. The box held a new pair of running shoes.

'Wow, they look great, but you know how hard it is to find shoes that fit me. Can I exchange them?'

'Trust me, darling. I *know* you'll love them.' She held one shoe up, triumphantly, like it was a glass slipper. 'Come on, Cinderella.'

***

I grabbed a few cotton shopping bags from under the sink, and ran out the door. If I kept a good pace I probably wouldn't be late to meet Theo. The shoes were perfect, like they were moulded for my feet. How did she do it?

The vibrant blue sky and contrasting white clouds looked just like Instagram; it was a perfect summer day. A little cold, but refreshing after a recent heatwave. I walked between beautiful old brick buildings, looming over tiny crooked lanes. The Shard pointed gracefully upwards, interrupting the skyline. Bermondsey had to be the best place to live in London.

We could have afforded a much more expensive place in Kensington. Jodie had wanted to move there for a long time, but I always preferred the great sense of community in Bermondsey, and how close it was to the centre. And on top of all that there was nothing to attract noisy tourists; no monuments of any sort. In the end, she gave up trying to convince me to move.

I turned the corner, and there were Theo and Anneli holding hands, waiting for me. Theo had changed a lot since he moved to London. He's much scruffier now, with patches of grey hair creeping down from his beard and head. He made no effort to cover them. His large framed glasses hid the bags under his eyes, which were getting darker and more pronounced with each passing year. He didn't care much about his clothes, either; jeans, a t-shirt, and a hoodie, and his dark skin and rough appearance contrasted vividly with Anneli, pale in her red polka-dot dress and a denim jacket. The shade of her slippers perfectly matched her dress. I wouldn't have been surprised if her outfit all came in one box. Theo lavished Anneli with attention; he loved her more than anything in the world.

Anneli saw me and dashed forward. She ran so fast that her hands flailed wildly in the air, almost seeming not to be attached to her torso. I knelt and opened my arms, waiting for that hug. She slammed into me full force, almost making me fall back.

'Ethan!' she screamed in my ear.

'Hello, my darling!' I gave her a big hug as I tried to stand up, playfully trying to shake her off. She laughed. Theo was standing beside us smiling. I was still shaking my shoulders, Anneli dangling from them. Slowly, we made our way to the shop.

Anneli was admiring the basil plants as Theo and I stood near the onions and potatoes, occasionally glancing at her.

'What are you planning for your wedding anniversary?' Theo asked, comparing two bags of red onions.

'I want to have a picnic in Southwark Park this afternoon. Then I have a reservation for a classy dinner at Clos Maggiore in Covent Garden, and after that, I guess I'll take Jodie for a romantic walk down the river.'

'Good effort, mate. She'll be thrilled.' He looked down at his feet, probably remembering how he used to spend his anniversary with Laura. 'Jodie is an amazing woman.'

'What are you planning for *our* anniversary?' I narrowed my eyes half smiling.

'They're releasing Resident Evil 7 in a couple of months.'

'Nerd.' I nudged him with my fist and Theo moved

down the aisle. Anneli followed us with a small, half-dead basil plant.

'I'm taking Anneli to Brighton tomorrow. We can swim if we feel brave enough.' He looked at her. 'Will we be brave enough to swim?' She aggressively jerked her head, making him laugh.

'She's so funny,' I said. 'And very smart for a 6-year-old!'

'Six and a half!' Anneli corrected me. 'Daddy, can we take this plant home with us? It's sad.'

'Sweetheart, we already have two basil plants at home; leave this for the other people, ok?' Anneli lowered her head.

'I wonder if I'll look back at my life one day and regret not trying harder to have children,' I said, turning to Theo. He was brandishing an amusingly-shaped potato. 'I'm so happy for you, you lucky fuck.'

Theo dropped the potato in his basket and moved to a box of aubergines. 'Lucky?' he frowned. 'Depends on who you're comparing me with.' He picked up the biggest aubergine from the crate and looked at me.

I shrugged. 'People like you?'

Theo narrowed his eyes. '*You're* the definition of luck, mate.'

'Come on.' I nudged him again with my fist.

'Ethan, please.' He looked mildly irritated now.

'I'm not lucky! Privileged - yes. But not lucky.'

He exhaled deeply before speaking. 'You met the love of your life when you were 16. You're the one Jodie helped with the rent all through university - you didn't need to work 30 hours a week in Wetherspoons serving beer to people who don't know when to stop.' I raised my finger to interrupt, but he continued. 'You won the lottery and then you used that money to travel the world!' He laughed, but now there was a bitter edge to it. He dropped his voice to a low, angry hiss. 'You've never had to deal with racist remarks. People eyeing me like I stole Anneli from a white family. You've never been really ill; you've never spent a night in hospital. *You think you're unlucky just because Jodie can't have kids?'*

I crossed my arms, angry now, as Theo continued to speak. 'You go skiing every winter, and yet you haven't broken a single bone. *Not even one injury!'* He sighed dramatically.

'I'm a good skier! What do you even want me to say?'

'Even professionals have more accidents than you, Ethan.' He waved his hand ambiguously and moved down the aisle. I followed. 'You've never been robbed, mugged, attacked, or scammed. You've never had a car accident or missed your flight. You've never lost your job. In fact, you were promoted faster than most of the other lawyers you work with—'

'Ok, but you can't say that me winning my cases is luck; it means I'm a good lawyer, a better lawyer than—'

'None of your family has died.'

'My father has.' I said it so quickly, as if I was proud of it, trying to win the argument, not thinking. My father died when I was eight. Laura died less than six years ago shortly after she gave birth to Anneli, and I instantly regretted my words. Theo recoiled in mock shock, pressing his hand to his heart, then grabbed a tub of hummus, tossing it angrily into his shopping basket and turning away.

I shouldn't have said anything. It hasn't even been six years since Laura's death, and it was still raw for Theo. He might never be okay with it. She was Theo's true love, as Jodie was mine. He first introduced Laura to Jodie and me back in university. He asked us both out for dinner and brought Laura along. I told him back then that she was totally out of his league. He agreed.

'I'm going to the deli section. Can you please stay here and watch Anneli?' Theo didn't wait for my answer and disappeared into the next aisle. Anneli came closer to me and took my hand.

'This plant is unhappy, Uncle Ethan.'

I crouched to meet her eyes. 'How about I take this to Aunt Jodie? She loves gardening, and I am sure she would be delighted to make it happy again. Then you can come and visit us!' I gently stroked her mop of curly hair. Anneli smiled and hugged me with one arm as she carefully held the plant with her other hand, looking more like her mother every day.

I missed Laura so much. After Anneli's birth, she and I had become even better friends. Our interactions had mainly involved picnics at Hampstead Heath, ski trips to Austria, or board game nights at Theo's. After Anneli was born, I would often visit them even when Jodie wasn't around. Sometimes Theo would be working late and it would just be the two of us playing games and nursing Anneli. We would stay up late, have dinner, and watch a movie. Theo and Jodie would laugh at us - asking if I wanted to adopt Anneli. I didn't mind it. I loved Anneli very much.

Then one day, to celebrate Theo's promotion to Chief Engineer, and head of the on-site engineering team, Jodie and I took everyone out to see 'Wicked'. Theo was working late and told us he would meet us at the Apollo Theatre. Jodie and I would meet Laura at 6:30 at our usual spot - by the Tesco, at the T junction. Jodie was running late, blaming an old mascara, and when we left home, it was already past the meeting time. We rushed, skipping every other step. The sun was almost down, just a faint light glimmering on the horizon. The first thing we heard was the siren of an ambulance. Then saw the blue lights flashing, getting brighter as we approached the T junction. Cries of despair louder than the siren itself echoed in the heavy, evening air. I let go of Jodie's hand and ran towards the voices and the lights.

My heart raced; my legs carried me much faster than I ever thought I could run. As I turned the corner, a paramedic was giving CPR to an older man on the pavement. Another was wheeling a child to an ambulance. The small body didn't move, not a single sound. A lady, maybe his mother, was running next to the trolley, shouting at him in vain. Another young man was hugging his boyfriend or younger brother by the side of the road. A few police officers were scattered and overwhelmed, trying to keep people away from the scene. The whole pavement had been destroyed, chunks of earth scattered everywhere, concrete pavers strewn over the road. A tree had been split all down one side. A stop sign had been knocked down. The benches were gone from their usual spot alongside the brick wall and the lamp post. At the end of the wall, I could see a truck turned sideways, partly on the road, its back wheels still on the pavement. It had driven into a group of pedestrians. The truck driver sat on the ground, gripping his head in despair, police standing close to him, trying to move him away from the scene. It had happened a few moments ago, we had barely missed it.

I shouted Laura's name again and again before my eyes finally found her. Jodie caught up with me. She grabbed my hand, but I tore away and walked towards Laura. She was lying on the pavement, her arms and legs straight, looking a bit like she was about to go down a water slide. Maybe it was the darkness, maybe the flashing blue lights, but I couldn't see any blood. She looked unharmed, just a couple of bruises, no more than if she'd fallen from a bike. Only after taking few steps closer I saw a small amount of blood, which lay delicately around her head. Her eyes stared into the sky. I knelt, lifting her shoulders; her head dropped back. I let out a cry. Laura was gone.

The rest of the night was a blur; I don't remember how I told Theo that his wife was dead. Maybe it was Jodie who called him. I can still hear his hysterical sobs and the next two years of pain and struggle. He didn't want to keep going. *What's the point?* He would ask me. *Do you think it would hurt if I jumped?* Listening to him talk that way broke my heart. At the same time, I understood him and his pain, his grief. I felt it too. I never let him see just how much Laura's death affected me; instead, I had to be there for him because he would have done the same for me. In a way, I also felt responsible for checking on Anneli. Laura would have appreciated it. Now, looking back, I'm almost positive that it wasn't me, or Jodie, or his family who helped him get through this. He lived only for Anneli.

I did have a wonderful life. I can't imagine how I would feel if Jodie died. Compared to Theo, my life was a walk in the park. Even six years later, his pain felt fresh.

Next to the entrance of the shop, Anneli kissed me, and Theo waved goodbye.

'I'm sorry, Theo.' I said, but he was too far away to hear it.

Anneli ran to catch up with her father and grabbed his hand. I prayed that nothing bad would ever happen to Anneli.

CHAPTER 2

I walked home, thinking about Theo. He knew I didn't mean any harm, but he'd probably say I deserved at least three dickhead points.

The weather had turned. Clouds blocked the sun, and the morning breeze had grown cold and uncomfortable. The chances of having a quiet picnic before our anniversary dinner were getting slimmer.

My phone vibrated. Jodie had sent a picture of herself, naked, stepping into the shower. Her breasts exposed and an angelic expression on her face. She followed a few seconds later with a message -

Ignore, wrong person.

I let out a huge laugh. She loved teasing me.

Ethan

***

I turned the key in my front door and headed straight to the kitchen. The sounds of a shower running came from the bathroom, and I imagined Jodie's naked body, the water running over her breasts.

Dropping the groceries on the kitchen counter, I went out on the terrace. The wooden decking was soft on my feet, creaking ever so slightly as I moved across. I carefully placed the basil plant from the shop next to Jodie's garden. She had turned this small outdoor area into a cosy spot where we both enjoyed spending our time. I liked lying on the hammock, watching as Jodie carefully measured out plant food and the soil's moisture level. She would pinch dead leaves off before they had a chance to fall, watching for any sign of disease. Once, shortly after starting her garden, Jodie had missed a scale infestation. By the time she had realised what had happened, most of her plants were dead. She was so angry that I thought she was going to launch the whole garden straight over the railing and into the Thames, five stories below.

With the shopping out on the kitchen counter, I ran about the kitchen, placing groceries where they belonged, my mouth filled with chocolate pastry. I grabbed the frying pan and started heating it over the flame.

In the top drawer, Jodie had neatly arranged our set of kitchen knives, and I spent a moment admiring them. I grabbed my favourite - *The Killer,* as Jodie called it. She had cut herself so many times when using it. I loved it because it was big and super sharp. Once, after she had cut herself again, she had wanted to replace it with something smaller. 'Don't worry, the man in this house knows how to use his weapons. Leave it to me' I'd laughed. She rolled her eyes, called me a dick, and stormed out of the kitchen.

Grabbing an onion, I peeled and diced it. Having no idea how long Jodie would be in the shower, I thought that if I moved quickly, I could get most of the food ready by the time she came out. Splashing some olive oil into the pan, I diced a second onion and added it to the first as the oil spat and sizzled.

Prepping the beef mince, breaking it down with my fingers, and kneading in chives, I remembered how Jodie and I would divide the housework back in university. She would pay for the groceries, and I would cook. It was my way of saying thank you. Over time, I became the cook in our family.

The onion was already burning. I grabbed the spatula and mixed it up. Garlic next. Three cloves, crushed with the side of the knife, and I started to slice them into thin slices. One. Two. The water in the shower stopped running. The onion was burning again. Not my best effort. I had to pick up the pace. I moved the onion around and went back to the garlic. Just before I finished slicing it, my hand jerked slightly.

My eyes dropped to the chopping block and saw red-like-tomato-juice blood running from the tip of my ring finger on to the garlic. There was a deep cut, just below the nail.

'Jesus Christ.' I inhaled deeply, put down the knife, and squeezed the cut with my right hand, slipping off my wedding ring before it got covered in blood. Did we have any plasters? When was the last time Jodie or I had needed them? We might not have any in the flat. 'Shit,' I mumbled, rummaging around the kitchen for alternatives with one hand.

'What's that smell?' Jodie shouted from the bathroom enthusiastically. Onions, and they were getting seriously crispy. I turned off the hob. I knew I'd be able to make the lasagna later. It was my fault for trying to rush things.

'Just some onion!' I shouted back, more cheerfully than I felt, still opening and closing kitchen cupboards.

'Do you need any help?' I heard the sound of the bathroom door opening.

'No, no, I'm fine.'

'It smells weird.' She laughed as she went into the bedroom. Her voice sounded sweet and happy.

I was still squeezing the wound to keep it shut, but the cut was much deeper than I had initially thought. Blood dripping from my hand onto our grey kitchen tiles, the deep red splashes contrasting nicely with the minimalist pattern.

'What are you cooking?' Jodie wandered into the kitchen looking blank, drained. She sounded so different and happy before. When I lifted my head, she was standing there, staring blankly. Had something changed? Her wet hair rested on her red t-shirt. She was wearing her favourite pair of white sweat pants.

'Lasagna,' I said, unsure if she'd already forgotten. Blood was running down my elbow in a steady stream. Jodie noticed.

'What happened?' she said, with an eerie calmness.

'I cut myself.' I said, lifting both of my bloody hands. 'Do we have any plasters anywhere?' I wasn't hopeful, but maybe she had a secret stash somewhere.

Jodie looked disappointed, shaking her head, almost angry.

'You cut yourself?' she asked. 'With *that* knife!' She pointed to *The Killer* resting on the kitchen counter, lying in a pool of light shining through the window. If we'd been in a video game, it would have been an interactive object.

Jodie shook her head, muttering, '... again.' Again? I frowned, confused.

She quickly stepped towards me and, without warning, slapped my face. Hard. The sharp pain in my cheek woke me up, and my face felt hot. I was speechless, not sure how to respond.

'Damn you!' she screamed. 'How many more times are you going to cut yourself with that knife?'

Instinctively, I hunched my shoulders against her sudden wrath, standing silently, entirely focused on Jodie. My face and my hand no longer hurt, even though it was now bleeding more. My heart started to pound, but I was frozen in place, still shocked. She picked up the knife and turned, throwing it across the dining room.

'Fucking knife!' It flew, hitting the wall, and, to my

utter surprise, it stayed there. It had landed, literally stuck in the wall, in between Jodie's canvas and the photo collage we'd made of our friends and us.

The whole scene seemed to drop into slow motion. My brain was trying to understand what was going on, and failing. Was it some sort of joke I wasn't quite getting? Was I missing a punchline?

She took a small step towards me and I reflexively took a step back. Then she followed with another step while raising her voice as if talking to a child.

'*Sure...* I guess *Jodie* should take care of everything, shouldn't she?' She still had that angry glare. 'Fine!' She spat the word at me. 'Jodie will fix everything!' She threw her hands into the air. 'Again!' she shouted.

I didn't understand what she was trying to say. I didn't recognise this Jodie. Surely a cut wasn't that big a deal.

I held onto the kitchen chair, now covered in bloodstains.

Jodie closed her eyes, her face relaxed, and all the anger disappeared from her face. I stood and waited, confused. She opened her eyes, and I could see something was wrong - she just stared at me, her face changing again. Her eyes traced around the kitchen, into the dining room, at me, and then out the window to the street. She reminded me of someone who had lost her friends in a crowd.

'Jodie? What's going on?' I said softly, as though I was talking to a wild animal.

She continued to stare *through* me, as if I wasn't there. Like she was looking at something I couldn't see. As my finger continued to bleed, still dripping onto the floor, Jodie moved her eyes to my hand.

'Jodie.' I repeated her name quietly. She still didn't respond, her skin grew paler by the second, the life literally draining from her face as I watched. I took a step forward and reached for her.

'No!' She screamed so loudly I leapt back. Jodie waved her hands in the air as if waving off a bee, backing into the dining room. I followed slowly, making sure to keep the same distance between us.

'What is going on?' I asked firmly, her mouth hung open, hands pressed to her stomach as she backed away.

'No, no, no.' She repeated over and over, pulling away from me until she was against the wall. As she looked around, she seemed to be seeing the apartment for the first time, seeing me for the first time.

Our bodies were trembling. I reached for her shoulder but she put her cold hands on mine instead - her hands were always freezing, no matter the weather - and gently pushed me away. She took another few steps back, avoiding the wall this time, reversing deeper into the living room.

And then almost like something passed through her, she stopped. 'Oh my god,' she whispered 'Laura.'

Suddenly, she let out a cry as loud as a mother might cry on discovering that her child had died.

'No!' She screamed again.

I started walking towards her, but she screamed, again and again, thrashing wildly against me as I tried to hold her. She grabbed our new picture frames and threw them at me.

They landed on the floor instead, shattering the glass.

'Jodie, stop!' I was shouting over her cries, no longer hiding the panic. My hands shook uncontrollably. The oozing blood no longer bothered me; the only thing I cared about was Jodie. I wanted her to stop, but she wasn't listening to my pleas. She kicked the armchair, still moving away from me. I followed her, not knowing what else to do. Should I call an ambulance?

I tried to say something, but I couldn't. Finally, I just froze, like I was watching a movie, like none of this was happening to me. I was just an observer. My vision narrowed. I could almost make out Jodie's shape in the living room. Her crying had quietened, as if it was coming from a long way away. Strange. Her ghostly figure moved from one side of the room to the other, occasionally throwing something at the wall. All my senses were slowly disappearing. The only thing present in this moment was a voiceless question: 'why?'

The sound of the bedroom door slamming into the door frame broke my trance. Jodie was no longer in front of me. Her cries now echoed from the bedroom, strangely muffled by the bedroom walls.

I had to do something. I ran back to the kitchen and grabbed my phone from the counter, smearing it with blood. I dialled 999. As I waited for the call to connect, I realised I had no idea what to say.

'9-9-9, which service do you require?' The operator had a deep, rich voice. I tried to collect my thoughts. I had the phone pressed to my ear, but I couldn't speak.

'Hello, is there someone there?' the operator sounded concerned rather than irritated. Perhaps he was able to hear Jodie in the other room.

'I–'

The sound of breaking glass echoed through the apartment, followed by a deathly silence. My hands stopped shaking briefly. There was a ringing in my ears, and it was getting stronger. I placed the phone on the counter and slowly walked to the bedroom door. In my heart, I knew what had happened. My entire body was shaking. I was almost at the door, but I didn't want to go inside. I didn't want to see what I feared. I told myself that my wife was in the bedroom, asleep and safe. I touched the door handle and pressed it down slowly, as if I was trying not to wake her.

The first thing I noticed was the windows - they were intact. Both of them. I had been sure that Jodie had jumped, and my knees weakened as relief flooded through me. My eyes followed the fragments of glass scattered across the carpet to the middle of the room and a bigger shard. It was just a drinking glass. There was Jodie, still as a statue, in the corner of the room. Her sad eyes were fixed on the floor like a guilty child's. She was no longer hysterical or disoriented. The relief of seeing her unharmed rushed through me. I couldn't remember the last time I was this happy to see my wife.

***

I don't know how long I stood by the door, neither of us moving. I was afraid to set her off again, but at the same time, it seemed the storm was over. I had no clue what had happened; it was simply up to me to help her. I slowly stepped into the bedroom. My foot pressed into something very sharp under the soft, deep-pile carpet, reminding me there were shards all over the floor. Luckily Jodie seemed unharmed; there was no visible blood.

Finally, I broke the silence. 'Sweetheart, please don't move; there's glass all over the floor.' She didn't. Not her body, not even her eyes.

I stepped carefully around the room, trying to avoid all the visible shards. With my hand on her shoulder, I couldn't believe how cold she was; she shivered under my touch.

'Jodie, you're freezing; let me put the duvet on you.' I tried to make eye contact, but there was still no reaction. I nudged her in the direction of the bed, and to my surprise, she didn't resist. She followed my lead and slowly sat down on the edge of our bed. I tucked the duvet around her shoulders, hoping she would feel a little warmer, a little safer, happier. I placed a hand on her thigh and the other around her waist.

Our flat was eerily quiet now. Raindrops began to fall gently against the bedroom windows, with a soft pitter-patter. It had all the hallmarks of a romantic moment, aside from the utter destruction in the room around us. And the blood on my hands.

Trying to find the words, praying this time she would hear me, 'I love you. Let me help you.'

Jodie moved her head towards me, putting her hand on top of my knee. Then she lifted her eyes to face me. She was as still and as pale as a ghost, looking up at me with big, sad eyes.

'It's ok, Ethan. I'll fix it.' She sighed, and said again, 'I'll fix it. I promise you that.'

Fix what? I wanted to ask, but she had already pulled away from me. She shook off the duvet, stood up, and gracefully stepped through the minefield of glass before disappearing into the flat.

***

I tried to talk to her that day, but she would just say 'leave it, please' or 'it doesn't matter, it won't happen again.' I was stunned.

Before clearing the glass from the bedroom, I went back to the shop to buy a first aid kit to fix up my hand properly. On the way home, I stumbled on a ridge in the pavement and sprained my ankle, a nice complement to my injured finger. By the time I'd returned, Jodie had already cleared up the living room, so we sat to have lunch. Of course, neither of us was in the mood for lasagna, so I made us cheese sandwiches.

As we ate, she seemed to be somewhere else entirely. Her eyes moved from side to side as if she was solving complicated mathematical problems in her head. When I asked her again about what had happened, she said, patronizingly, 'You wouldn't understand. Drop it, please.' It made me furious. I couldn't remember the last time - if ever - I had been so angry with her. I stewed in silence.

She moved around the house, avoiding any interaction; if we happened to be in the same room, she didn't acknowledge me. At one point, I watched her biting her nails, something I hadn't seen her do in almost eighteen years.

By the end of the day, I was no longer making any effort to speak with her, and she seemed almost relieved that I'd stopped trying. I went to bed early, wanting the day to end, but I couldn't fall asleep. My heart pounding, I lay counting hours, staring at the bright light seeping in from underneath the door. I wondered what Jodie was doing, and more importantly, what she was thinking.

I watched my wedding ring resting on the nightstand, the symbol of our marriage and our love. It wouldn't fit over the bulky bandage.

I don't remember how long I lay there before sleep finally took me.

CHAPTER 3

I opened my eyes to grey light, filtering in through the window. Heavy, dark clouds hid London from the sun. I lay in bed, not moving, still annoyed with Jodie and how she had treated me the day before - but my anger was less raw. My mother had often said that a good night's sleep puts things into perspective. I hoped Jodie felt better too; she rarely cried and I never seen her so distraught - not even when Laura died.

Not even when the doctors told her she couldn't have a baby. We tried for four months - special diets, looser underwear, careful timing. Then, one day, returning from work, I found her sitting motionless on the couch, gazing off into space. She looked up the second time I said hello.

'The doctor called,' she said, her voice flat as she explained that her fallopian tubes were completely blocked. An infection as a child.

'An infection? That's all it takes?' I'd asked in disbelief.

Her parents hadn't cared much for her. She'd been very sick before they finally took her to the hospital. *Your treatment was started too late*, the gynaecologist had told her. Jodie had only just found out because our doctor had suggested an ultrasound, and I knew she hated her parents for what they had done to her.

I told her that there were still options, that maybe we could extract eggs and try IVF. Money wasn't an issue, but she had said no. Jodie hated pain, and she preferred to accept that she couldn't give birth. I tried to reassure her, to persuade her - I didn't understand why she would just give up - saying that the procedure wouldn't be so bad, but hell, what did I know?

I was devastated, but not Jodie; she coped through her art, and a few months after the news, I came home after an intense day in court to see that she'd finished a new painting. Two children, a girl and a boy, both looking out over the landscape on a bright sunny day. The girl was slightly taller, with a pink headband, holding the boy's hand by her side as he clutched a small toy robot. We hung the painting in the middle of the dining room, and sometimes I would catch Jodie looking at it, wistfully.

It was getting warm under the duvet, and it was time to get up. I rolled over, but Jodie wasn't there, which was strange. She loved lazy lie-ins, and I was usually the one who got up early. Her pillow lay neatly arranged at the pretty 45-degree angle to the bed frame that she liked, almost as if she hadn't come to bed. My heart pounded - there was no reason to assume anything - but something deep inside me knew. I wasn't even out of bed yet, and the drama had already started. Was she still mad with me? Did she sleep in the guest bedroom?

I got out of bed, quickly pulling on my boxers, and crept to the door listening carefully. Silence. Opening the bedroom door and walking to the dining room, I scanned the kitchen, the living room, the guest bedroom. I peered cautiously into the study. Empty.

'Jodie?' I shouted, still hoping for a simple answer. Maybe she was in the bathroom or the storage cupboard. Nothing but silence. Could she have gone to the shop? It was possible, but still early, really. Picking up my phone, I checked Maps to see if her shared location came up, but she was offline. The last known location was here in the flat, ten hours ago. Maybe her phone was flat. Maybe she did go to the shop.

I made myself coffee and sat down on the couch to shoot some zombies.

When I looked at my watch again it was almost midday. I grabbed my phone and called Jodie, worried now. It rang until her voicemail kicked in, her funny Scottish recorded greeting. I dialled again, but it went straight to voicemail. I sent her a WhatsApp message. Delivered. Which meant she had internet and her phone was on. I checked back on Google Maps. Her last location was still in the flat. Twelve hours ago now. She had deactivated her location sharing last night. Why? Did she leave? Nothing was making sense.

Had she taken anything with her? I looked first for her purse, rushing through the flat, but it wasn't in any of the usual places. In the hall cupboard, my small green backpack was also missing. She had left, and it wasn't an impulse. I had been so frustrated that I must have missed something. I must have. What had she been struggling with that she didn't want to tell me? Had my insistence on questioning her pushed her away? She clearly hadn't been ready to talk. But none of that mattered; I had to find her.

Taking a deep breath, I closed the door to the walk-in wardrobe. Overreacting wouldn't help the situation; I had to slow down and think clearly. Jodie might have gone to see Amy, so I should start there. And if she hadn't, then perhaps Amy could help me to understand what was going on. Jodie wasn't a dramatic person; this was not how she behaved. She wouldn't just leave me, running away without telling me. Amy had to be my first stop.

I dialled Amy's number. Like Jodie's, after the 4th beep it went to her voicemail. I re-dialled. Voicemail again. My stomach felt like it was filled with lead. Amy lived nearby; a fifteen minute walk, five in a car. I had to go.

Stepping into the bedroom, I grabbed the first pair of jeans I found in the wardrobe. As they came up over my right leg, I stepped on the carpet, and a blinding pain shot through my foot. I fell backward, grasping the bookshelf for support, causing all the books and ornaments to fall to the floor. I shouted in frustration: a glass shard protruded from my right foot, and blood was dripping on the carpet for the second time in as many days.

'God damn!' I shouted again. There was no one to hear me. I had to get this piece of glass out of my foot.

The nurse that had led the first aid course at work had said that you shouldn't try to remove anything sharp from your body - something about causing more harm in the removal. I took a minute running through alternatives, but lying on the floor surrounded by orange & cinnamon candles and books about female empowerment wouldn't help anyone. There was no way I could get to the hospital on my own, not with glass sticking out of my foot. Theo was in Brighton. I called Amy again, but she didn't pick up.

'Fuck me!' Inhaling deeply.

I took another deep breath. It would probably be easier to use one quick motion, though looking at how much blood there was, I guessed that making an even bigger wound wouldn't be wise.

My hands started to shake, like my brain was shouting 'don't touch it, you fool!' I took hold of the shard: instant, agonising pain.

'Fuck!'

Hitting the floor with my hands, just to get the anger out of my system, blood splattering on the carpet. The whole room was starting to look like a murder scene from CSI Miami. My heart was pounding, sweat ran down my face; I could feel the pressure deep in my head. Taking a couple more deep breaths, I gripped the glass again and pulled. It was like my foot was being held in a furnace. The pain was so intense that for a moment, I wanted to throw up. I shouted again, and suddenly the pain was gone.

'Thank God for that.' I leant my head against the side of the mattress.

Bandaging my foot, I slid it carefully into the most comfortable trainers I owned, then grabbed my coat and car keys, hopping out the front door as fast as I was able.

Stepping carefully down the stairs, I considered where else Jodie might be staying. Amy seemed like the best possibility - she must know something, and there was still hope that I would find Jodie there.

A rainstorm had just started as I limped and hopped pathetically to my car. Water trickled into the collar of my jacket. One more thing to add to the mess of the day.

The car was still a few metres away, and the rain was already seeping into my trainers. I unlocked it and watched it flash joyfully, as if inviting me into the cosy, dry interior. Yanking the door open, I finally fell into the car.

The rain hitting the car's roof made a deafening, pounding noise as I backed out of the parking space. I was surprised that my right foot felt ok on the pedals. I gave the engine a little more power and was thrown back in my seat with a sudden crash. For a moment, there was silence. I turned, barely making out the silhouette of a car through my back window.

'God damn!' No freaking way. What were the chances? Seriously? *When it rains, it pours.*

I took some deep breaths, counting slowly from one to ten; a tip from my mother. I found some paper in the glove box and wrote a few apologetic lines under my contact details, then I pushed it into a plastic sleeve and stepped out into the rainstorm, limping back to examine the damage. It was just a scratch, but I left the note under the other car's wiper.

'Having a bad day?' A woman's voice, barely audible over the storm, came from behind me. I turned, and made out a baseball cap over fiery red hair. She was slim, maybe in her 30s or 40s, and wore a shiny yellow raincoat over jeans and dark boots. A huge umbrella shielded her from the rain. She had a broad, friendly smile, the kind that could persuade you to join a cult.

'Excuse me?' I yelled. I was angered just by her standing there, smug and cosy. I wanted to get back inside the car.

'I can see you're having a bad day.' Shouting, she pointed at my car.

'Thanks for noticing.' I gave her a thumbs-up and turned back to check that the note hadn't been washed away.

'Do you need an umbrella?' She shouted again.

'Why? Do you have another one?'

'No.' She paused, then apologised.

'Cute,' I retorted. It wasn't.

I went back to my car and returned it to my space, ordered an Uber, and limped back to the shelter of my building. I was starting to shiver from the cold now. It would have been smarter to go upstairs and change into some dry clothes, but the idea of climbing those stairs again felt worse than the prospect of hypothermia. I lifted my head to watch the rain falling and noticed the woman with the umbrella reading the note I'd left on the red car.

'Oi!' I yelled. 'Leave it be!'

'Ethan?' She shouted back. 'Nice name!' Anger coursed through me. Jodie was missing; I had a bleeding foot, and it was all topped off by this car accident - she had *no right.*

'Miss - leave it! It's for the owner of the car!' I shouted louder this time. Abruptly, she turned towards me, and gave me a *teasing look* as she swung her hand slightly. The car I'd collided with beeped and flashed.

'Fucking hell,' I muttered to myself.

'Are you ok with me taking this now?' She had my plastic sleeve and note in her other hand. I nodded, trying not to make eye contact.

'I'm sorry! I'll pay for the damage. I live here.' I pointed to the building behind me. 'Apartment 17.' She didn't say anything. 'I'm so sorry!'

If she wanted to, she could be a right bitch, call the police, make me wait here. She could make my day even worse.

'It's ok, Ethan. I can see that today is not your day.' She raised her voice as the rain stepped up another notch. 'I'll give you a call in a few days to talk about the damage. I'm not in a rush.'

She took something from her car, locked it, and walked away, waving at me. I didn't wave back.

CHAPTER 4

The Uber pulled gently to a stop just outside Amy's house, with a soft whine of electric motors. She lived in a beautiful, rambling terrace in Rotherhithe, and I could see why Amy and Julie moved here after adopting Emmet. Ducks bobbed on the glittering lake nearby, and a few regal white swans during the summer months. I eyed their wooden front porch, evergreens in clay pots on either side of the door. No toys, or mess, no sign that a child lived here.

'Is everything ok?' the driver asked. He seemed worried, but I sat in silence, hoping to see Jodie walking past a window. This was surely the first place she would go if she wanted to get away from me for a bit. But then she knew that this would be the first place I would try looking for her.

The rain hadn't stopped, but at least it wasn't pouring now.

'Sir?' The driver was probably starting to get nervous. I asked him to wait for me while I checked with Amy. Stepping out of the car, my trainers squelched on the tarmac.

I limped to the front door. As I moved closer to the house, a light flicked on upstairs. There was no doubt they were home, and then I heard noises, the sound of a child's laughter. Emmet. Synchronised clapping and singing; I was obviously about to interrupt a lovely afternoon.

The door knocker clattered, the sound of playtime stopped, and footsteps could be heard approaching until the door finally swung open.

As soon as Amy saw me, her smile faded. I guess she was expecting a delivery man or a *good* friend. She had her hair tied up, a jam stain on her yellow t-shirt and checkered PJs.

'Ethan,' she said, her voice flat. 'How're *things?*'

'Amy, hi, I called you.' My smile faltered under her stony gaze. 'Is everything okay?'

'I'm not attached to my phone, you know,' she crossed her arms. 'But yeah, I'm fine. Better than Jodie anyway. She told me what happened.'

'Oh, she's with you!' I hesitated again. 'Wait, told you what? What's happened to her? I've been so worried!' I tried to move behind her, looking around Amy to catch a glance of Jodie.

'Nope.' She didn't budge. 'She's not here. Not anymore, anyway.' The hostility was unmistakable.

'Amy, what the hell is going on? Please can you tell me

what's happening? I've been losing my mind with worry.'

'She left early this morning.' Jodie spending the night at least meant she was safe, which was a relief. Amy was staring at me.

'Did she tell you why she left our house? I can't reach her. I don't understand.' I could feel my throat constricting, my voice about to catch. I swallowed and took a breath. *Calm down. She's safe.*

Amy glanced behind her to make sure Julie and Emmet weren't catching wind of the doorstep drama. She waved her hand at me, motioning that I should step back, and closed the door behind her. We stood under the small porch, barely sheltered from the rain, almost breathing on each other. Standing so close together, I can't help but notice how much shorter she was than me.

'What do you mean she *left your house?*' She was talking more quietly now.

'Well, we had a bit of a fight yesterday, and –'

Amy interrupted, 'Look, Ethan. I know all about it; she told me! I honestly thought better of you, but you're an absolute pig. Of course she came over - she needed some space.' Amy was furious, her eyes narrowed, and she was breathing heavily.

I pulled my head back, and some drops of rain hit the side of my cheek.

'Wait; *what?*'

'I can't believe you!'

'I don't know what's going on. I cut my finger yesterday, and she got so mad. It was so... it was stupid. She

42

was irrational yesterday, all over the place, throwing things around the house, breaking stuff. She just kept saying she needed to fix something. But I don't know what she meant, and I thought it would be easier just to sleep it off and talk this morning. I woke up to find that she'd gone.' I couldn't wrap my head around what was happening. Why was Amy so cross? What had Jodie told her?

'Right.' Amy was cold. 'So you just handily forgot to mention the yoga teacher – Stacey.' It wasn't a question. She held my gaze, jaw tight. I stared in shock, unable to comprehend this twist in our conversation. 'How could you just do this to her? To *our* Jodie!' She uncrossed her arms and crossed them again. 'Sometimes, Ethan, I swear to God...'

My body stood stock still, but I certainly wasn't cold anymore; in fact, I'd started to sweat. I didn't even know where to begin.

'A yoga teacher? I don't know any yoga teachers. What the hell, Amy? I would never! Come on, you know me.' A headache came over me, creeping in from my temples. I took a steadying breath to stave off the anger. I felt like I'd been losing my footing for so long that at any minute, I would explode.

'Are you seriously going to deny it? Why would she make shit like that up? To me, of all people?' She was shouting now. 'Honest to God, I expected more from you.'

'It's a lie,' I said slowly, almost to convince myself. 'It just *isn't true*, Amy! I swear it.'

'Please don't even–'

'I don't even go to yoga classes.' Amy stared at me and pulled her head back. She had opened her mouth for a retort, then shut it again. I felt a tiny glimmer of hope.

'What?' She was confused by my remark. She'd realised that there was more to it than what she'd heard from Jodie the previous day.

'I don't go to yoga classes.' I repeated it slower. 'About two weeks ago, Jodie suggested we try yoga together. There was this thing called acro yoga, where you do poses as a couple. I just rolled with it. We were going to try our first class tomorrow.'

Amy stood there, silently digesting what I'd said. She was Jodie's best friend, and she would always pick her side, but I wasn't backing down.

'Just because you haven't been attending classes doesn't mean you couldn't have whored around with this *tall, brunette, Stacey person.*' It was apparent she wanted to believe that Jodie had been telling the truth. It would be much easier if I were that *absolute pig.*

'This is ridiculous.' I didn't know who this Stacey was. 'I never cheated on Jodie. Ever.' Amy raised her index finger and her eyebrow.

'Ever?'

'Amy...' I sighed. 'It was like eighteen years ago.'

'Seventeen.'

I raised my voice. 'It didn't mean anything, drunken mistake, come on!' She was just trying to make me feel bad.

'Blame it on alcohol, or maybe your testosterone. Yes, of course it wasn't your fault. How could it be? I'm so disappointed with you right now, you know.'

'Look, since then I haven't kissed anyone but my wife. I have been faithful for every single moment of our marriage.' I could see Amy wanted to interrupt, so I spoke louder and quicker. *'No matter what you think!'*

Amy sighed but I continued.

'And frankly, it hurts that Jodie said something like this, and you don't even want to listen to me - when I say nothing happened.' I took a deep breath. 'I promise.'

Amy shrugged. 'Then I have no idea why she would say something like that. She spoke with incredible certainty, telling me about the 30-year-old brunette, tall, with short, fashionable hair. Her high-vis jacket made her stand out from the crowd.' She was watching me for some sort of reaction. 'Jodie thought she must be one of those girls who runs every other day, cycles to work, and eats salads for lunch.' Amy looked into my eyes and took another breath before she spoke again. 'I don't think Jodie was lying, Ethan.' I shook my head, and she touched my arm with her hand, though my wet jacket. 'And it blows my mind because you seem like you're telling the truth too. You two finally found some drama in your life, and hell! It looks like it's a whopper.' She looked away.

'Where is she?' I just wanted to speak with my wife.

'Home. She said she was going home.'

'Home?' I asked in disbelief.

'That's why I was surprised to see you, you know. You would have crossed paths. She must be back at your flat.'

I was overwhelmed with relief, though I was still angry

with Jodie for lying to Amy. I kept telling myself there must be some reason for all of this, some misunderstanding. I just needed to speak with Jodie. No matter what, I wasn't going to let this marriage crumble.

I thanked Amy and waved goodbye as I limped back to the car. I could feel Amy's stare burning a hole in the back of my neck. I would bet anything that she was dying to know why I was limping. I climbed into the back seat and asked the driver to take me home. Amy was still standing on her porch watching me leave, arms crossed.

CHAPTER 5

The door to the apartment was unlocked, and I shouted Jodie's name. There was no response. I walked through the empty apartment remembering the times when I'd come back home late from work and she would hide somewhere in the flat. It was her way of teasing me for being late. It wouldn't be obvious at first, but after a few minutes of complete silence, I could sense she was somewhere, waiting to leap out. But now, she wasn't here; she hadn't come home. Maybe I had just left the door unlocked.

It was only about twenty four hours since I had seen her, but I already missed her silliness, her love.

I called Nancy - Jodie's friend from work. As I expected, she knew nothing about Jodie's disappearance, but in our short conversation she succeeded in stressing me out - saying that she read that the first 72 hours were the most important when someone goes missing. I hung up the phone. Thanks for nothing, Nancy.

Next I called my mother - careful to avoid using the word *missing*. Jodie treated my mother as her own and I had hoped she might have said something. Nothing.

Fuck this, I'm calling the police.

Though I'd never reported a missing person before, it felt like the right thing to do - maybe Amy thought everything was ok, but I had to believe what I'd seen with my own eyes yesterday afternoon. The dispatcher answered on the first ring and quickly redirected me to the police.

'I need to report a missing person - Jodie, my wife.' I said it confidently. The dispatcher asked for her full name, date of birth, and a lot of other information.

'Jodie Page, her date of birth is 24th of September 1980, the last person to see Jodie was her friend, Amy Hale.' It made Amy sound a bit suspicious.

'Is there any immediate danger to this person?'

They needed something to take the case seriously. 'She might be suicidal,' I lied. I didn't feel good about it. But if I told them the truth, they might have waited some time before they started a search. I didn't want to wait.

The officer told me they would contact me if any information came in.

It was only lunchtime, but I needed a drink, so I grabbed a beer. Time was passing too slowly; as a distraction, I called Theo. As soon as he picked up, he started talking about his gadget.

'You know my face motion tracking -' he paused, not knowing yet what to call his invention '- motion tracking robot camera. I think it might have huge potential.'

I knew he'd been working very hard to develop his idea and was super excited to tell me about it, but I just couldn't pretend everything was normal.

'Jodie left. I don't know where she is.' I interjected, and he fell silent.

We remained that way until Theo spoke. 'What?'

Not knowing where to start, I told him everything; about our fight, Jodie spending the night at Amy's, me reporting Jodie as a missing person.

'But why would she leave?' he asked and I told him what Amy had said, about this Stacey person, someone who I'd never met and probably didn't exist. 'Did you kiss her?' His question was ridiculous.

'Of course not! She's not real!' I shouted.

'There must be something you don't know. If I'd finished my motion tracking robot camera we could find Jodie in no time!' He was trying to make me feel better.

'If only.'

'It's been less than twenty-four hours, mate, we need to wait and see. Jodie is upset. Give her time. You can come here if you'd like; you know you're always welcome at our house.'

'I do.'

My Wife Jodie

***

I needed a distraction, and so I started fixing the mess from earlier. On my knees, I dug through the carpet with my fingers, hoping to find more shards of glass. I found two more; satisfying and terrifying. In the process of fixing the fallen shelf, I hit my thumb with the hammer and it started to swell. I got another plaster out of the kit.

The bloodstains on the carpet proved more difficult to clean than I'd thought. I scrubbed and scrubbed with a sponge, but the rust-red stain remained. I just wanted it gone. The frustration built and built and overflowed, and I screamed into the empty flat.

Fuck this! I grabbed a bottle of red wine from the kitchen cupboard and filled two glasses, went back to the bedroom, poured one of them on the stain and downed the other. I opened the bedroom window to try and clear the smell.

In the kitchen, I cleaned all the counters. Emptying the cupboards, I wiped every item one by one until they were perfectly clean again. Tears rolled down my cheeks, tickling my nose. *Damn it!*

The local DIY shop sold me some filler after I described the hole in my living room wall. It repaired the hole, but not perfectly; like a wound, there would always be a scar.

By 7 pm, everything was done. I got some food and turned on the TV, though I couldn't relax. Hundreds of questions were spinning through my head.

One after the other, they demanded to be dealt with. I

tried to focus on them in some sort of order – yet still, my head spun. What had triggered all this? I hopelessly tried calling Jodie again. It went to her voicemail, after the fourth ring this time.

Even if - *if* - I had somehow kissed Stacey and Jodie was furious, it didn't explain why she'd waited till night to sneak out; as if she was running away.

Darkness had descended, the fourth beer was almost finished, and I sat in the living room studying Jodie's painting of the two children. Jodie was a talented artist, who had been able to pursue her twin passions for art and teaching with her parents' support. She described them as the kind of people who had separate quarters for the servants. I'd never met them, and Jodie rarely talked about it, but she seemed happy enough to take their money. Something was badly wrong with that family.

Next to the painting of the children holding hands, on the other side of the fireplace, hung my favourite piece of Jodie's. Twins, she called it. It showed a happy family - a father, mother and a young girl having a picnic, while an identical twin woman watched them from a distance - alone. Even though the colours were bright and vibrant, this painting felt sad.

She was talented, there was no doubt about that, but now more than ever, I believed she deserved to be recognised. Her art should be hanging in galleries across Europe. She had been painting less recently, and maybe I should have supported her more.

My phone rang, causing me to jump. An unknown number and my heart leapt.

'Hello?'

'Good evening, this is Sergeant Michelle Gasser from Southwark Police Station. I'm calling about your missing person report, for Ms Jodie Page.'

'Yes, that's correct.'

'According to the notes I have here, you were the person who made the report?'

'Yes. Do you have some news?' I could tell from the policewoman's tone of voice that the news was good.

'We were able to locate Jodie based on the information you provided. She is safe; however, she does not want to be contacted, and I'm afraid I can't disclose any further information.'

'Doesn't want to be contacted?' What did that mean?

'Is there anything else I can help you with?' she asked.

'Wait a minute, Jodie is my wife. What does it mean that she doesn't want to be contacted?'

'It means that she is no longer a missing person, as we were able to speak with her. She was asked if she wanted us to pass on her location or contact information to the person who reported her missing. She said no.'

'She said no?'

'That's correct, sir.'

'But, I need to know whether she's safe. I don't want Jodie sleeping on the streets!' I needed her to give me something more, a bit of information. There was a patient pause on the other end of the line. 'She has to take medication every day! Someone has to look after her.' It was a lie, but the situation was getting desperate.

'Sir, you don't need to worry. I can tell you that she is not alone and will be looked after.'

Not alone? It meant she was staying with someone. Had Amy lied to me? Not Theo. But who?

'Thank you, Sergeant. Thank you for your call.'

'Have a good day, sir.' The line crackled and the call ended with a beep.

She is no longer a missing person. When was she coming back? What about her job? She loved the kids she looked after more than anything. At least she was safe, but I couldn't let it go; I needed to find her. She'd run off without saying anything. Did she expect me to do nothing? Was I to wait patiently until she returned?

The light flickered in the study, where she kept her laptop. I prayed she hadn't taken it with her. Finding it in the second desk drawer, I took it out and opened it on the desk. Luckily I knew her password - *LadyBird.* She had deactivated the location sharing on her phone, but maybe something would still be syncing from her phone to her laptop. I opened the browser and found the web history for all of her devices, all conveniently time-stamped, right up to this afternoon.

Today 15:22 - Google search: Sensory deprivation Edinburgh
Today 08:32 - Google search: Meditation benefits
Today 08:14 - https://harvard.edu/how-memory-works
Yesterday 20:55 - Google search: London to Edinburgh trains

'Edinburgh?' Amy had seemed positive when she'd told me that Jodie was going home. *Home.* That word floated for a second in my head before I made the connection. She meant she was going back home to Edinburgh. Was she going to stay with her parents?

When I proposed to Jodie, she called my mother right away. It seemed a little strange that she didn't call her own parents, but when they didn't show up to our wedding, I realised that her relationship with them was much more strained than I had originally thought. Jodie had never spoken much about why; she had always been much more mature and independent than the rest of us. It seemed we were the only family she had. I was happy to be close to her and did my best to fill that void in her life.

Now, after all these years of never speaking about her parents, after twenty years of silence, she suddenly decides to go back? And all this triggered by her thinking I'd kissed a yoga teacher?

The problem was, I didn't know where her parents lived. Jodie was from Edinburgh, but she'd somehow managed never to tell me exactly where. The only information I had were their names: Derek and Denise Brown, and they were wealthy, thanks to some sort of successful business that Jodie had also failed to talk about.

I closed the browsing history and went straight to Google, typing in *Derek Denise Brown.* Nothing related to business owners from Edinburgh came up. But on LinkedIn I found a Derek Brown, originally from Scotland, now in

London - but he was married to a Sarah. Another Derek Brown was a musician in America, but he was too young to be Jodie's father. I closed the laptop and limped out of the study.

I needed Amy's help. When she picked up, and I'd filled her in, she expressed surprise that Jodie hadn't come home. She told me that Jodie had replied to a text asking if she was ok, with a simple *I'm fine*. When I told Amy I'd reported Jodie as a missing person she snorted in amusement.

'Well, someone is clearly a bit melodramatic.' I imagined she was rolling her eyes as she said that. She was more interested when I told her about Jodie going to Edinburgh. She wanted to know how I knew, but I changed the subject. Anything that was said to Amy would most certainly be reported back to Jodie.

'Do you think she really went to Edinburgh? You both are such drama queens! Are you going to chase her all the way there, keel before her, and beg forgiveness?'

'What the hell? I don't have anything to apologise for!' Clearly, she didn't understand how much distress this was causing me.

'Ethan.' She sounded disappointed. 'You *seriously* need to relax. She is fine. We had a good chat yesterday - she was upset, but nothing more than that. She is not suicidal; she wants some time to herself. Can you respect that?'

No. Amy hadn't been there when Jodie'd hit me or thrown that knife into the wall. She wasn't there when Jodie had said, 'Don't worry, I'll fix everything.' Amy only saw what Jodie let her see. I know Jodie, and she hadn't been faking it. She was in some kind of trouble, and she wasn't talking to me about what it was.

'Do you know where her parents live?' I spoke calmly.

'No. I'm in the same boat as you. I've never heard her speak much about her parents. Once, she told me her father said that he'd never wanted to have children, that Jodie was a mistake.' I sighed at Amy's remark. *What a dick.*

Saying goodnight, I hung up, sitting in the darkened room. I remained for a while, not thinking, just watching the light from the window illuminating the pictures on the wall. We had created so many lovely memories; there was even a picture of our first dance together as newlyweds.

We'd been married in the forest just outside London. A picturesque nature-wedding had proven to be more complicated than our collection of Instagram photos had indicated. There'd been tents, generators, transport, permits to organise; we'd had to make sure the roads were wide enough for vans. But the moment our wedding song came up, Jodie and I came together on the dance floor as everyone stepped to the edge, and it was the perfect moment. We had placed hundreds of small lights in the trees so that they illuminated the dance floor. I grabbed her waist and swung her around me, people cheered, and then our bodies touched. We moved in sync. The night was clear, a million stars above us. My eyes were filled with tears. I couldn't help myself; I wept, letting them fall on Jodie's shoulder. She laughed and told me I was cute. My mother was beaming as she watched. She didn't need to say that she was happy; she had worked meticulously on our wedding arrangements. We'd given her a sheet with the details of all 57 guests, and she'd written the names and addresses neatly on each envelope. Jodie had drawn a small heart on the envelope addressed to her parents.

I bolted upright; the list of addresses my mother had used! It must be somewhere. My heart started to pound.
I limped back to the study and started opening and closing drawers as if I was a thief searching for valuables. There was nothing in them, but there was one other place we kept various important documents – in a box under our bed. I dragged myself to the bedroom, adrenaline counteracting the pain. I lifted our bed, seeing the box still there, next to the extra sheets and duvet. One folder was for finances: flat ownership papers and P60s, national insurance contribution papers, and private pension care plans. The yellow folder I was holding seemed to be all Jodie's freelance work.

Going through everything reminded me how long we had been together. At this point, our lives had become one. I couldn't bear the thought that we might fall apart. One after the other, I pulled out folders and stacked them beside me. Maybe Jodie tossed it out years ago. I certainly hadn't seen it since the wedding.

I had to make sure; it might be my only chance to find Jodie. But the box was empty now, with nothing but a few scraps of paper at the bottom. The address sheet I was looking for wasn't there. There was another box next to it, one we used to fill with sentimental things. I took it out and opened it, photographs spilling from the top onto the floor. Of the two of us, Jodie was the one who liked taking pictures. There was a picture of me leaning against a palm tree on a perfect, white sandy beach in Vietnam - one of the islands called Phu Quoc. Aside from an overwhelming number of drunk Russian tourists, that holiday had been amazing. A picture of us in Lithuania, standing on a strange hill full of old crosses. A photo of St. Abb's Head lighthouse in Scotland. I'd taken Jodie there shortly after I'd won the lottery. We were sitting on a bench looking into the depths of the North Sea when I asked her if she would marry me. She wasn't shocked. Maybe the carefully planned romantic trip had given it away. She'd only said *yes*, hugged me, and called my mother. She laughed and screamed with joy, telling my mother to stop the car - she had some amazing news to share.

Photos of our wedding surfaced next, one of them taken just after the ceremony. When we'd exchanged rings, and the celebrant had told us we were officially husband and wife, all of our friends and family had lined up neatly along the path in the forest. Jodie had jumped on my back, making me carry her along the hard earth path while people laughed and clapped, throwing rice and seeds. Jodie threw her bouquet into the air, hanging on to me with her other hand. At that instant, the photographer snapped the picture and froze the moment forever. I smiled and put it carefully in my shirt pocket.

Seeing all the happy memories we had shared broke something inside of me. I desperately wanted her back. Tears spilled down my cheek as I smiled, remembering these little snippets from our life. One by one the pictures came out, and my eyes went automatically to the next thing in the box, resting on top of the pile. The small green notebook somehow felt out of place; it wasn't as dusty as the other things. I took it out and looked more closely. A dark green, hardcover A5 notebook. There was no branding on it, maybe it was even handmade. Posh. I opened it and on the first page in Jodie's handwriting was the word 'Remember.'

I quickly flipped through the pages, but it was mostly empty. There were just a few pages filled at the front and a few more at the back. The back pages, titled *happiness,* were neatly ruled into three columns and were filled with names and dates. The middle column listed a profession or some other form of identification.

Happinesss

Jordan	Student	17-03-1998
Camilla	Student	15-08-1998
Kate	Lesbian	03-12-1998
Taylor	Runner	29-07-2000
Drew	Magazine	16-05-2001
Victoria	Actress	10-08-2002
Jamie	Whore	02-08-2003
Remy	Motorbike	16-10-2004
Alex	Starbucks	30-09-2007
Charlie	Neighbour	14-03-2008
Laura	Baby	17-09-2010
Riley	Accounts	13-05-2012
Stacey	Yoga	22-08-2016

Life

Gary	22-07-1999	02-05-03
A-levels	16-04-1999	12-00-00
History degree	02-03-2000	02-03-01
Martha's death	10-07-2003	
Bike	14-03-2004	02-07-00
Burglary	29-04-2006	05-00-00
Depression	23-06-2006	12-04-02
Money	02-04-2007	01-07-00
Cancer	12-02-2007	02-11-00
Tony's case	07-02-2009	16-03-00
Jill	11-05-2009	02-05-07
Truck	01-03-2010	03-10-00
Adoption	07-07-2011	18-01-00
Car crash	01-09-2013	02-00-00
Marathon	08-06-2015	05-10-00
Motorcycle	11-11-2015	02-08-00
Amar	27-07-2016	

I stared at the *happiness* list for a few minutes, trying to make sense of the names. Laura - that was probably most familiar to me. I'd had two flatmates back in university who were called Jamie and Remy. Last time I saw Remy was when he'd finished university in 2003. And I hadn't seen Jamie since he moved out of the halls in 2001. Maybe these were different people. The dates, on the other hand, made no sense to me - but the last entry sent cold chills down my spine. *Stacey 22-08-2016.* That's tomorrow's date. Tomorrow?

Jodie's writing was neat and precise; this was important to her, and she'd cared enough to keep it carefully hidden. I couldn't stop thinking about Jodie and her secrets; I needed answers. I flipped back to the front of the notebook, to the other list titled *life*. The layout was similar, though this time, they seemed to be events and dates.

This list made even less sense than the other. It seemed that the first column was just keywords - things Jodie wanted to remember but not intended to be seen by anyone, probably including me. Some of the keywords and dates made sense. I recognised my failed investment in Kodak in 2007 and Amy trying to adopt Emmet in the summer of 2011. In 2007 I had been diagnosed with cancer but had been lucky enough to catch it early, avoiding serious treatment. My mother had gone through breast cancer in 1995 and had also been successfully treated. But other things like *depression* or *Martha's death* were mystifying. The only Martha I knew was my mother, but she wasn't dead. I didn't know anyone who had *depression*. Those keywords could mean something else, a code of some sort; I didn't know anyone called *Jill* nor anyone who had studied history.

I held the small green notebook in my hands as my grip slowly tightened until my knuckles were white, trying and failing to calm my breathing. I had no idea what to make of this. It felt as if my life was unravelling, and I didn't know what to do.

There was a pain in my chest, and cold beads of sweat pricked at my temple. My mouth was dry, and I realised I was aching for Jodie. I wanted to hold her tightly in my arms until it felt like we were becoming one. We would talk, and everything would make sense again.

Shutting my eyes, I took a deep breath in, holding it to feel the beat of my heart slow slightly. Exhaling, I crossed my arms and held the book to my chest. Slightly calmer, I had just reopened my eyes when a light blue folder caught my attention. It had been hidden under the notebook, and with black marker in my handwriting was labelled, "Wedding Stuff".

CHAPTER 6

It hurt to look at the empty side of the bed. Since Jodie and I had first moved in together, fresh out of college, we'd barely been apart. A few people questioned the rush to move in together - including me - but Jodie assured me it would be fine, and she was right. Though we attended different universities, we had found a small town between Leeds and York called Micklefield, and the commute for each of us was less than half an hour. We settled in. It was working out for us. Now it was only the second day waking up without her by my side, and there was nothing I wanted more than to feel her soft touch.

The sheets didn't feel quite right. They were stiff over my legs, like I was lying on a sheet of paper. I hesitated for a moment before pulling the sheets aside; there it was, blood. I stared at it, frozen - *what the hell had happened?* The blood covered the sheets around my feet. I slowly started to move my legs, one at a time. There was no pain, good. Now there were two bloodstains in this room, on the mattress, and the carpet.

I moved my feet down to the floor, the stinging sensation in my left foot making me flinch. The bandage must have moved during the night. I could replace the mattress, but it was time to go and see a doctor. An infection now would prevent me going to Edinburgh, and I couldn't risk that.

I called work and told them I'd be late, happy that there were no client meetings scheduled for today. I put another plaster on the wound for now to stop the blood and went straight to a private clinic I'd found online. I didn't fancy going to the hospital and waiting for hours in A&E with other people. It was easier to pay and skip the queue.

It was a beautiful fresh morning with an icy blue sky - no hint of yesterday's downpour. It was unusually cold for this time of year, but most of the people I saw en-route to the clinic were still wearing colourful shorts and light summer dresses.

I had to use the railing outside the clinic to pull myself up the four small steps. Inside, a young receptionist smiled brightly at me.

'Hello sir! Do you have an appointment?' She half stood to greet me, her voluptuous breasts bouncing slightly from the movement.

'Hello–' I forced myself to read her name tag, slightly disconcerted '–Emily. No, I don't. But I'd like to see a doctor if that's possible.'

She took my details, and we discovered I was in fact a registered patient. Jodie must have done it ages ago. She guided me to a seating area, where there were already three people waiting: a hipster-looking guy in his mid-twenties and a father with a toddler.

Since I didn't know how long the wait was going to be, I had brought the wedding folder I'd found. I had spent some time going through it yesterday, and had just about memorised its contents. The first few plastic sleeves contained magazine clippings and a few sticky notes with scrawled messages in capital letters like *white lilies?* The next few pages were dedicated to an outdoor layout with white chairs. Others were about Jodie's dress and the bouquet, which Laura had been determined to catch. As it turned out, she didn't - but she laughed it off and got married the next summer anyway. There was a numbered list of eighty-nine songs for the DJ at the reception. "Coolplay - Yellow" had a star next to it; the song for our first dance. I laughed when I spotted the spelling mistake I'd made. The clippings continued: cake and menu options, seating plans, accommodation notes. Towards the end was a section that held the contracts with the band, the venue, catering, and many other suppliers. And finally there was the guest list, including the names and addresses we'd sent invitations to with their RSVP noted. Next to Derek and Denise Brown, there was no mark; they had not responded. I brought the book closer, rereading something I had already read many times yesterday. Next to their name, an address was printed in Jodie's handwriting: *183 Constitution St, Leith, Edinburgh.*

I had done it. I had found something which might lead to Jodie. I felt a warm sensation passing through my body, like after a successful day in court defending a client. Pride and a sense of accomplishment. But this wasn't some video game where you gathered clues until you had enough to unlock the next door. It was real life.

'Mr Page?' The receptionist called from behind her desk. 'Dr Leigh will be with you in a few minutes.'

I thanked her with a quick wave. A little girl - no more than three - was enjoying the sliding doors that led to another area. She would walk slowly towards the door, and as soon it slid open, she would shriek, spin around and run back to her father, already with his arms spread wide to catch her, both of them laughing. By this point, it was clear the receptionist and the other patients in the waiting room weren't finding it very amusing. I chuckled at the girl's surprise every time the door opened. She was lovely.

'Mr Page? I'm Dr Leigh.' It was a soft, familiar voice. I jumped slightly and turned towards her. She slowed down as she recognised me.

It was the lady whose car I'd driven into yesterday. Dr Leigh was wearing more official clothes now: she had a light blue checked shirt under her white coat, black trousers, and matching flats. She was a lovely woman, her wavy red hair complementing her brown eyes. Her hair was in a low bun, neatly tied.

'Hello.' I was slightly embarrassed, but she grinned.

'Come through,' Dr Leigh waved ambiguously and turned towards the consulting rooms. I followed her, limping, each step more painful than the last. Now I just wanted to get this over and done with.

Dr Leigh opened the door and a strong scent of sanitiser hit my nostrils. It was a relatively large room, with a hospital bed, a desk, a few chairs, and quite a few well-looked-after plants. A tall bookshelf stood in the corner and was filled with colourful books, giving it a homey feel. Dr Leigh sat at her desk and invited me to take a seat.

'So, Mr *Ethan*, how can I help you today?' She was still smiling.

'Look -' I wasn't quite sure what to say. 'This is quite a coincidence.'

'Indeed.' It sounded like she spoke in slow motion.

In one breath, I explained. 'I will get back to you about your car - I had an emergency to deal with.'

'I'm not judging.' She placed her hands carefully on her desk and looked at me. 'How can I help you?'

I explained to Dr Leigh how I'd broken a glass, leaving Jodie out of the story. As I was talking, I realised that telling Dr Leigh that I had thrown the glass at the wall made *me* sound like a lunatic. Dr Leigh listened quietly, occasionally interjecting with words like *blimey* and *ouch*. Then I told her how I stepped on the shard, fell, and then to top it off had backed into her car. 'Gracious, you were having a bad day!' Dr Leigh said as I finished. I nodded.

'Shall we have a look at your foot then?' She asked me to lay on the bed and remove my shoe and sock. Maybe I should have taken a shower this morning after all. She lifted my leg and examined the cut closely.

'We-eew!' she exclaimed loudly.

'Do you usually react like that when you examine a patient?' I asked, as I counted the number of hooks holding up the privacy curtain.

'Reacting out loud like that is extremely unprofessional.' She shot back. 'Though the rules change after someone *destroys* your car–'

'–barely a scratch,' I interjected, cheerfully.

'–and it wouldn't start yesterday!' she continued.

'Did it have any petrol in it?'

'Oi!' She lowered my foot. 'I can hurt you!' From her position at the end of the bed, she looked up at me with a mock glare.

After a moment, we smiled at each other, for slightly too long. Dr Leigh went back to being a doctor.

'The good news is, it doesn't look like you need stitches. The bad news is that it's a very tricky area to heal, and if you flex your foot too much, you will make it bleed again.' I nodded. 'I'll put the bandage on - try to be extra careful with this foot for the next few days.'

'Noted.' Dr Leigh got some bandages and lifted my foot again before washing, covering, and bandaging it. She was very gentle.

I put my shoes back on and limped painfully over to the chair. Dr Leigh watched my performance with a grin.

'Ok, drama queen,' she rolled her eyes.

'I'm surprised that you're a doctor!' I genuinely was surprised.

'Considering the quantities of drugs and alcohol that

I consumed in my student years - me too.' She'd said it under her breath while typing something on her computer. When she glanced at me blankly, I was still staring at her. I couldn't decide if she was joking or serious. She looked away, continued typing, and mumbled '...drugs which helped me focus and study hard, of course.'

'Of course,' I nodded in agreement.

She printed a few sheets of paper, stapled them together, and signed the top page. After giving me a few more instructions - don't let the bandage get wet - I was good to go. She waved as I closed the door, and a faint 'see you soon!' followed me down the corridor.

***

I drove straight to work, though based on my colleagues' reactions when I arrived I probably should have cleaned up a bit first. I hadn't shaved in two days and the limp finished off my derelict look nicely. I went straight to my desk and pulled out the topmost file, just to work on something. Luckily, the case was straightforward and I was pretty confident that when this matter came before the court next month, it wouldn't take much to convince the judge that my client had been provoked into violent retaliation. After jotting down some notes for my closing remarks, I dragged myself out of my chair to explain to my boss that I'd need some time off work this week, because of a family emergency. I expected her to ask me to work from home, but seeing how rough I looked, she just said.

'Of course. Take your time.' And gave me the afternoon off. I must have looked *really* bad.

Stopping by Pret on the way home, I seated myself by a window with a warm falafel wrap, a smoked salmon and cream cheese sandwich, and a bottle of water. The wrap in one hand, I searched for travel options to Edinburgh. It was looking a lot like a train would be best: slower than flying, but at least I wouldn't be queuing in airports with an injured foot. Less hassle. Near me, two young girls wearing bright cycling jackets shrieked, looking at something on a phone.

Drama queen. Dr Leigh's phrase popped into my head. It made me chuckle between bites of the wrap. I realised I felt pretty normal - not happy, just ok. It was the first time since Saturday. A small distraction and the beginning of the understanding that even if Jodie wasn't here, life went on.

The shop was starting to fill with hungry people looking for lunch. I found myself drifting into dark thoughts again. What if Jodie had left Edinburgh by now, and was somewhere else? Hey - worst case scenario, I could still meet Jodie's parents, look them in the eye, and ask them why they had neglected their child.

The queue was getting longer and the tables began to fill with rubbish as the staff took orders. The same two girls were still laughing loudly. A lady in the queue sighed, visibly irritated by the noise. One of the girls, wearing a pink vest, reached down and grabbed her backpack. The other, with brown hair, grabbed her rolled yoga mat and started playfully poking her friend with it.

'Come on, tell me if you fucked him!' The brown-haired girl continued to poke her friend.

'Stacey shhh!' shouted the girl in the vest, grabbing the hand of her friend, dragging her away from their table and out the door.

As they were leaving, the girl with brown hair turned to check she hadn't left anything behind. Lifting her head slightly, our eyes met for no more than a moment. Beautiful, wide, hazel eyes. And then her friend pulled her out of the shop.

CHAPTER 7

The train pulled smoothly out of King's Cross station shortly after lunch. I had a rental car booked in Edinburgh, though the address was only a few minutes from the station. Beyond visiting Jodie's parents, I didn't have much of a plan, and I wasn't sure what I would do when I met them. My priority was to find my wife. I hoped that she would be at her family home; meeting my parents-in-law for the first time hadn't really crossed my mind. I'd booked a hotel nearby, and I was hoping I could persuade her to stay with me. She had to be there. The alternative was unthinkable.

I'd taken pictures of Jodie's green notebook with my phone, just in case. It wasn't a great thing to do, but I just needed answers. Watching my reflection in the train window, I could see the story of the last three restless nights in the shadows under my eyes. At least my foot was feeling better.

My seat in first class was comfortable, and I closed my eyes for a few seconds, soothed by the motion of the train. I'd hopefully be seeing Jodie in less than six hours. I was slowly drifting off when my phone jolted me awake. Theo.

'Are you on a train?' He sounded a little worried. I explained I had discovered Jodie was headed home and that I had decided to follow her.

'How's the leg?'

'Much better, I can walk again - just about.' I said, stretching it out gently.

'I'm worried about you, Ethan.' He sighed. 'Really.'

'Thanks. I just... I have to make sure that Jodie is okay.'

'I messaged and called her yesterday, but she didn't respond. Amy told me that Jodie's keeping her whereabouts a secret. Though she's still chill - very relaxed about the situation.'

'I know! Amy's too relaxed. I don't get it.'

'She told me Jodie just needs some time.' I shook my head as Theo was talking.

'Trust me, that's not it.'

'What the hell happened between you two?'

'Man! I wish I knew myself.'

'Amy kept talking to me about you kissing this other woman.'

'I told you, that's bullshit. It's a lie. And it's one of the reasons I'm going to Edinburgh. I want to know the real reason Jodie left.'

'Mate, you don't need to prove anything to me, I believe you. Tell me if there's anything I can help you with.' I was at rock bottom, and Theo made me want to cry. I could always count on him.

'Please don't tell Amy that I'm going to Edinburgh. I don't want to risk her saying anything to Jodie before I find her.'

'I won't.' No one talked for a few seconds. 'By the way, if Jodie is stupid enough to stop loving you, just remember Anneli and me are always going to be here for you. You are our family.'

The call disconnected, and my chat with Jodie appeared on the screen. I swiped up, looking at the messages I'd sent her in the last couple of days - pleading with her to talk to me. She hadn't responded to a single one. She hadn't even read them.

***

'Sir?' A male voice floated down from somewhere above me. And again, 'Sir?' My eyes opened and light flooded in, blurring everything for a few seconds. It was the conductor. 'Sorry to wake you, sir, we're just pulling into the last stop.'

'Edinburgh?' Still feeling dizzy from being awoken, I muttered a hasty thank you as I tried to fully wake up. The train was just settling into the platform.

Gazing out the window, I could see heavy clouds sitting grimly over the city, the train station starkly bright against the darkness outside. There might be rain soon. I closed my laptop, stood up from my seat gathering my belongings, and left the empty train carriage.

I entered the address into the GPS in the rental Audi. I found an odd comfort in its rich, freshly cleaned smell. As expected, Derek and Denise lived only an eight-minute drive from the train station, and it was just one straight road, so using the sat nav felt a little much. Still. I wanted to be sure. As I made my way along Leith Walk, my mood deepened, reflecting the sky outside. I tried to picture how this would go. Even the idea of introducing myself as Jodie's husband sounded silly - we'd been married for twenty years! In no time at all, I was close. The traffic light in front of me changed suddenly to red, and I stopped just in time. I was happy to have the extra few seconds to gather myself.

'I'm here to see Jodie.' I said out loud to myself, trying to sound firm. 'I want...I demand to see my wife.' I stared at the road ahead. *Why had they never wanted to know who their daughter had married?* Another red light and I screeched to a halt, pedestrians flooding into the street. A small girl wearing a bright pink jacket and holding a colouring book waved at me. She must have been no more than three years old. Her mother noticed and gave me a little smile; I took this as a good omen. A few minutes later, the GPS announced that the destination would be on the right. I was approaching the marker on the map, but I couldn't see anything that looked residential. I slowed down and parked on the side of the road, feeling self-conscious at how luxurious the Audi was compared to the surroundings I'd parked in. I'd imagined Jodie's parents living in a beautiful terraced house on a street with plenty of well looked after trees. This road was loud and dirty.

I stepped out of the car and checked the address in the *Wedding Stuff* folder. I knew I had typed the postcode correctly. 'Okay, then.' I muttered to myself. I took a breath, put away the papers, and started looking for the entrance to the apartment.

It was a bustling intersection. A large monument on the other side of the street attracted a few tourists, but no one seemed too excited. A couple of middle-aged men passed me and went into a grimy pub. None of this was right, considering Jodie's wealthy upbringing. What the hell was going on? The address was correct; I was here. I walked across the front a few times, trying to understand the order of these old buildings. Not all the houses had clear numbers attached to them, and many had peeling front doors and a worn, blank look. Another man, balding and with a considerable gut, was shambling towards the pub. Waving awkwardly, I asked for his help.

'183 Constitution St?' He repeated slowly in his thick accent, eyeing me suspiciously. He looked around, down the street, and then back at me. 'You're standing in front of it.' He pointed to the pub.

'I'm looking for a reside–' but the man interrupted me.

'See?' He said, shortly. He pointed a sausage-shaped finger, and my eyes followed. There it was, in faded lettering - number 183, over the entrance of the pub. It slowly dawned on me. *A fake address? What the hell, Jodie?*

'You alright, mate?' the man asked.

'Yes.' I thanked him absently, and he walked into the pub.

***

I don't know how long I stood there. It could have been a minute; it could have been ten. My mind was spinning. The fact that I'd been stupid enough not to check the address online and had come from London to Edinburgh for a pub didn't bother me as much as the lie. It meant the lies had started much earlier than I'd realised. If she wanted to, she could do a great Scottish accent, but apart from that, I knew nothing about her past. Could Jodie have written the wrong address back then? She might have the house number wrong, one digit on the postcode, but the address was correct. The postcode matched the street and the number. There was no mistake. Fifteen years ago, Jodie had told me she would have loved to have her parents at her wedding, but that had been a lie - she hadn't sent them an invitation.

Though this pub certainly wasn't the kind of place where I'd wanted to spend my evening, I was exhausted and back at square one. Just a beer and some chips. I placed my order at the counter, grabbed my beer then found a table next to the window. For a few minutes, I wanted to stop thinking about Jodie and her lies. The drama was getting too much. Could I manage to just have a drink? People were walking outside, minding their own business, and getting on with their lives. Any one of them could have the information I needed. I considered showing Jodie's picture; maybe someone would know something, remember her growing up in the area, or knew her family. It was only a slim possibility; too slim to proceed. She had only arrived here two days ago, and there was nothing about her that particularly stood out. No crazy piercings, no face tattoos. She dressed well. But was it enough for me to go around asking people if they have seen a beautifully dressed blond woman? I took a sip of my beer as a plump waitress approached my table.

'Your chips, sir.' She was young and had a sweet voice. I thanked her, and she walked back to the bar, swinging her hips from side to side. The crowd in this place was rough; middle-aged, working-class men wearing work clothes who sat by themselves, drinking their sorrows away. Apart from my organic wool jacket, I blended in here perfectly.

Drinking and driving wasn't my style, but then today wasn't a normal day. Time seemed to speed up after the third pint. It was getting dark, and the street lights turned on one by one, illuminating the road with an orange glow. More people were in the pub now, and the solitary drinkers at their small tables had found a way to connect. The place was getting louder, too loud for me.

I went back to the car, closed the door, and listened to the sound of people heading home outside. What were my next steps? She must be here, must be somewhere nearby. This city was much smaller than London - maybe I should just drive around, maybe I would see her.

I drove for more than two hours, down every street I could find, turning left and right, searching, eyeing every single pedestrian. Edinburgh was an extraordinary city with well-lit monuments, surrounded by buildings from two, three, even four hundred years ago. But then it was getting late, and the pints were taking their toll. I closed my eyes to rest while waiting for a green light and jumped as the car behind me beeped; I'd been sitting there, blocking traffic, for some time. I finally admitted defeat.

I had booked a cosy room in the Malmaison, overlooking the docks. The clouds had cleared, and the shimmering water reflected a huge, silver moon. It was hard to believe I was in Edinburgh, this beautiful city; alone. *Where are you, Jodie?*

My phone started to vibrate on the table and I jumped – Amy.

'Hello.' I heard my voice, unmistakably tired.

'Where are you?' Amy sounded concerned, something I rarely heard from her. There wasn't much point in keeping the secret.

'Edinburgh.' I said in a flat voice. I was exhausted.

'Jesus, really? You found out where her parents live?' She sounded excited.

'I found an address in our wedding planning folder, so I came.'

She raised her voice. 'And?'

'The address was wrong. It ... it led me to a Wetherspoons.' Amy's laughter crackled down the phone line.

'Seriously?' I asked irritably. I was no longer feeling sleepy.

'Sorry ... sorry. But this is *so* Jodie.' She was barely

holding herself together. 'This is her sense of humour!'

'Why aren't you worried?' I snapped, 'Jesus, she's your best friend!' Amy could always push my buttons.

'Yes, but I'm not worried that she's in danger or anything. I told her the other day; I understand if she wants to be left alone. Maybe it's not the approach you or I would take, but we have to respect her. Jodie hasn't been anything but a great friend to me *and* you. She hasn't done anything to hurt me; she has always been there, caring for me and wishing me the best. I respect her decision if she wants to give herself a break.'

'Yes, but –' I tried to interrupt, but Amy persisted, raising her voice.

'Jesus, Ethan! She was sixteen when she moved to Leeds. Do you think she killed her parents or something and ran away with their money? You didn't respect the decision not to talk with you about her family. And this is what you get. A 'spoons, to be exact!' There was a moment of silence.

I took a deep breath and spoke calmly, 'Equally, she didn't respect *me* by just walking out and telling you a pack of lies!'

'Yes, a lie,' Amy murmured.

'I don't want to argue with you.'

'Well, don't. Be the bigger person here. Let her be. Trust for a moment that maybe she knows what she needs – you should chill out a bit. If you're heading back tomorrow, we could have a smoke if you need to unwind a little?'

I sighed. 'Do you know anything which might help me

find her? I just want to talk to her. You don't understand - the way she left things on Saturday, she was scared, not angry.'

Amy was silent for a minute that stretched; I almost asked if she was still there. 'I don't think so.' she said quietly.

'Are there any old friends of hers who might know where she lived, any place she used to go when she was a teenager, the name of her high school, anything about her parents' business?'

'James Gillespie's High School.'

'What?' Her answer was so quick it threw me off balance.

'James Gillespie's High School was where she went in Edinburgh. I think.' I was quiet as Amy spoke. 'I remember it because we were at my place, and she liked the music I was playing so I told her it was James Gillespie, this indie artist from London. She laughed and told me she went to his school.'

'James Gillespie's High School,' I repeated slowly.

'Yep. Now, don't say I never help you.' Even though I couldn't see her face, I knew she was smiling.

CHAPTER 8

The high school was founded in 1803 by James Gillespie and it was a short drive from the hotel. It was a long shot coming here, especially during half term, but I took my chances. It was either that or harass strangers in the street.

The school parking lot was almost empty, with only a few cars parked close to the main building entrance. I was surprised to see such modern-looking architecture, remembering the year the school had been founded. I'd assumed it would be one of those stunning old buildings; Edinburgh had so many of them. I was wrong. The school seemed newly built, but cheaply. It didn't look like it would last hundreds of years.

I stepped out of the car and made my way to the front entrance. The peeling sticker on the glass window told me to pull.

Inside, the sun filtered weakly through a skylight, the only illumination. By the reception desk, a man and a woman were having a relaxed conversation. As soon as they saw me, the lady touched the guy gently on the shoulder and walked away, saying she would see him later. Were they flirting? I confidently approached the desk and tried to speak as if I belonged there.

'Hey, man!' I only had one shot at making this work. 'I was wondering if you could help me out. I'm doing a class reunion next year, and I wanted to get some of the info on my old classmates.' He looked at me blankly, and my palms started to sweat. 'I wondered if I could take a look at some of the old Alumni records?'

He finally opened his mouth to speak. 'Well, I'm just covering today, so I'm actually the wrong person to ask.' He shrugged.

'Should I try the admin office, perhaps?' I kept my confident tone. I didn't want him to ask any questions I couldn't answer.

'Aye, you can try that!' He sounded relieved, gesturing to the right.

I had no idea where the admin office was, but judging by the exterior of the building, it was clear it had undergone a relatively new restoration. I used this as my excuse.

'And where is the admin office? I guess the location of it changed.' I gave him a polite smile.

'Aye, sorry...' He paused for a moment. 'Take those stairs up, and turn right, then look for the office on your left.'

I gave a thumbs up and climbed the stairs to the next

floor. The first floor had another large bright open space. There were sounds of people talking, somewhere. I turned to the corridor and walked, reading nameplates as I went; on the left-hand side, the sign on the door read *207, Admin Office*. I took a deep breath and knocked. I could hear a low woman's voice saying to come in; so I opened the door and stepped in. There were two small rooms inside, each of them occupied. A middle-aged lady with glasses was sitting in the slightly dimmer room to my left; a younger woman sat in the room by the door.

'Hello there. The man at reception told me you could help me. I'm looking for information on some old classmates.' I was trying to keep eye contact. The lady in the room to my left gave me a big smile and waved me inside.

'Come in, come in!' This looked promising. 'It's so nice when graduates come to visit us.'

I swallowed and sat where she had indicated. I feared being busted, so I kept my smile up, hoping she would want to help me.

'The school looks great!'

'Oh yes, we had major work done a few years ago.' she waved her hand behind her. 'Looks smashing, eh?'

'It sure does.' I nodded, letting the pause stretch until she spoke again.

'So how can I help you?'

'I'm working on a reunion; it's twenty years since we finished school.'

She clapped her hands. 'Twenty? That was a wee while ago,' she put both her hands on the desk and looked at me.

'I'm sorry, we have so many pupils coming and going, I don't recognise you.' She was apologetic. 'What is your name?'

'Theo, Theo Page.' I had to say something, but using my real name didn't seem like it could benefit me anyway.

'Oh..' her face was thoughtful. 'I'm terribly sorry I don't recognise you. I've seen so many students pass through these halls! Although I'm usually quite good with faces.' I nodded and smiled again. She adjusted her glasses and smiled back.

'When did you graduate?' It took me longer than it should have, and she noticed my pause.

'I left here in 1996.'

'I see' she typed something on her computer. 'Is this the first time you've been back since then?'

'Yes,' I nodded.

'Which class did you attend? Or who was your headteacher at the time of graduation?' I froze. She suspected something and I knew there was no way to get this right.

'Ms ...' I paused too long and she frowned.

'You don't remember the Head's name?' She was less friendly now.

'Er … Can you find it by the pupil's name?' I finally said, ending the silence, 'Jodie Brown.'

'What was the name of the Headmaster when you *studied* here?' There was a clear emphasis. I ignored her question.

'Please ... is it possible to just search for Jodie Brown? It's important.'

She ignored my question. 'You didn't go here, did you?

I never forget a face.' There was not a trace of a smile left on her face. Now she just wanted me to admit what we both already knew.

'I'm trying to find my missing wi–'

'Please leave.' She wasn't having any of this.

'I'm sorry I lied but–'

'Leave right now, or I'll call security.' A woman from another room peered in and asked if we were okay. 'Don't worry Sophie; this man is leaving now.' I stood up. I couldn't leave; this school was my only hope for finding Jodie.

'Please ... I'm trying to find my missing wife.'

The other younger woman, I guess her name was Sophie, looked scared. 'You heard Ellena... please leave now.' She stuttered, her eyes darting between mine and her colleague.

I tried to say something, but Ellena stood and told Sophie to fetch security. As she left, I followed. I was desperate and needed them to listen to me. I grabbed Sophie's arm and her eyes widened with fear. The door opened, and a much older woman entered, carrying a few large notepads. She stared in shock at the scene - first at me and then to Sophie.

'Is ... is everything okay in here?'

I realised what it looked like and let go of Sophie's arm, backing towards the door.

'Just tell me if Jodie Brown ever went to this school? Please! Please tell me that much!'

'Leave.' Ellena was behind me. The game was up. I stepped reluctantly past the two ladies and left the room.

My Wife Jodie

***

I hit the steering wheel until I finally started to feel the pain. 'God damn it!' A poisonous mix of frustration, anger, and sadness coursed through me, tears flooding my eyes. The pints of cheap beer the night before weren't helping; my head ached. Would they have reacted differently if I had explained everything honestly from the beginning? Was there anything I could do to salvage it? I rested my head on the steering wheel, furious with myself for getting so close to answers only to fail.

A knock at the car window made me jump. Sunshine was streaming in, and I couldn't see who it was, so I lowered the window a crack. It was the elderly woman from the admin office. There were a few seconds of hesitation before she cleared her throat and spoke.

'Jodie Brown did attend this school,' she paused and smiled, 'but it was a long time ago.' I could feel myself smile, despite everything. I opened the car door and stepped out. She was much smaller than me but kept her back perfectly straight, making the difference seem less.

'Do you ... do you remember her?' I asked eagerly. 'Jodie's my wife.' I added, so she wouldn't think I was some sort of psycho; that she'd caught me grabbing her colleague's arm earlier probably wasn't helping my case.

'Oh aye, she was an excellent student,' she coughed. 'One of the best this school has had,' she pressed her hand to her heart. Though I'd known Jodie was smart, she hadn't seemed particularly academic. 'She represented this school in many competitions, different ones too: Maths, English, Science.' It was a strange feeling of relief to hear about Jodie's youth. The lady moved around the car, and I followed her.

Some pupils were walking down the street and waved. 'Morning, Miss!'

She waved back.

'Did you teach her?' I wanted to keep the conversation going.

'Yes, I was Jodie's old Maths teacher. I'm Ms Farrel. She was a wonderful pupil, terribly bright. Shame it was so awful for her at home with her parents. I never felt happy with the fact we couldn't help her.'

'What about her parents? She told me they were never there, she was brought up by a nanny.' Ms Farrel stopped and took a good look at me.

'Never there?' she frowned, perplexed. 'What nanny?'

'What do you mean?'

Ms Farrel stood in front of me, hesitating as she had after she'd knocked on my car window.

'She never told you?'

'Told me what?' My heart started to pound harder.

'Maybe I shouldn't say anything, I'm sorry,' she waved her hand. I took a photo from the pocket and showed her the wedding picture of me and Jodie, the one where Jodie had jumped on my back. She squinted, looking at the picture. Then her face lit up.

'Oh, Jodie! Oh, she looks wonderful, what a beautiful dress! You both look so happy.' She touched the photo with one finger smiling.

I watched her face. I knew this was my only chance. 'Please. Can you help me?'

Ms Farrel sighed. 'Well, no one knew how bad things really were.' She spoke slowly, thinking about events that happened so long ago. 'There were rumours some of the girls saw bruises on Jodie's body in the changing rooms, but she never admitted anything. She would often stay late after school and do her homework, and we would end up talking, just the two of us. But as hard as I tried to convince her it was safe to talk to me about anything, she never said a word about what was happening at home. She had explanations for everything, and then she would change the subject.'

'Jesus, do you think her parents were abusing her?'

She was quiet for a moment and watched me. Quietly she said, 'I know that look when someone's afraid to go home.' I swallowed.

I hadn't expected this, Jodie being abused by her parents. Things were bad, yes, but this was a completely new level. Jodie had always seemed so happy, I'd never thought that she might have had a traumatic childhood. Not wanting to talk about her parents made sense, and them sending her money too. Probably feeling shitty about how they'd treated their daughter. My heart raced, knowing she'd had to carry this by herself.

'Anyway, how is she?' Ms Farrel's eyes brightened. I could tell she was excited to learn about Jodie's life as much as I was curious to learn about Jodie's past.

'She's an artist!' I said proudly. 'She is in the process of opening an art gallery.'

'An artist.' Ms Farrel pressed both of her hands against her heart again. 'Well, isn't that a lovely surprise!' That made her happy.

'We both live in London, surrounded by a lot of friends, we are very happy.' She smiled. 'But she's missing, and I'm trying to find her.' My lips started to tremble as I heard my words.

'Missing? Oh, dear God,' her hands covered her mouth.

'She came to Edinburgh from London; I had reason to believe she was coming to her family home.' Ms Farrel didn't say anything. 'I just need to know where her parents lived and those ladies weren't helpful.'

'Ellena and Sophie?' she paused for a second. 'Yes, they can be ... difficult sometimes.'

'Could you help me? Could you somehow access the database for me?'

'I'm sorry, but I shouldn't really–' She shook her head, and I interrupted quickly.

'She is in a very dark place, and I'm afraid she might hurt herself.' The lie came from nowhere, but I couldn't stop; I was so close.

'Jodie? Oh no,' she opened her eyes slowly. 'How? Why?'

'Our son died, and she's absolutely despondent.' I'm such a pig.

'Oh my God. I'm so sorry,' Ms Farrel gently placed her hand on my shoulder.

'I ... I can't lose her too.' Even though all of it was a lie, I felt a shiver go through me. For a moment, I believed it.

Ms Farrel stared at me, silently shaking her head, unsure what to say.

'Poor lass.' She lowered her gaze at the floor, eventually. For a few minutes, no one said a word, but her face was determined when she finally looked back up at me. 'Let me see what I can do.'

I waited patiently by the car while she went back into the school. After ten minutes, the door swung open again. She had a folded sheet of paper in her hand.

'Here.' She gave me the sheet, but before I could unfold it, Ms Farrel placed her hands on mine. 'In '96, at the end of summer, Jodie came to see me.'

'To say goodbye?'

'Yes. I was worried about not seeing her through the long summer break; I'd told her that if she needed anything, or if she was scared of her parents, she should come back to school and ask for me.'

'And?'

'She replied - *I should set an example by leaving my own abusive husband.*' My eyes widened. What? 'I don't know how she knew - I never told her anything about it, but that day was the day I left my husband. When I came back to school the following September to tell her, she had already dropped out and moved on.' She paused, her eyes bright. 'If you see her, please say thank you.'

I unfolded the sheet and there it was, Jodie Brown's Alumni record. It had her home address and parents' names. David and Kathleen Brown.

CHAPTER 9

I sat in the car long after saying goodbye, clutching Jodie's alumni records. It was hard to believe that she went as far as changing her parent's names; she'd done everything she could to keep her past hidden. After her teacher's explanation, it was clear why she didn't want me to know. I was sad that she hadn't felt she could trust me with this information after we'd spend so much of our lives together. Maybe she just wanted to forget the past.

The biggest question remained - why did Jodie come back to Edinburgh? I couldn't believe she'd come to visit her parents because she missed them. Did she need more money? The GPS was now displaying directions to her parents' real address, the destination – twelve minutes away. What would I find there? Her parents must have moved out long ago. I could only hope that the new owners might have something to tell me.

I used the car's phone system to call Theo. He answered straight away.

'Mate, you're joking. A fake address?' He squeezed in a few words as I unloaded two days worth of stress and emotion.

'Yes. Jodie planned everything to ensure I'd never meet her parents. In a moment of desperation, I called Amy and she managed to remember the high school Jodie went to.'

'Ten points go to Amy Hale for providing crucial information in the time of desperation!' He tried to sound like a presenter on a gameshow. I chuckled, appreciating that he was trying to lighten my mood.

'Anyway...' I paused, waiting for him to become serious. 'I went to the school, and after a few failed attempts I was able to get her records. So guess what.'

'What?'

'Derek and Denise Brown turned out to be David and Kathleen Brown'

'Er. Why? Why did she hide them from you?'

'I think.' I stopped myself, unsure if Jodie, who had for so long tried to hide this secret from me, would be happy to share it with Theo. I continued. 'I think they were abusive.'

'No way. They hit her?'

'Yes.' Every time I thought of them hitting Jodie, my blood boiled. 'I can't *wait* to meet those sons of bitches.'

'Bloody hell.' I imagined him shaking his head, thinking about anyone laying a finger on Anneli. None of us spoke for a while.

'I'm going to the last address the school had. I doubt

that they would still be there after twenty years, but could you do me a favour and just check for me; find out who owns the property, try to locate any information about where they moved – anything, please.'

'Leave it with me, mate.' He sounded excited to help, wanting to be there for me as I had been for him when Laura passed away.

'I appreciate it.'

'Don't mention it. I love you, Ethan, I hope you know that.'

'I do.' I smiled and hung up the phone quickly, so Theo wouldn't hear my voice crack.

The GPS led me to a suburb called Niddrie. Two teenagers were urinating on the wall of a corner shop, their stare following me as I drove by. Something wasn't right - I was only two minutes away, and this neighbourhood was getting rougher with every turn. Ripped bin bags spread across the street, the wind blowing the contents into someone's front garden. A woman pushing a pram stared too; as if they all knew I didn't belong here.

My plan was simple. Check out the property and find out if the people who lived there had any information on the previous owners.

'Your destination is on the left,' The GPS announced in its cheerful, robotic voice.

As I stopped the car, I leaned forward to get a better look through the rear window. It wasn't what I'd been expecting to see. It wasn't glamorous, expensive or well maintained. In fact, it was a bit of a shithole. I imagined it must have been a very different place twenty years ago when Jodie had lived here. Now someone else had taken over - the pretty green wall had faded, the chipped roof tiles hadn't been repaired. A storm had loosened the fence, and now it wobbled slightly in the breeze.

I stepped out of the car, locking it behind me, and walked across the road to push the gates open. They creaked, making the fence tilt inwards. It wasn't clear if anyone lived here, but I knocked anyway. Nothing. I knocked again. More silence. The streets were almost empty in this neighbourhood; every third house was abandoned. As I closed the gates behind me, I glanced back once more, in time to see a curtain twitch on the second floor. I kept my gaze steady for a few minutes, but the curtain remained still. It had probably been my imagination.

While sitting in the car, I couldn't stop looking at this sad house. The house where Jodie and her parents had once lived. I put the radio on and waited for Theo to call me back. Music hummed from the speaker while I looked at the old alumni record again. It had a black-and-white photo of Jodie attached; she would have been no more than 14 or 15 years old in it. Her smile hadn't changed after all these years. It reminded me of the time we first met on a college campus in Leeds.

It was the last day of September in 1996; the girls were still wearing colourful summer dresses. I was sitting under a tree reading *GamesPro* magazine, waiting for Theo to grab a chocolate bar from the canteen. We had celebrated his brother's birthday the weekend before and his parents had given him *'Resident Evil'* so we had played it all night, shooting zombies in a huge mansion. The following day Theo and I had pooled our money to buy the magazine. The magazine which had led Jodie to talk to me.

'Have you played the game already?' A voice came from behind me; soft and enthusiastic. I stopped reading as soon as I realised the question was meant for me; slightly annoyed that a stranger was interrupting. When I turned my head, the sun shone directly into my eyes so that I had to shift to see who it was. That was the first time I saw Jodie. Her long blonde hair in a pigtail; she held her books in front of her, covering the thin jumper. Her faded blue jeans looked very fashionable back then. It took me slightly longer than usual to start speaking.

'You know this game?' I frowned.

'Of course, I do! God! Chris' playthrough was so much harder than Jill's, but I loved it!' It surprised me just how enthusiastic she was. Not many girls I knew were interested in video games, let alone horror. 'I was sad when the game finished. Now I'm playing Mortal Kombat 3.'

My body twitched when I heard the name of the game. 'You play Mortal Kombat too?' I asked slowly, just in case I'd misheard. She nodded. 'That's like my favourite game!' I shouted, maybe a bit too excited. 'Finish himmmm!' I said in a deep rumbling voice. Jodie giggled.

'Well, maybe one day I can play you.' Her smile turned into a cheeky grin as she walked away.

She knew I was fascinated. My heart pounded as she walked away, turning back to see if I was still watching. When Theo returned from the canteen, I told him about her, saying that if you gave Lara Croft two books instead of her handguns, that would be Jodie.

Voices from outside woke me up; I took a deep breath and stretched my hands up, touching the soft fabric roof of the car. Looking at the forest ahead - illuminated by the last of the sunlight - I guessed it was around eight o'clock. The golden hour. The chatter of two older people who had parked next to the house had woken me. They were both around sixty, both wearing denim jeans and oversized sweatshirts. The man had a belly so big that he barely fit behind the wheel, and he squeezed out grunting, slammed the door of the ageing blue Toyota, then went to the trunk and took out some plastic grocery bags.

'Move your fat ass!' He shouted at the older woman - he wasn't trying to be playful. She waved her hand and turned away, clearly infuriating him, and he took a few of the bags and made his way to the front gate, kicking it open. The fence wobbled, straightening itself after a few seconds. The woman followed him, struggling silently with the remainder of the shopping.

My phone rang, loud over the car speakers. The screen said 'Theo'.

'Did you find anything?'

'It was easy. I paid £3 to access the title register for the address you sent me.'

'And?' I waited to hear the good news.

'It says it still belongs to Kathleen Brown.'

The old man opened the door to his house and turned on the light. The woman followed him in, and just before closing the door, she looked at me for a minute, as if to warn me she knew I was there.

'No way,' I couldn't believe Theo's words. I almost wanted him to tell me he was messing with me. 'I guess I've just seen my parents-in-law.'

'And?' He waited for my answer patiently.

'Their house looks like it's about to collapse. They're not rich at all.'

'Could it be just a facade?'

'No. No, it can't,' I exhaled deeply. 'Let's just say I'm not looking forward to meeting them.' It was true; they were part of a world with different rules.

'Let me know how it goes, ok? Kick their ass.' He wanted to put a funny twist on it, but I was having trouble seeing the humour. Though there had been many different ways I'd imagined Jodie's parents, this wasn't one of them. It was no secret that her family had troubles. But I'd imagined they were people who thought they were better than everyone else. People who only flew first class and drank the finest scotch. I imagined them used to being treated like kings, having an aura of entitlement. But the people who just walked into that house were people whose entire lives had been dedicated to following the simplest path.

I locked the car and walked hesitantly towards the house. The fluorescent light filtering through the small, dirty window set in the front door gave the place a slightly spooky air. After a moment of hesitation, I approached the door and knocked. The muffled conversation from inside the house stopped suddenly. The sound of footsteps grew louder, and as it reached me, the door opened just enough to show David's head.

'Yes?' He had a deep voice, a bald head, and unruly eyebrows. He was glaring at me, teeth clenching, challenging me to answer him. I had disturbed him. But I was angry, now - I knew he had hit my wife, the woman that I loved. Scumbag.

'Hello, do you happen to be David Brown?'

'Who's asking?'

'I'm Ethan Page, your daughter's husband,' and with that, I raised the wedding picture. He glanced at it dismissively.

'I don't know who you are. Good day.' He tried to slam the door, but I'd already blocked it with my foot. His eyes narrowed, dangerously.

'David, I was just wondering when you last saw your daughter?' I spoke with cheery confidence, not letting my feelings show.

'Move away from the door or I'll break your leg and you'll have to drag yourself away to your *fancy* car.'

'If you break my leg - you'd be charged with assault.' His hand was forming slowly into a fist as his breath intensified. 'It's not worth it, David. I just want to ask a few questions.'

'Go fuck yourself you bloody eejit–'

'It's fine. I can wait until you're ready to talk, but I'm

not leaving until I speak to you or your wife.'

'I'm going to call the police!' Why didn't he want to talk to me?

'And tell them what? That someone is outside your house, eating a sandwich in their car? I'm not the one threatening to break your leg. I'm just here to talk.'

David slammed the door in my face, and I just managed to withdraw my foot in time. Fuck this! I exhaled deeply. I could hear Kathleen whispering inside, then footsteps. I didn't know what the hell I should do. I turned around to walk back to the car when the door opened again.

'You've got five minutes, and then you're out,' he muttered, not looking at me, and opened the door slowly. Kathleen was standing right there holding a large, very grumpy-looking German Shepherd. I lifted my hands - slowly and carefully - and put on a very big smile.

'You must be Kathleen!' Don't think about the dog. 'It is so great to meet you!' I walked towards her, and the dog snarled. I stopped, still smiling. Hands still up. Kathleen nodded, ignoring my hand and stepped deeper into the kitchen. David closed the door behind me, and it was now four of us in their old dim kitchen with the smell of rotting wood.

A bare fluorescent light glared over the small table in the middle of the room. There were only two chairs.

'You can sit here,' David said, pointing to one. I sat down, my shoes sticking to the floor. Kathleen walked behind me to grab a dirty water bowl for the dog, filling it in the sink.

'So?' David asked, sitting down in front of me, resting one of his arms on the back of the chair.

'Right. When did you last see your daughter?'

'Her?' It was an ugly sound, barely a word. 'I haven't seen her since she walked out on us twenty years ago.' His fists were still clenched; he wasn't trying to hide his anger, now.

'And what about you, Kathleen?' I turned in my chair to meet her eyes. They were dead, expressionless.

'Kathleen hasn't seen her either.' David answered for her, and Kathleen turned away to unpack the groceries.

I sighed. 'Have you been in any contact with her since then, or–'

'No.' David interrupted.

'Ok. And Kathleen?' I turned back again.

'She hasn't been in contact with her either.'

'I asked your wife, David.' I turned around to meet David's stare, and watched his blood pressure rise another notch.

'No. I haven't been in contact with Jodie,' Kathleen said, quietly, behind me. Her voice was soft, musical.

'Thank you.'

'Any *more* questions?' asked David, resentfully. All I wanted was to ask him what it felt like to beat a little girl, his own daughter. I dug my nails into my thigh, as uninvited images played in my imagination.

'Have you been sending any money to Jodie since she left?'

'Why would I?' David seemed surprised by this. Of

course he wasn't sending any money. They barely seemed to be scraping through life as it was. So where was Jodie's money coming from?

'So, that's a *no* then?'

'Aye.' David glared at me.

I turned again to look at Kathleen, but she hid her face from me, pushing rubbish into an already overflowing bin. There was a pause.

'No, I didn't send her any money.' She placed the dog's bowl on the floor and kicked it into the corner, water splashing on the floor. I turned back to look at David, looking at his watch, counting the few remaining minutes. The dog stared at me, waiting for his master's command to rip my throat out. He completely ignored the water that Kathleen had given him.

'Are you aware that Jodie's a millionaire?' I lied now, trying to get some sort of reaction, anything. David crossed his hands and shook his head once.

'No.'

I expected at least a flash of surprise, but he gave me nothing. Time for a change of tactics.

'What are you two into? I'd love to get to know you better.'

'None of your goddamn business,' David stroked the dog, which was growling, now, a continuous low noise. Kathleen walked past me, carrying a two-liter plastic milk carton. She opened the fridge.

'Would you like tea?' she started at my face, almost as if she was trying to memorise it. The light in the kitchen was dim and I could barely make out her facial features, but there was no doubt that she was Jodie's mother.

'Yes, please I–'

'The five minutes are up,' David stood suddenly, knocking his chair back.

Kathleen closed the fridge door and walked deeper into the long kitchen. I tried to follow her with my eyes, but instead I noticed the fridge. It was old and made unpleasant sounds. A magnetic Edinburgh ornament held a piece of paper that listed "cheese, tomatoes, orange juice, milk" in neat handwriting. It was undoubtedly Jodie's handwriting. She was here somewhere, being held by these people.

I jumped up. 'Can I use your bathroom, please, before I go?' David frowned. 'I'm bursting, and it's a long journey back.' David and Kathleen exchanged looks. God knew what they were thinking.

David turned to face me. 'After that you're done here, do you understand?' I nodded in agreement, and David pointed back down the hall. I walked slowly, passing what looked like a living room; the powerful stink of stale beer hitting me. An empty bird cage sat by the television. The bathroom door was open further down, but I grabbed the bannister and started climbing the stairs, slowly. The old tread creaked slightly.

'The toilet isn't upstairs.' David's voice came from behind me, firm and suspicious. I turned around. His expression was openly hostile now.

'Thank you, I was a bit confused.' I laughed uncomfortably, but he didn't smile. I stepped down the few stairs and walked into the bathroom. As I turned around to close the door both David and Kathleen were right there, staring at me, the dog licking David's hand. I shut the door in their face.

'What the actual fuck?' I whispered to myself. That man was fucking nuts. I just wanted to get Jodie out of here, as far as possible away from him. I lifted the toilet cover loudly, deliberately making noise, and the smell of urine filled the bathroom. I leant towards the half-open window to get a breath of clean air. The window wasn't big, but I managed to squeeze my shoulders out, as far away as possible from that horrendous smell. Their back garden was in even worse condition than the front. I took another deep breath, looking at the sky as my eyes caught an open window on the first floor. Next to it, there was a drainpipe leading up. The idea formed in my head. Too crazy to attempt, surely. But this was my only chance. Either I leave the bathroom and get kicked out, back to London, or I attempt the climb and maybe save Jodie.

I opened the window as far as it would go, then squeezed silently through it. Before standing up, I coughed loudly in the direction of the bathroom door, to make it sound like I was still doing my business. I gripped the drainpipe and stood on my toes on the windowsill, grasping the brackets, and pulled up. My feet slid - I had no grip on my shoes - and my hands got tired almost instantly. I reached for a mount closer to the first-floor window and used all the strength I had to pull myself up. I swung my leg and placed it on the windowsill, then carefully, hanging on to the side of the window frame, I pulled my body inside.

I presumed I was in David and Kathleen's bedroom. Though the window was open, it still smelled like laundry left too long in a washing machine. Staying on all fours to avoid creaking boards, I crawled slowly along the floor, proud of my stealth skills. I checked under the bed before moving closer to the door to the hall. An old exercise machine of some sort stood in the corner, covered with years of dust. The door to the room was ajar, and I could hear David whispering something to Kathleen downstairs.

My hands started to shake uncontrollably as the reality of what I was doing sunk in. I left their room, staying in a half crouch, carefully placing each step to prevent floorboards creaking. The door ahead was slightly ajar, and I peered inside. It looked like a storage room filled with dusty jars and bags. At the end of the hall, the other room's door was wide open. The moon shone brightly outside in the fading light, framed in the room's window, calling me towards it. Apart from David and Kathleen whispering downstairs, the house was dead silent.

It was a combination living room, bedroom and junkroom; there were quite a few boxes, a two-seat sofa which faced nothing, a single bed with a duvet, and something that looked like an old picnic blanket. Jodie was surely here, but where? Was she hiding? If she was, she could be anywhere; crouching in her parents' wardrobe, maybe in one of these boxes in front of me.

I had an idea: I took my phone out and dialled Jodie's number, and three things happened at once. First, my phone made a soft ringing sound; second, I heard a phone vibrating from behind the door, only a few centimetres away; and third, David's voice. Right behind me.

'The fuck are you doing in here!' His face was red, veins popping in his forehead, eyes wide, and ready to attack. I'd jumped back in surprise and the door to the room slammed shut, leaving me and David on the landing. 'Kath! Release Buck!'

I shouted Jodie's name. As David leapt towards me, I tried to open the door, but it was either locked or jammed. I managed to bang on it twice before David's hands gripped my shoulders and slammed me into the floor. He stood between me and the locked door.

I knew now that he was lying, and Jodie was here, in that room. So close to me. I slowly stood up again.

'Get out of the way, David!' He spat at me. In any other situation, I would have been horrified, but this close to finding Jodie and I was flying high on adrenaline. I took a few quick steps back and rushed towards him. Gathering all my strength and power in the few meters of space I had, using my hands and head, I crashed into him. He fell back, and the door burst open, both of us rolling on the floor. The window, closed when I had first seen it, was now open.

David was on his knees but I was up faster, and I used the extra second to leap towards the window, and I saw her. Jodie had jumped to the ground, unmistakably Jodie. She was wearing her yellow hoodie, gym pants, and trainers.

'Jodie!' I screamed as she looked up to me, her eyes meeting mine, and I could see the tears. I read her lips as she silently mouthed *I'm sorry.*

A sudden, excruciating pain in my left calf brought my attention back into the room, and I collapsed to my knees. Buck had his teeth excruciatingly deep in my leg, and he maintained eye contact as he dragged me backwards. Kathleen stood in the corridor, now, and David sat on the floor panting, watching the dog attack me.

I gathered my strength and dragged myself slowly to my feet. Using the radiator for balance, I kicked the dog as hard as I could and heard a satisfying yelp. It let go. There was no fear now. I turned around and faced David and Kathleen, both horrified at what I'd just done to their dog. David lunged towards me, screaming wildly. 'You cunt!'

Before he could reach me, I ducked, and with one fluid, instinctive motion I hit David hard on the nose with my open palm. It cracked under my hand, and I knew I'd broken it from the way he instantly recoiled, grabbing his face. I'd never hit anyone in my life, but I wasn't stopping now; I kicked him in the stomach for good measure. It felt good to see him defenceless.

'That's for raising your hand against your child, you prick!' The words poured out of me, and with them the raw anger.

'How dare you!' Kathleen yelled, awkwardly slapping the back of my head. I pushed her back towards the wall and raised my fist, and saw how she lifted her hands to defend herself. Her forearms were bruised and scarred, and I could see her frightened face, and the marks there. Jodie was not David's only victim.

I had suddenly run out of anger. David was rolling on the floor, screaming and blaming Kathleen, who was sobbing desperately. I felt bad for the dog, and for her. They'd both been unfortunate enough to end up here, with this man.

When I stepped into the street the last of the evening light was fading. I ran to the back of the house, trying to figure out which way Jodie went. Through the dilapidated houses, a small yellow dot was disappearing into the darkness of the forest up ahead. Was that her? The trees were a few hundred meters from the house. No time to think. I sprinted in that direction, my breath coming in ragged, broken bursts. The wound on my foot broke open, it stung with every single step, but I kept the pace steady.

The forest was dark, with hardly any sunlight reaching the ground. I ran into it and kept on running for a minute before leaning against a tree for support. This was it for me; I couldn't go on. The only positive was that Jodie's fitness level wasn't as high as mine. Which meant she would have struggled to run much further. Was she hiding? I was still, calming my breath, preparing, if necessary, for the next burst of running.

I tried to listen to my surroundings; the wind rustling in the leaves, the crickets chirping. My eyes were slowly adjusting to the darkness, but there was nothing to see. Just eerie shadows created by the trees. As I had done in the house, I placed every footstep carefully, trying not to give away my location. But every movement caused the leaves to rustle; every second step seemed to snap a small branch.

I walked around the trees slowly, systematically searching the area. I took my phone and rang Jodie again. Her phone was off. I moved from one tree to another so slowly that I made no more noise than the leaves rustling in the wind. I reached another tree, and drifted around, and there she was. Jodie stood silently in front of me.

CHAPTER 10

The forest was quiet, the trees casting long shadows that stretched into the darkness. A low light obscured Jodie's face, just her silhouette visible, outlined by the soft glow of the moon.

Standing right here, seeing her in front of me, I felt like I'd won. I'd done it. I was thrilled that she was safe and unharmed, but the anger still remained - for what she had put me through. The game was up and we both knew it. She had a lot of explaining to do; I wanted answers.

I stepped forward as my eyes adjusted to the night. She was staring at her trainers. I took one step closer, but she was so still, she seemed to be an illusion, standing in the darkness. Neither of us spoke.

I moved closer. I could reach out and touch her, but I didn't. 'Jodie?'

'Why did you come here?' She lifted her head, revealing

her tearful eyes.

'Because you left, without explanation.'

'I needed to be by myself,' she was clenching her fists now.

'You disappeared the day after your outburst.' As I spoke the words brought back bad memories. 'Why didn't you text me back? A simple message like: "I need some space, please don't be worried, love Jodie," would have made all the difference.'

She continued standing there, fists clenched.

'I'm sorry,' she finally spat out. 'I messed up; I should have taken your feelings into account.'

I couldn't remember the last time Jodie apologised. 'You need to tell me what's going on. Do you have any idea what I've been through?'

Jodie watched in horror as I took another step forward.

'Ethan, please trust me. I'm doing the best I can. I am *sorry*,' she grabbed my hands, held them tight.

'Talk to me! Let me help you.'

'Please. I love you so much, I will do anything else you ask but don't make me do this,' she pulled her hands back to hug them around herself. Jodie's teeth chattered though the night was warm.

'No, Jodie. If you want this marriage to work, you have to talk.' At first, I thought she hadn't heard me, then Jodie fell to her knees crying. I knelt next to her, and this time, I took her hands.

'Jodie, I respected your privacy when you said you didn't want to talk about your parents, or about your infertility.'

I took a deep breath. 'But after this, after you lied to Amy about this Stacey girl, then me finding out the truth about your parents,' I grabbed her by her shoulders, 'after finding out that you never sent them an invitation to our wedding! And then there's the money. *Where is the money coming from, Jodie?*'

'You won't be able to cope if I tell you the truth.'

'You have to trust me. We have to trust each other.'

She was still avoiding my eyes. 'Tell me!'

'No!'

'Tell me, Jodie!'

'*Please* no!'

'Jodie!' After a pause, she looked into my eyes.

'I won the lottery.' She wiped her tears and took a deep breath.

'What do you mean? I won the lottery–'

Jodie interrupted. 'No! I won the lottery… twice.' She repeated it, slower, more clearly this time, leaving no space for another interpretation.

'When? How much?'

'The first time when I was 16 and then again when I was 26.'

'Come on,' I snapped at her. She was playing with me again.

'I'm telling you the truth.'

'You are more likely to be struck by the lightning than win the lottery. Winning it twice would put you in the history books. Tell me the truth.'

She lifted her eyes and looked at me. 'I have the ability,

to... to go back. To change the future.' I snorted, but she didn't smile. The words repeated in my head. Was she serious? I wanted to laugh, but I smiled. It didn't make any sense. Jodie saw me smile and her jaw clenched, eyes fixed on mine.

'You predict things?' Hoping for some clarification. Jodie shot up and looked down at me.

'No! I go back, to *fix things*!'

Why did she keep saying that? A minute ago, I'd screamed at her to tell me the truth, and now I was kneeling beside her like a guilty puppy, trying to understand how this was supposed to explain anything. Was she inventing this story just so she could hide the source of her wealth?

Jodie's face slowly relaxed, the muscles releasing one by one. 'I can go back in time, Ethan. Sometimes I take advantage of it, like the times I - and later you - won the lottery.'

Those winning lottery numbers on the card inside the frame in our flat in Bermondsey, it hadn't been me who came up with them. I remember Jodie had told me to start with nine because it's her lucky number. 'Use twenty-one because we spent the night at the casino playing blackjack,' Jodie had said. 'Thirty-three because three is your favourite number, isn't it?' She told me which numbers to put on the ticket. I had never given it much thought; I'd been overwhelmed with winning.

'Is that supposed to explain everything?' I asked.

'Yes.'

'But it doesn't! It's insane.' For a brief moment, I had

almost believed her.

'What do you want to know?' She sounded defeated.

I stood up slowly. I wasn't sure how to continue this conversation. Jodie got up as well and turned away from me, walking a few steps, towards the moon.

'How does it work?'

She spoke quickly. 'How do you maintain your balance when you walk?'

'Excuse me?'

'Try to explain something that you've done as long as you can remember, something you can't imagine your life without, like walking, breathing, understanding a language.'

'I don't know,' I said. 'Have you always had this,' I hesitated - '... this ability?' This was insane.

'I guess the earliest memory of me using it was trying to find a hiding place from my father. I had done something bad, and he was angry. He'd be stomping towards the closet to get his belt, the one with the metal buckle. The first time, I tried hiding under the bed but he just dragged me out. I remember screaming, and then the next time, I hid in the closet. He would search under the bed, in the bathroom, storage room, and the closet. He would slap me; I would scream, go back and hide again, better this time.' As I walked towards her, she gazed at the sky. 'After that, I used my ability to get myself out of trouble, instead of hiding. I would try to prevent him from getting angry. Well, that's what I thought I was doing, anyway. The truth is no matter what I did, I always got punished.'

'What do you mean?'

She turned back to me only for a second and then turned around to gaze at the waxing moon, low on the horizon now. 'When I would bring good grades home, he would call me a smartarse; if my marks were bad, he would call me a dumbarse. If I decided to tidy the house, he would say I was complaining and I didn't like the way we lived. If I didn't clean, then I'd be called a selfish bitch.' Jodie took a deep breath. 'When I tried to tell him he was being unreasonable, I'd get slapped or worse. Sometimes, he just locked me in a tiny cupboard for a few hours.' Her body was shaking even more now. 'The truth is, when I was younger, I tried to help my parents, to make things better for us, but I was naive; what I didn't understand then is that it wasn't possible to fix anything, no matter how much I tried. My contribution … my real contribution to that household was to be someone he could humiliate, for him to put me down so he could feel better about himself. Nothing else I did mattered.'

'Jesus Christ.' I walked towards her, trying to hug her, but she pulled away, holding me back with her hand.

'When I got slightly older, I realised that the best thing I could do was to keep myself out of that place as much as possible. But when I started spending too much time at my friend's house, their parents figured it out and called social services. I was taken away and put in an orphanage, which was all the more horrible. People there were trying to look after me, talking to me as if I was sick, like I was broken. They said I had to stay until I turned eighteen. I only wanted to get the hell out. So I went back to when I was younger again, and learned to be more clever. I hid all my bruises and had a lie ready every time someone would ask me about them. The one that worked best was that I was an aspiring dancer, and I had been bumping into things in the house while practicing.'

'So you can ... move through time?'

'I can only go back in time, not forward.'

I was trying to understand what she said while Jodie continued.

'School was easy; I repeated the lessons as much as I wanted 'til I knew the subject by heart. If I didn't know the question during the exam, I would ask my teacher for the answer before the test. The hardest times were when I had to go back home to my parents. Sometimes I would relive the same hour after school over and over again, too scared to open the front door. When I found the courage to go in, the shouting would begin. I would travel back in time and try again. I would act sadder, to make him feel guilty. But the outcome never changed. The best thing I could do was to sneak into my room and not leave until the early morning. I ate food that I bought at school, making sure to hide it because if I was caught eating anywhere but the kitchen, that would be another unforgivable mistake.'

Not in a million years would I have imagined Jodie's childhood like this.

'Do you know what the worst thing was?'

I shook my head. I knew nothing any more.

'My father would think he only hit me once, and yes, my body, in theory, would have only have been hit once, but I experienced it over and over and over again, each time I went back to make it better. I understand this now, but I exchanged the physical scars with mental trauma. Trying to make it better just made the outcome worse.'

'Jodie, I am so sorry.' She stepped back. She was keeping a distance between us, on the verge of bursting into tears again. I gave her time to collect herself.

'I waited till my sixteenth birthday and then convinced my parents I could find a job in a coffee shop and pay rent. David seemed thrilled - me finally doing something for him. It was the happiest I had ever seen my father.'

'But,' I said, already feeling what was coming. The pain vanished as if into thin air, and she became cocky.

'As soon as I got my bank card, I coerced an older boy at the school to help me, to get-'

'Coerced how?'

She just smiled and waved her hand, eyes still red. 'Knowing the future can be very scary for certain people. I gave him a winning lottery ticket, and every month, he would send me a payment. I let him keep 10% till I turned 18.'

'So your parents never had-'

'Money?' She asked in high-pitched voice. 'Nooo. As soon as I could survive on my own, I ran away and moved to Leeds - and started my new life.'

'And then you met me...' My voice faded.

There was a slight pause. 'No, I met Gary before you; he was my first boyfriend. About three and a half years into our relationship, I realised I had made a mistake, so went

118

back in time and tried again. It was only then that I met you. You were such a sweet boy with a gorgeous smile.

'So you were older when we met, even though we were both sixteen?'

'I was around twenty, in my head.'

My jaw was wide open now. It was all too much to comprehend. I let out the breath I'd been holding. I wanted to ask questions but was unable to put anything into words. The whole thing was ridiculous.

'Jodie, you can't expect me to believe this!' Stepping towards her again.

'I don't need you to accept any of this, Ethan. Earlier you asked a question, and I gave you an answer.' Her voice was firm now, back in control.

'I need the truth -' but she shouted over me.

'When was the last time you were injured? You go skiing at least three times a year, always off-piste, always recklessly fast.'

Theo had made the same remark a week ago. 'I'm an excellent skier.'

'How many times have you crashed your car? How many times have you burned or cut yourself while cooking? When was the last time you sprained an ankle? Do you think spotting your colorectal cancer early was just a coincidence too?' Jodie had insisted on me checking after I had difficulty in the bathroom. I'd laughed at her for being paranoid, until the results came back.

'How long have you been doing this?'

She was silent.

I asked again, more calmly than I felt. 'How long?'

'Every time something bad happened, eventually, news would reach me. I would gather information about when and where it happened, and then, a simple phone call to that person at the right moment would be the difference between them falling off a cliff and safely reaching the campsite.'

'No,' I shook my head. This can't be real.

'Do you think losing that wealth investing in Kodak was an accident, a bad decision?' She started to lose her control again, lashing out at me, mad because I was making her talk about this.

'What do you mean?'

'I made a mistake giving you that lottery ticket. You had too much money, so you took things for granted. It bored you; you had no more passion or ambition. You needed to be brought back to earth.'

Was my entire existence fake, a carefully choreographed dance? 'Am I just supposed to accept all of this? Do you see yourself as some sort of superhero?'

'I could have been,' she turned away from me again and gazed into the distance. 'But I fell in love with you.' Her words trailed off and disappeared into the forest. Then she continued. 'I suffered so much when I was younger that I told myself I would have the perfect family when I grew up.'

'But this,' I didn't know what to call my life now, 'this life. It's fake.'

'Fake?' She turned to face me, surprised by my reaction. 'What if you had been born into wealth, inheriting billions?

Would you say that your life was fake because you were born privileged?' I wanted to interrupt, but she wouldn't let me speak, 'This is my advantage, *my privilege.* I can't ignore this power, because it's part of who I am.'

We stood in silence for several minutes, just staring at each other, not knowing how to continue.

'You said that I never hurt myself.' I spoke quietly now. She looked at me. 'But I did. I did cut my finger, the day you left. I sprained an ankle too.'

'Because I lost it.'

'Lost what?'

'I can't go back in time any more. I can no longer help you, or anyone, and that's why I left. I was so scared.'

'Jodie, but that's not a big–'

'Not a big *what?*' she spits out. '...deal?' I stared at her. 'No, Ethan, it is a pretty huge fucking deal because without my power, I can't protect anyone.'

There was a pause. 'And you decided to just leave me?'

She lifted her head again, frowning. 'Imagine you couldn't swim and someone pushed you out of a boat in the middle of a lake. The rational thing to do is float calmly on your back, just relax and float, slowly making your way to the shore. But in that moment of terror, there is no rationality. There is only panic. Obviously, the best action for me was to stay calm, stay at home, and tell you that I needed to visit my parents. But I was embarassed; the way I acted - I hit you, I screamed, I told Amy you cheated - all of that is permanent, it can't be undone. The more I hid here in Edinburgh, without my power returning, the more

I thought of the damage I'd done, and the deeper the hole became.'

'Jodie.' I rushed to her and hugged her before she could push me away. 'Don't say this. Seeing you makes me happier than anyone else in this world. I love you with all my heart.'

She covered her face with her palms, but she didn't cry. Instead, she took a deep breath, moving her hands away from her face, simply staring at me.

'Now you know everything, Ethan. What do you want to do?'

Was there anything I could do? These stories were unbelievable. But Jodie was with me, it would be fine; we could work through it.

'Let's leave this place.'

We walked out of the forest into the tall grass at the edge of the development. The only light guiding our way was the moon ahead of us, and the night air was filled with chirping crickets. We walked in sync, lifting our legs high, skimming across the sea of grass. The adrenalin was wearing off, and the pain where that dog had bitten me was getting worse.

'Do your parents know?' I asked.

'No.' She gazed at me with the hint of a smile. I thought about it some more, still finding it hard to begin to believe what she'd told me in the past hour. But now, she said her powers were gone. We would have to learn to live together again.

'What about Stacey?' I asked casually.

'Stacey?' It took her a minute to register what I was asking. 'The yoga teacher?'

I nodded. 'Amy...' I shrugged my shoulders like it shouldn't be a surprise. Jodie rolled her eyes as if she didn't care, but I saw her tense. I felt like I knew what was coming.

'Stacey was someone who you thought was worth cheating on me with.' She kept walking, her pace even, not looking at me.

'Because you think you saw me in the future with her?' She was silent. 'Jesus!' This couldn't be true. I wouldn't cheat on Jodie.

I stared into the long grass illuminated, by the moonlight. Since I had met Jodie twenty years ago, I'd never even considered cheating on her. I couldn't believe that this was something I was going to do. Stacey's face in the coffee shop earlier this week flashed before my eyes, her lean body, her laughter, her cheekiness with her friend. She had a gorgeous smile. Very inviting body language. Yes, of course she was charming and attractive. But aside from admiring her from a distance, there was nothing I wanted from her. The thought of leaving Jodie for some bimbo was foreign, almost sickening to me.

'Well, Amy, thinks I am cheating on you now.'

'I'm sorry, Ethan. I panicked. Amy was scared for me, I shouldn't have said anything.'

'You could have said *anything* else.'

'I was afraid she would call you, let you know I was staying at hers. I couldn't explain the truth to her. Can you imagine?' Jodie imitated a dumb bimbo. '*Hey Aims, so you know that thing about me going back in time? I can't do it any more, but the last thing I saw was Ethan making out with this slut, the home-wrecker Stacey from Yoga.'* She took a deep breath and rolled her eyes, flicking her hair with a hand. *'So, anyway, I'm going to run away because I don't want to deal with this mess right now. Catch you later, babes.'* She turned to me with her head tilted to one side.

'Well, you kinda did that, just without the weird voice.'

Moonlight fell on Jodie's face, casting hard shadows, and her profile looked like one of her paintings. Magical.

'The memory of seeing you kissing Stacey will never fade. Just so you know, I'm not blaming *you* for anything. I understand the cost I pay, and it's my burden to carry, not yours.'

I didn't say a word. I wanted to say that I was sorry, but it was ridiculous. Apologising for something that hadn't happened yet, and never would? It would be like apologising for a dream.

Jodie's parents' house was now close enough to be able to make out its ugly shape. We were about fifty meters away from it. The lights were on in almost every window. My breath failed again at the thought of seeing them after everything that had happened.

'Jodie?'

'Mhm?'

'I think I broke your father's nose.' Jodie snorted with laughter in the darkness beside me.

'You did *not?*' Her eyes were wide, carrying the smile across her face. I found it strange that she was so excited about it.

'And then I kicked him, and his dog.'

'Oh my God!' She covered her mouth with her hands.

'He attacked me! I was defending myself.'

'I'm sorry. I'd told him I'd wire them both half a million pounds if they could keep you away from me.'

'Jesus Christ. Are you mad?!' She shrugged and looked at her parent's house, which was just across the road. 'I'm sorry about them. About your family.'

'David had this coming for quite some time now.' Though she was smiling, the pain inflicted by him so many years ago was still present in her eyes. Things like this might never go away, but I could be there for her now, and help her cope. I brushed my hand down the length of her arm, and when I reached her hand, I found it cold; instinctively, I squeezed it tighter to warm it up. It had been almost a week since I had held her hand.

'I care about you, Jodie, and Amy, Theo, Anneli do as well.'

We stepped on to the road; my shoes were muddy. My car was just up ahead and I continued to walk towards it, but Jodie's hand let go of mine as she stopped in front of her parents' house.

'Are you getting your stuff?' I asked.

'No, I'm going back to stay the night.' She lowered her eyes onto the ground. 'I guess he'll be pretty pissed off.' She spoke so casually, as if all that talk earlier about her being abused had never happened.

'You are not spending the night, surely. I booked a

hotel in the city.'

'No, I'm staying here.'

'What?' I shook my head in disbelief. 'What do you mean?'

'Listen, I don't know what's happening, but I have to do everything I can to at least try to get it back.'

'Get what back?'

'My power!'

'What the hell, Jodie? You can't go back in there! Jesus! Are you insane? That man! It makes no sense.'

'My power doesn't make sense either; the only thing I know is that I had it. I learned I had it while living here; I don't know if that's related to anything, but I have to try. I have to try for both of us.'

I was speechless. For a moment I stared, trying to understand if she was serious.

'Jodie, this is ridiculous. You don't need your... power, and you don't need to stay here. We love each other - that's all that matters. Come with me, and we'll get through this together... but in London. At home.'

'No, Ethan.' She was firm. 'You fell in love with a woman who looked after you, who protected you. Without that power, I'm not her. I'm not the person you fell in love with.'

'I don't care!' We stood straight, facing off on the road, staring at each other.

'If I get my power back, we can go back to normal. You won't even remember we had this conversation. You will wake up on the 20th of August and leave the house to buy groceries for lasagna. You won't cut your finger, and we'll have a beautiful lunch. Then we'll have sex, and I'll persuade you to do some painting with me. You will hesitate at first, but I'll convince you, eventually. Then in the evening, you will take me to this Clos Maggiore restaurant you booked. I'll act all surprised and hold your hand the entire time we're there. There will be a small string orchestra in the corner, and after we share dessert, you'll suggest walking home. Fairy lights will light the way, and street performers will entertain us all the way to Tower Bridge. Tired from walking, we'll jump in bed, and you will tell me how excited you are to replay Resident Evil before the release of part 7.'

Now I didn't know what to do, what to say. My vision blurred. I had listened to her stories about time traveling without believing them at first, but now it all sank in at once, crashing down around me like an avalanche. I couldn't breathe. Jodie was able to travel back in time.

She had already experienced our anniversary dinner, and she knew every detail. The perfect day I had planned was somehow tainted, somehow wrong now. How could I enjoy life knowing that no matter what I do or how much I try to surprise her, she will always be one step ahead of me? Just pretending to be surprised, like you might for a small child.

'I don't want that. I want to remember this, to remember what happened. I want us to be closer than before. I don't want a perfect fairytale version of our anniversary.' I walked towards her and took her hand in mine. 'Jodie, don't go back in there; I love you.' She tilted her head to meet my eyes; her eyes reflected the moon. She let go of my hand and took a step back.

'The thing is Ethan, you say this is what you want - but I can tell you, that's not true. I have seen much more than you have, and I know exactly what it takes to make you happy.'

I just stood there.

'I'm sorry, Ethan.' She turned away from me and walked to the house, waving her hand once. When she closed the door, I stood illuminated by the streetlight, alone, surrounded by darkness.

***

My vision was clouded, and the road signs ahead had lost their sharpness. I squeezed the steering wheel tighter with every turn I took. After I put all this effort into finding her, taking her out of that house with that horrible man she called her father, still she went back. All to keep this ability that she was using to twist our lives together. I took a turn, ignoring the signal for the pedestrian crossing, causing a few people to jump out of the way and shout. The city lights became brighter, which affected my vision even more. I had never had a car crash - maybe this was my only chance before Jodie's powers returned and she turned my life back again, turned it into the fairy tale she desired. I yelled again and again, accelerating down the street.

The sign of the bar up ahead read Juniper. Slamming on the brakes, the traction control kicked in and the seatbelt pulled harshly against my body. The car behind me beeped, wanting me to move. Flashing my middle finger from the window, I ignored the woman's gestures and parked the car right in front of the bar, taking up one-and-a-half spaces.

As I opened the door, it was wrenched out of my grip as a passing cyclist slammed into the edge, somersaulting in the air, leaving his bike on the ground next to the now-dented door. He landed on his helmet. The street stopped for a moment, then people began running towards him, and me. He sat up. I didn't move.

People stepped aside as the cyclist staggered back to his broken bike. Stepping into the light, he shook with anger.

'Idiot!'

PART II

CHAPTER 11

I wasn't thrilled to be back here. The receptionist, Emily, I think her name was, recognised me and asked if I was in for my follow-up visit. I mumbled something about it being a different issue. She pointed to the seating area and asked me to wait. My head was heavy with a hangover.

Yesterday, when I woke up in the hotel, my anger was still raw. I tried to make sense of my emotions, but it was a mess: anger, confusion, disappointment, sadness. I thought about divorce for the first time. Something that had never crossed my mind in all the time I'd known Jodie. I immediately dismissed it. I loved her, and she was my wife.

I had started drinking early in the afternoon, kept it up during the train journey to London, trying to mute the voices in my head: *'I can go back in time.' 'You won't be able to cope with the truth.' 'Idiot!'* I continued drinking once I was home, finally passing out before dark. It was the only way to make myself stop thinking. To stop overanalysing. About Stacey, Jodie and her ex Gary. To stop myself from believing that me cutting my finger, stepping on the shard and hitting that poor cyclist were all things Jodie would have fixed, if she had been there. How many times had she stopped me, just before I did something stupid? How many times had she turned back time to warn me? Truly, what kind of person was I?

This morning, I couldn't find my wedding ring.

I touched my bandaged finger where the ring was supposed to be, and thought back to when things were so much simpler - before I knew about this *superhero* I had married.

'Dr Leigh has one person before you.' The receptionist called over to me with a gentle smile. I wasn't in a hurry; in fact, I was more than happy to wait. Since Jodie had refused to come back with me, I'd spent all that time trying to understand her. When she went back to her parents' house, she did the same thing she had done at home after that episode. She just went on with whatever she thought needed to be done. It was all about her. There were too many questions waiting to be answered, but Jodie wasn't here to address any of them. Turning back time? How did it work? Was there even a point to me visiting the doctor now, if she would just erase all of this pain when she got her powers back?

The clinic was empty, and I was drifting back into unpleasant thoughts. I reached into my backpack, hoping to find an old snack bar I might have forgotten weeks earlier.

Instead, my fingers came across something hard. The green book ... I had been so preoccupied that I'd forgotten I had it with me. I took it out and held it in my hands for a few seconds before opening it. With everything Jodie had told me, this slender notebook took on a completely different meaning.

The first entry said 'Gary 22-07-1999; 02-05-03' - earlier than the day we had met. This must have been the date she went back to. And what about the second date, 02-05-03. If it was the same format as the first one - *dd/mm/yy* - then it would be the 2nd of May 2003. Could this be the date she came back from? No, that wasn't right. Jodie had told me she'd been with Gary for three and a half years. I took another look, and realised it wasn't a date, but rather a length of time. Two days, five months, and three years. That made more sense, and it meant she had left Gary sometime around Christmas Eve, 2002. *Christmas.* Jesus, that guy must have messed something up if she had decided to end their relationship and *erase it from time* at Christmas.

The next entry in Jodie's diary was *History Degree.* I couldn't think of anything for this one. Back at college I'd loved history classes - I spent days watching documentaries about World War Two and the cold war, the Great Depression, the spread of religion, and the Holocaust. Was this somehow linked with that? *Martha's Death - 2003-07-10* was another entry. Did my mother die in 2003? A chill ran down my spine. That was the day I'd proposed to Jodie. I laughed when she told me she would call my mother straight after to announce the news. Did that somehow have something to do with this entry? I squeezed the book in my arms. Losing my mother thirteen years ago, on the day I'd proposed to Jodie, would have destroyed me. Not having her at my wedding - even trying to imagine that day without her - froze my heart.

The entry *Cancer* must have been the time I was diagnosed with colorectal cancer. The doctor said I was fortunate, because it was one of the cancers middle-aged men often get - but they don't often visit the doctor in time to be treated. Once - once! - I had some bad constipation and had spent longer than usual in the bathroom. Jodie *insisted* on me checking with my doctor. I thought her reaction was weird, and I attempted to laugh it off, saying I ate too many nuts the day before - but she wasn't laughing. Jodie booked the appointment with the specialist for me, and a few weeks later I was having surgery to remove the tumour in my intestines. If she hadn't said anything, I'd probably be dead by now... resting next to my father in a graveyard in Leeds.

Is this what it's like to have a guardian angel? She was there protecting me all the time, granting me the kind of life most people dreamt of - but at the same time, did it mean I relinquished all control? If all the major decisions in my life were influenced in some way by Jodie, was I still in control of my own life?

I really wanted to see Theo and talk through all of this with him. I valued his opinion, and the last time I'd spoken to him was when I told him I'd seen my parents in law. He had messaged me a couple of times to ask me about what had happened, but I told him I wasn't in the mood to talk. He must be worried sick. Amy was also desperate for information. She'd called me four times the previous day until I'd finally sent her a message:

> *Found her.*
> *Jodie is staying with her parents, and she is fine.*

I regretted sending it as soon as I read her response.

> *Told you she was fine!*
> *You should listen to me more often, you know! xx*

Sometimes, in order to not lose my temper with Amy, I had to imagine she was my teenage daughter. Most of the time, it worked like a charm. Most of the time.

'Mr Page.' The receptionist caught my attention, leaning over the reception desk. 'Dr Leigh is waiting for you in 106.' I nodded and left the reception area.

I opened the door to Dr Leigh's office just as she was screwing the top back on a polished silver hip flask. She gave me a big smile and waved me in. Was she drunk? She raised both her hands.

'He's *baack!*' Her voice echoed in the hall. I closed the door quickly behind me, as if to protect her secret.

'I have a few interesting ways to greet my patients.' She laughed at herself and directed me towards the chair by her desk, and I sat down.

'So, Mr Page. What's bothering you *now*?'

'You mean besides this?' I pointed to the flask, which

remained proudly on her desk. It looked expensive.

'Oh?' She was surprised by my question. 'Have a sip.' She grabbed it, placing it right in front of me and nodded firmly. Did she really expect me to drink it?

'Anyway.' I couldn't help but roll my eyes. 'This dog bit my leg, and I think it's swelling up.' I pointed to the wound.

'Mmhmm,' she nodded. 'It seems like you're getting into all kinds of mischief these days.' She raised her eyebrow, and I replied with a shrug. 'What happened?' I'd really been hoping she wouldn't ask.

'I attacked the owner, and his dog bit me.' Now I had finally managed to shock Dr Leigh, and she was staring at me with a strange expression on her face. It took a few seconds for her to start speaking again.

'I see … take off your jeans and lie face down on the bed, please.' Her tone became professional.

I wasn't a timid person, but there was something about Dr Leigh. It felt as if she might be enjoying this. As I lay on the bed, which smelled of disinfectant, a pair of disposable gloves snapped and I felt her cold fingers examining my leg. I turned around to look, but she didn't raise her head. The expression on her face was intense, like she was examining something very small.

'You have an infection, and you'll need a course of antibiotics.' Her voice carried a lot of authority, 'It doesn't look fresh. Make sure you come in sooner the next time it happens.'

'"The next time?"'

She ignored me as she gathered items from her

neatly organised set of drawers and began to bandage my calf, changing the bandage on my foot as well. There was something very comforting about lying on this bed and letting Dr Leigh fix me. Somehow, I trusted her, and apart from the drinking she seemed to be a pretty good doctor.

There was something about this moment that made me think of my conversation with Jodie in the forest. She had asked me to do the same thing, to trust that she knew what was best for me, to let her help me. The only thing I was being asked to do was to let go, not intervene, and enjoy my life. Dr Leigh, in a way, was doing the same thing now.

'Job's done!' She announced in a sing-song voice. 'You can cover your ice-cream print underwear now.' I did just that, whilst shaking my head, wondering how much more uncomfortable she could make me feel.

Once I'd finished dressing, she printed a prescription for the antibiotics she had mentioned earlier.

'Once a day for seven days. Please take them and don't miss any; otherwise, things might get nasty. Do not stop the course early, even if you feel the leg is back to normal.' Then she handed me the prescription with an *NHS is here to help you* leaflet. Dr Leigh grinned as she held it towards me. 'Because of the whole *attacking* thing.'

I smiled, not being entirely sure if this was another joke. It all went into my backpack and I shook her hand. As I reached the door, I turned around.

'About your car–'

Dr Leigh raised her hand and smiled. 'Honestly, don't

worry. It was just a scratch. Forgiving you can be my good deed for today.' She bowed slightly.

'Oh, I can't allow that - I have to do something!' I wasn't going to take *no* for an answer. I was pretty sure that I could afford it.

'Honestly–'

'I insist.'

She shrugged. 'How about you take me out for dinner? I love free food.' Her eyes were avoiding mine. 'Most of my friends are married with kids, now, and they just seemed to have moved on with their lives. So I guess I'm searching for new connections.'

I stood there, my eyes fixed on hers. It felt unethical for her to offer, but surely saying *no* would be rude, especially considering how nice she'd been to me. Even if it wasn't a date, it was still strange.

'A meal?' My face must have given away my surprise.

Dr Leigh shrugged again. 'Yes, just dinner.' Her level gaze met mine.

'Oh ... ok. I guess that's fine.' The voice in my head said it wasn't fine, but I ignored it. It was just dinner. Dr Leigh smiled suddenly and turned away to use her computer. I stood there for a few seconds, still unsure of what had just happened. Was this the cue for me to go? I turned to go.

'You sure you don't want any?' She pushed the metal flask across the desk. I hesitated before picking it up. The contents sloshed slightly as I unscrewed the cap and raised it to my nose. Water.

'I take pride in my work.' Dr Leigh gave me a strange

look. 'I just like to have some fun on the side. I hope you won't judge me.'

I said that I wouldn't as I placed the flask back on her desk. 'Good day, doctor.'

'See you *soon*.'

Her smile was burning a hole in the back of my neck as I left the room.

***

Le Pont de la Tour served decent food, and on a warm Friday evening it was almost full. I was happy to get the last seat outside overlooking Tower Bridge. Though I could see it from my living room window, the bridge somehow felt different when I was on the ground and it soared overlead. It was far-reaching, graceful, royal. Hundreds of fairy lights stretched along the riverbank, illuminating the boulevard where people leant over the railing, straining to take a selfie with the bridge in the background.

Theo was late. 'Anneli decided to give herself a haircut. No surprise, it didn't go as she had planned!' He'd called to let me know, and I'd laughed. He was less amused; perhaps he wasn't looking forward to being a hairdresser for the next 20 minutes. 'I'll sort this out and drop Anneli at Amy's, be with you by half eight.' I was happy to wait and ordered another beer.

When Theo had moved to London, we'd established a tradition of meeting once a month, just the two of us. People had occasionally mistaken us for a couple, and we'd started calling them our "anniversary dinners." After Laura's death, I used this time to help Theo work through his feelings. If he wasn't in the mood to talk, we would just share a comfortable silence watching people strolling on the Thames path. It was a good tradition, and Amy was thrilled to have Anneli as a regular playmate for Emmet.

I was finally ready to talk to someone about everything that had happened. The events of the last two days had consumed me, and been emotionally exhausting. The only time I hadn't been thinking about Jodie was when I had visited the clinic this afternoon. Dr Leigh - with her jokes and her flask - was a welcome distraction. She kept me on my toes, and I admired her: she didn't care much about what other people thought of her, and she just wanted to have a bit of fun - she'd said so herself. Then I caught myself thinking about the doctor, and a chill went down my spine. I rejected the idea that I had cheated on Jodie before, but Dr Leigh had invited me to dinner and I certainly hadn't said *no.* Is this how things start? No. I'm not that kind of person.

In some sense, Dr Leigh reminded me of Jodie the first time I'd met her; she was confident in who she was, she'd made me laugh by calling me *lover boy* every time another woman would look at me. Jodie cared for me, and I missed her. I'd texted her, asking her to come back. Her reply was a long message explaining why she couldn't: she was determined to wait in the hope her power would return. I didn't know what else I could say. The idea of Jodie getting her powers back, and then simply erasing my memories and everything that had happened bothered me deeply.

I flipped Jodie's green notebook back and forth; I'd been staring at it a lot these past few days. There were still so many questions to be answered, things which couldn't be discussed over the phone. I regretted not asking her when I'd had the chance, back in the forest. It hadn't felt like the right thing at the time. The vibe was different then; Jodie was already upset, and talking about scribbles in a notebook after you've just been told she turns back time seemed ridiculous.

One of the biggest questions for me was the name, *Jill.*

| *Jill* | *11-05-2009* | *02-05-07* |

There were two reasons why this name stood out. First, why it wasn't in the section at the back with all the other names. Sure Gary wasn't there either, but I knew about him. Also, if the second date is the length of time before Jodie travelled back in time, it meant whoever Jill was, Jodie had gone back almost seven and a half years. It was an enormous gap, by far the longest when compared to the others.

Theo's hand landed suddenly on my shoulder, making me jump.

'Sorry, mate,' he said as he sat down in front of me. 'Anneli was pretty upset about her accidental makeover!' He shook his head and tried to attract the attention of the waitress. A young, skinny girl in her early twenties approached our table.

'Can I get a 2014 Piedlong, please? My boyfriend here

will take the BrewDog you have on tap.' Theo went the extra mile by rubbing my hand as he smiled at the waitress. I was too exhausted to play along as usual. As soon as the waitress left, Theo faced me, and from the look on his face it was clear he was anxious to know what had happened in Edinburgh.

'So ...? Hit me with it.'

'Prepare for crazy, ok?' I exhaled deeply, preparing myself to tell him something I didn't fully believe.

'How crazy?' He grinned at me.

'Donald Trump running for election crazy.'

'I'm *all yours,* baby!' He threw his hands into the air as if he was surrendering.

I started with how creepy Jodie's parents were and how much they had abused her when she was a child. Then, told him about climbing into their first-floor bedroom using a drain pipe. Throughout, Theo was silent except for an occasional gasp or *maaate.* He laughed when I reached the part about kicking Jodie's father in the stomach. Telling him everything that had happened, actually hearing words like *sneaking, hiding, attacked, Jodie jumped, broke his nose,* made me question my sanity. Had this really happened? It sounded like I was describing a movie. I told him about chasing Jodie into the forest. All Theo said was *unbelievable.*

'For the next part, you'll need to be *extremely* open-minded.' Theo nodded cautiously, and I struggled to find a place to start, telling someone like Theo about Jodie's ability. He lived for science and didn't understand people who believed in God. There had been a few very heated arguments about religion in the past - with Laura and myself on one side and Jodie, Amy, Theo on the other.

He wasn't impressed. I watched the disappointment on his face change slowly to concern as I tried to convince him that Jodie could control time. I showed him the notebook and explained what I thought the words and dates meant. He studied it for a few minutes, then returned it without comment. I told him about Jodie deciding to stay in Edinburgh rather than coming to London because she thought it would bring her ability back. Theo was looking at me intensely like he was analysing my face, trying to figure out how much I believed it myself.

Our drinks were on the table now, but I had no memory of the waitress bringing them. My cheeks were burning by the time I finished talking.

'What do you think?' I asked Theo hesitantly, sipping my beer.

'Time travel?' He asked slowly, almost like he had to check he had heard me correctly. 'It's completely bonkers. Secondly, it's impossible. Did I mention bonkers?' He took a deep breath, working himself up, 'to *begin* with, it breaks the laws of thermodynamics. Secondly... I mean... Ethan, how are you even considering this?'

'Right. What about the book, the dates, the thing with Stacey? How did she know which restaurant I had a booking for on our anniversary, or that I was planning to play Resident Evil this week?

'Mate, are you seriously taking a few coincidences as proof of time travel? The book doesn't prove shit,' his voice was raised now, and there were scandalised expressions at the tables around us. He moved his head closer and dropped his voice to a whisper. 'What if I were to tell you that the time we went to Paris two years ago, the trip *I arranged* saved your life.' I took his point, but he continued. 'Yes, I saved your life, because if you had stayed in London that week,' he paused, trying to come up with an ending, 'you would have been *stabbed*,' I raised my hand to interrupt, '*multiple times*!' he added a few quick, jerky hand motions as if he was stabbing someone with a certain flourish.

I exhaled. 'And the restaurant reservation?'

'Did you make the booking online?'

'Over the phone.'

'Did they send you an email confirmation? Does Jodie have access to those emails?'

'Yes.' I lowered my voice in defeat. 'And yes.' I didn't like where this conversation was going. Theo was opening the door to doubt, but I wasn't ready to consider this as a solution to Jodie's behaviour.

'What about the game?' I demanded.

'Did you buy that game recently?'

'Yes.'

'Do I need to continue?'

'No.' I shook my head and paused. 'How did she know that I wanted to take her for a walk? Or cancer? Stacey? Or winning those lotteries?

'Couples going for a walk on their anniversaries? Wow, that's completely unheard of.' I shook my head at his sarcasm. 'Cancer? You must have had symptoms...' He hesitated slightly.

'Stacey?'

'She described the teacher of a yoga class you were planning on attending, and then told you that you would have kissed her? Are we seriously having this conversation?'

'And the lottery?'

'Has she shown you *any* proof that she actually won the lottery twenty times, or whatever?'

'Twice and no, because we were in the middle of a bloody forest!' Now I was the one making a scene.

'Convenient,' he shrugged. 'As far as we know, she could just be dealing drugs on the side to make some cash.' I exhaled, searching for some sanity. 'And you know what's even more convenient?' he continued. 'She says she just lost her powers, so now she can't prove *anything*.'

Theo shrugged his shoulders again, as if to continue, but something changed in his face and he stopped. Could he be right? If Jodie were making everything up, then it would mean she was crazy. Not just a little bit crazy, but certifiably insane. Had I somehow failed to see it?

I looked up at Theo, who was still silent, his face stony.

'If you honestly believe this bullshit, then ask Jodie the next time you see her …' he gathered himself. 'Ask her - how come Laura ended up under the wheels of that lorry?'

CHAPTER 12

The basil plant on our terrace had died, and the leaves crumbled and fell to the floor under my touch. I could imagine Anneli's disappointment if she saw it. But the basil wasn't the only dead plant in here - the orchids were long gone. A small ficus tree looked a little like autumn had come early, and the ornamental cumquat had its leaves all pointed towards the ground, as if it had just given up on life. A small smile formed as I realised that I knew most of the plants' names. This was Jodie's space, and she could talk for hours about how the rhododendron needed humidity, and how the calathea couldn't survive with soil that was too wet or too dry. *It had to be just right.* I picked up the basil plant and chucked it into the compost box.

Ethan

***

Even in the warm, early morning sunlight through the frosted bathroom window, my skin looked pallid and wan. The person in the mirror didn't look like a high profile lawyer. It had been a whole week since I last shaved; a week since I had a real night's sleep; one week since my perfect life had shattered just like that glass Jodie had thrown at the wall.

Most of the evening before had been spent thinking about what Theo had said to me. Could this all be in Jodie's head, a figment of her imagination? There were only two options: either Jodie could go back in time, or she was a crazy lunatic; neither was great. Just thinking about it again made my head hurt. I missed our old life when Jodie was just Jodie and nothing more.

On one of the walls in the bathroom Jodie had hung a painting of a man standing on a tall building looking out over the city at dawn. He had his arms spread, forming into wings, and black feathers were sprouting from his fingertips. *Freedom* - Jodie had called it. She'd painted it soon after Laura's death, and I'd asked if the man in the painting was an angel. 'No,' she had said, hesitantly. 'Just … a man wanting to escape.' Now I wondered - was this me in the painting, trying to escape the life Jodie had created for me?

My phone buzzed in my pocket. A message from an unknown number.

Good morning, criminal.

There was a certain familiar humour.

Dr Leigh?

A speech bubble appeared. I waited patiently.

Mr Page.

I was still smiling, but the longer I looked at Dr Leigh's message, the stronger the guilt grew. A slight thrill. A long-forgotten feeling.

I replied, *Yes sir :)* and stared hungrily at the screen.

Madam … [Accompanied by an eye-rolling emoji.] I'm going to Spain today for a long weekend but back on Monday evening. Fancy that <u>dinner</u> Tuesday night?

Dr Leigh was always direct and to the point; there was no fakery. I read her message a few times, smiling at the emphasised *dinner*. Almost as if we both felt uncomfortable about it, and so that was why she highlighted it. Was I crossing a line? I reminded myself that we were just acquaintances. Friends *maybe*. There was no harm in making new connections. My heart was pounding. I'm not someone who cheats, and besides Jodie wasn't here - so what harm could it do? And if she did get her powers back, then nothing else would matter, everything would be erased, reset, and dinner with my doctor would be the least of my problems.

Sounds good. I'll see you then :)

I checked again to see if there was a missed message from Jodie. But there was nothing, as expected. In the bedroom, I put the notebook carefully back in the box under the bed, so she wouldn't know I had seen it, and made my way to the kitchen.

As soon as my bare feet stepped on to the cold kitchen tiles I stopped. Something was out of place. There was a pot that hadn't been used in a week on the stove; the bin was fuller and had an egg carton in it. I hadn't eaten eggs in the previous three weeks.

'Good morning!' I jumped as a familiar voice filled the kitchen.

'Jodie?' I turned around, and there she was in the living room, standing near the dining table. She had two plates of breakfast laid out ready. From where I stood it looked like three eggs, soft boiled, were balanced on top of a stack of smoked salmon on rye, spread with guacamole and nigella seeds. We called this the perfect breakfast. Jodie cooking for me - especially something as nice as this - would normally have been a pleasant surprise, but after the past week it jarred.

Jodie gazed at me with her innocent look that I adored so much. I rushed into the living room and hugged her. I held her tight, and her hair smelled of apples. We spent a moment in silence, her hands wrapped tight around my neck. Eventually she let go and took my hands.

'Ethan, I'm sorry,' as she squeezed them tightly, like she was never going to let go again. 'I'm sorry for behaving like a total fool. I was wrong to stay with my parents, especially after everything -'

'Jodie, I ...'

'No, let me finish.' She was barely holding herself together now. 'I betrayed you, so I decided to come back because I -' her voice was breaking '- I would rather have you now, even if it means never going back in time again.' She burst into tears.

'Jesus, Jodie.' I instinctively hugged her again, as her tears soaked my shirt.

Theo's voice was in the back of my head - *It's completely bonkers, how are you even considering this* - was he right, was Jodie crazy? How could I believe that all this, our whole life, could be her delusion?

'I'm sorry, Ethan, I'm so so sorry.' She spoke while still pressing her face to my chest, like she was afraid to look up at me. I held her in my arms.

'Jodie, you're my true soulmate. You are my life.' She wept even more now. Time slowed down. It was healthy for her to cry, to know I was here for her, here to support her. She pulled back to look at my face, her face red and her cheeks shiny with tears. I smiled, hoping to make her feel better. I felt her pain and shame, and I wanted her to be happy.

'Thank you, thank you, thank you,' she repeated and added, 'I'm so sorry and thank you.'

I rocked her gently from side to side until her sobs eventually subsided.

'Is this breakfast for us?' I asked.

'I was waiting for the queen, but you showed up so–' She lifted her head, her face still red - but she smiled now, and it was all I needed.

We sat at the places she'd set; the meal looked delicious. I cut the egg in half, the runny yolk covering the smoked salmon and bread; Jodie had timed them perfectly. It was exactly what I loved, and Jodie looked like she was enjoying herself now too. We ate in silence.

By the time we'd finished, Jodie's colour had returned to normal, her tears dry. She laughed when I told her she could have outrun me in the forest if she'd kept up her training. But she was less amused when she noticed my missing wedding ring, and I had to explain that I had lost it somewhere in the house in a drunken blackout two days ago.

I took our plates to the kitchen and started washing them, the cold water fresh on my hands. Just being together with Jodie again made me more relaxed, but I had to know the truth about her power. As Theo had said yesterday, it was all too convenient for her ability to disappear right when she was asked to prove them.

When I returned to the dining room, Jodie had her hands placed in front of her on the dining room table.

'Jodie?' She flinched ever so slightly as I spoke. 'How can I trust you're telling the truth, that you had these powers you now claim to have lost?' Was there now a slight tension in her jaw? She spoke calmly.

'You don't believe me? Maybe I shouldn't blame you. It must sound crazy.'

'It does.'

'I grew up with this. I am not lying to you.'

'Can you prove it to me?'

Jodie looked around the room like she was searching for something.

'I know there will be a huge storm on the 9th of September, next Friday. Worse than the forecasts are predicting. There will be two casualties here in London, many more taken to hospital.'

'How do you ...' It was instinct. I already knew what she was going to say.

'Because I already lived through this when I went back from the 12th of September,' she lowered her hands nervously. 'Stacey.'

The mention of the name irritated me, with the implication that I should have to apologise for something.

'The storm's almost a week away. Is there anything sooner you remember happening?'

She glanced at me, then stood up and disappeared into the study. A few minutes later, she returned, carrying her laptop, placed it on the dining room table, and entered her password. The first thing that appeared on her desktop was the list of train times from London to Edinburgh. She stared at it for a few moments, confused.

'Did you use my computer to access the browsing history on my phone?'

'Yup.'

'Smart,' she nodded, genuinely impressed. Then she connected to her bank, entering a password sent to her on her phone, as well as taking a photo of her face. There seemed to be a lot more security than on my account. It was the first time I'd seen her do this.

'Jesus Christ,' my jaw dropping as I saw the balance. It was more than six million pounds. 'Jodie, this is—' my voice broke. Then she showed me the monthly payments of £23,524 from a reference NL10058. It was the same one they'd used when I won the lottery.

Jodie's face was unreadable when I looked at her. She shrugged, shut down the laptop, and took it back.

She could see the future. I was grappling with the fact that everything she'd told me was surely true. How else could she have won that money?

I stood where Jodie had left me, still working to digest this new reality. The sound of the bedroom door closing startled me. Following Jodie to the bedroom, I saw she was lying in bed, facing the wall, but I slid in next to her. She didn't move, so I wrapped my hand around her waist, watching the back of her head and listening to her deep breathing; her chest moved up and down rhythmically, her hands resting under her face.

I tried to imagine what it would be like to have powers like hers. It would be lonely, having no one to talk to about this. She'd have memories no one else would. Now with her powers finally gone, there was no longer a safety net, no one to protect us any more. I thought of my mother dying, and my heart constricted. The thought scared me; Jodie had made my life what it was today, peaceful, comfortable, maybe a bit boring, but nevertheless good and happy. If I had lost something by not experiencing the pain Jodie had tried so desperately to protect me from, I didn't know it.

A note jarred. What about all those other timelines, that pain and sorrow and happiness and frustration Jodie had experienced, and that we would never share? She would always know things I could never know, or understand. For the last 20 years I thought we had been growing together, but she had an entirely parallel life. Who was this person that I thought I knew so well?

My breathing intensified as I watched her sleep. But it was all over, now - I had to remind myself that chapter of our life is gone. She had made mistakes and I was willing to forgive her, as long as we moved forward in love and trust, as partners together.

***

SUNDAY 28 AUGUST 2016

By the following day, everything was like it was back to normal. When we woke up, Jodie noticed the blood/ wine stain on the bedroom carpet and asked me if I'd had my period while she was away. She laughed until she heard that I had stepped on one of the shards from the glass she'd broken. Jodie was quiet for a few moments then quickly dismissed it. We both agreed the glasses were ugly anyway.

I turned on my PS4 to play Resident Evil and asked Jodie to join me. The original game, after all, was how we'd met. But today she just couldn't catch a break, and the words JILL IS DEAD were sprayed across the screen, the game taunting us.

Jodie leapt up, irritated, and ran to the bathroom. When she didn't return, I found her hunched on the floor, sobbing. She explained that she would need some time to get used to her powers being gone.

She seemed happier when I proposed we paint together. When I struggled to get started, Jodie suggested I place a dot in the middle of the canvas. 'This way, you break the whiteness of it, and you can't turn back.' We painted in a companionable silence for a while, with Jodie nodding at my progress and making occasional encouraging noises.

'Do you know why I choose to paint?' she asked, but didn't wait for an answer. 'Everyone starts with a blank canvas and if you mess up, you throw it out and paint another one. This way I didn't have an unfair advantage compared with other artists. We all have the power to start over.'

'Did it bother you, having an advantage over everybody else?' I asked.

'Yes. It's hard to resist not using a power like this... and I abused it.'

'How?'

'Winning the lottery. Passing my exams at school and university ... knowledge.'

'Knowledge?'

'Well, yes. If someone would ask me a question I didn't know the answer to, I could always just Google it and go back.' All those impressive pub quiz rounds we'd shared had been fake, it seemed.

'What about that time with your plants? The infestation of scale insects you had. You were so angry then.'

She looked out through the window, where you could just see the corner of the terrace.

'That was one place where I could use my powers, but I chose not to. I wanted to have hobbies - some part of my life where I wasn't constantly going back and fixing every little thing. And those scales that time ... well I took it as a defeat.'

I failed to impress Jodie with my portrait of her, so I cooked some gnocchi for lunch. She set the table and poured us drinks; red wine for herself and a beer for me. As we took our first mouthful, Jodie's phone buzzed. She laughed as she read the message, pushing her phone over to me. The text from Amy read:

Are you back in London, or are you still going through menopause? If not, it would be great to see you TOMORROW for Emmet's birthday at 2PM sharp. If you're still angry at Ethan, then come alone. xx

I made it very clear to Jodie that she'd need to explain about Stacey. 'You trashed my good name!'

'Can we just say that you did kiss Stacey, but I forgave you?'

I laughed. 'Definitely not. You will just have to admit to Amy you're delusional,' Jodie wasn't thrilled, but I wasn't taking no for an answer.

Later that afternoon, we had sex. Twice. As we lay in bed afterward, I asked about her parents and how they were. David was apparently more ashamed than angry. Jodie explained to me that during the week she had stayed with her parents, David hadn't been as bad as they'd used to be. 'Getting old slowly takes your pride away.' She was still hurt and had no intention of forgiving him. That was fine with me.

We ended up having dinner that evening at the turkish grill across the road. It was a swanky place, but Jodie didn't make an effort to look presentable, and neither did I. The waiter haughtily made it clear we were bringing down the tone of the establishment, and my grilled fish was slightly overdone. Jodie's Tavuk Gogsu chicken was just awful. 'If something like this had happened before, I would've turned back time and ordered an ice cream instead,' she laughed and I joined her, hiding my flash of anger. Everytime she spoke about her powers it was a constant reminder of how she had controlled my life. All I wanted to do was forget about it and move forward.

We were walking back after the sun had gone down. The sky was still bright, but only for a few minutes more.

One after the other, the street lights turned on, gently illuminating the old cobbled streets. Jodie told me she wanted to stop past a shop to get herself some tampons and I waited outside, appreciating the view of the Shard. Only the tip was visible, surrounded by brown-brick council buildings, but it was still beautiful in the summer night.

Laura had always thought that the Shard was so pretty. Under the big sycamore tree sat a bench, in her memory. I approached it slowly and touched its slightly faded paint. It flaked as I brushed it with my fingers.

'I miss her too.' Jodie's voice came quietly from behind. I took a moment for myself before turning to face her.

'Jodie, I have to ask you something.' I'd avoided asking too many direct questions about her other … lives, but I had to know what happened here, that awful day.

'You want to know why Laura is dead?'

I didn't move. The street around us was busy, and people were still going in and out of the shop, but everything felt suddenly numb. She went around and sat on the bench; I joined her, waiting patiently. She was looking at the houses, cars, and people rushing home. My heart was pounding, and Jodie exhaled deeply.

'If Laura hadn't died on that day, our life would have carried on. We would have gone to see Wicked, and then gone back to their place to celebrate Theo's promotion with ice-cream on the balcony.' My teeth were clenched, trying to hold myself together. Part of me was so, so jealous that Jodie had experienced the day we should have had, that wonderful other future. But it seemed there was more she wanted to say.

'Five months after that day, Laura would have come home from work and told Theo she was in love with another man. I went back several times to try talking her out of it, preventing her from dating him, dropping hints that it wouldn't end well, but nothing helped. The outcome was always the same. I realised this was something I wasn't able to change. All of us - me, you, Amy, Theo, and Laura - were torn apart. Of course, everyone rallied around Theo. He was devastated. He took Anneli and prevented Laura from seeing her. It was at that point that Laura filed for divorce, and custody. She was angry at him for trying to take Anneli from her.' Surely Laura wasn't capable of something like that. In the weeks leading to her death, I had spent so much time with her, and there couldn't have been anyone else in her life. She only cared about baby Anneli.

'No, this isn't–' I tried to say something, but Jodie wouldn't stop. She kept her voice level.

'She argued in court that Theo was incapable of looking after Anneli. She was just mad, because he was bitter, and he did everything he could to make her life difficult. I can't blame her; she was right; he was too. And she won, and the judge gave her full custody of Anneli. She told Theo that he could visit whenever he wished, that she was more than happy to have him in Anneli's life, but he couldn't. All he saw was his white wife, running away with a white man and taking away his daughter. It was too painful. He jumped from the crane on the construction site he was working on at the time.'

I squeezed my eyes tight, but a single tear escaped and rolled down my cheek. This was horrible. 'But... but you knew he jumped, you surely could have saved him!' I spoke as if it had really happened, as if Theo was dead today, and Laura was alive.

'I tried to save him, to be there for him, telling him we would get through it together. But if I talked him out of it on Tuesday, then it would just happen on Thursday, Friday, or Monday.' Her voice finally gave way to the emotion. 'Of all of us, you were the most devastated, even more than Laura. He was your best friend, and you cried more than you had cried when Laura died.' I remember how I'd felt after Laura's death, but the idea of Theo being there in her place was just as unbearable to imagine. Jodie squeezed her eyes shut, her facial expression eerily calm, and I was afraid that if I touched her she would burst into tears.

'Ethan, when I decided to go back that time, it was one of the most difficult decisions I've ever made. On that evening in our past when Laura died, I had to pretend everything was fine, smiling, joking, acting as if nothing was unusual, though I knew that she would be run down by that truck.' Jodie turned her head slightly to one side and her eyes moved slightly, like she was weighing probabilities. 'I knew what was going to happen to Laura, and I could have stopped it, but this time around I chose to save Theo instead.' She looked at me, and I stared back at her agape, horrified by what she was telling me and by her cold calculation; horrified that Laura left Theo for someone else. I felt sick. 'Theo was broken after Laura's death, and so were we, but we all looked after each other and managed to pull ourselves together. If Laura hadn't died, we would have ended up losing both of them.'

'So you just made a decision to save Theo instead of Laura?'

She raised her voice slightly. 'What Laura did - leave her marriage for another man - was so incredibly selfish. No one was better off, including Laura herself. Do you think she enjoyed her life after Theo committed suicide? All her friends and family - everyone was horrified. Anneli would have grown up and asked questions about her father.'

Jodie closed her eyes, and the tension was vibrating from her in waves. 'Yes, I let Laura die,' she finally spat out. 'It was her destiny, and I didn't stop it! Does that make me culpable? There was no other way, and *I had to choose.*'

Neither of us spoke for a few minutes.

'I have seen many people die, Ethan. Where I could, I have always prevented them from dying. Those I could not, I knew one day I would see them again. One day when I got old, I would have gone back to 1996, college, and start my life again. And then we would all be alive again, together, happy and innocent. I never intended for Laura to stay dead.'

'But ...'

'But now it's all over. I can't go back, I will never be able to go back. And I'll have to live the rest of my life with this choice, knowing I let her die. That it was my fault Anneli grew up without her mother,' banging her hands on her thighs, 'all because she wanted to have a bit of a thrill, *the bitch!'*

I recoiled from the word. Surely people were staring at us by now, but we both just stared into the distance. I didn't know what to do or say and I searched for something that would help me relate to Jodie, to her pain, but there was nothing.

How could *I* go on? How could I face Theo knowing this, that Jodie took this decision, that she was deciding who lives and who dies.

After a moment of silence, Jodie continued talking, calmer now. 'I had a difficult choice to make. Both options were horrible, but I had to do something, and before you go and judge me–'

'I'm not judging,' I said quietly, but Jodie spoke over me.

'Before you judge, think about what Amy would have chosen. Or Theo himself. What would you have chosen if you were in my position?'

I ignored her question. We sat in silence for a few minutes, just listening to the outside world.

'Is there anything else I should know?'

'What do you mean?' Her eyes widened.

'Is there anything else I should know about, that you've done, that would turn my world upside down?' She lowered her gaze to her lap, squeezing her hands together hard. After a moment she looked back up at me, but didn't meet my eyes.

'No.' She paused. 'There's nothing more.'

CHAPTER 13

Amy

My knees were aching as I rushed back home, last-minute pack of birthday candles in hand. It was already a few minutes past two, and Jodie was always early. People who come early to parties are the *worst*. But I loved her.

As I hurried along, the sun pierced suddenly through the clouds and the day brightened. I was excited for all of us to be together and clear the air a little and I prayed the sun would stay. Hopefully, we could enjoy a bit of it before Theo made us play his board games.

I pushed the door open with my foot and hurried in, passing Jodie and Ethan in the living room, talking to Emmet. I called out greetings on my way to the kitchen, where Julie was making her famous hummus - a recipe she'd stolen from her ex-husband. Throwing her the candles before Emmet could see, she caught them deftly and grinned, tilting her head slightly towards Jodie and

Ethan. I knew what the look was for as I kicked off my flats and went back for a proper greeting. At first glance, the lucky couple seemed perfectly happy together, beaming at each other and chatting cheerfully with Emmet. However, something was not quite right. I thought Jodie would be more distant, given she just caught her husband cheating on her. But Ethan was the one that seemed distant, and he flinched every time she touched him.

'Guys, you made it!' I gave Ethan a brief hug, then an extra hard squeeze for Jodie. Ethan was his usual, casual self. Jacket and jeans, but a certain something that made him look cool. Jodie, of course, looked stunning. Her wavy blonde hair, worn as waterfall braids, set against her deep navy dress. Always flawless makeup. Dressed to kill for a 5-year-old's birthday.

'You look amazing, Jodie.' I smiled at her. 'How have you been since I last saw you? Everything okay?' Jodie smiled back and nodded but said nothing. When I caught her eyes, they widened slightly, and I got the message. We would talk more later.

'And how's *the whore* doing?' I said, eyeing Ethan. Jodie nudged me with her elbow as he shifted uncomfortably.

'What's a whore, mummy?'

I crouched to meet Emmet's eyes.

'A whore is a woman who–'

Julie swooped in and scooped up Emmet before I could finish my sentence.

'A woman who loves...' Julie hesitated for a moment,

'everyone.' She looked relieved, shot me a glare as she returned to the kitchen, and I grinned. Emmet had so many questions, and Julie and I were in constant battle about how to answer them.

'Well done with all of this,' Ethan gestured around the living room, which was covered floor-to-ceiling in decorations. 'It looks wonderful, doesn't it, Emmet?' A big and colourful happy birthday sign draped from one side of the wall to the other, balloons were drifting into corners of the room, and we had put some bright flowers on the side table.

'Well done to both of you. And whatever that is, it smells heavenly,' said Jodie, as Julie came into the room with a bowl of blueberries in one hand and a large frosted cake balanced in the other.

'Can't expect anything less from lesbians, y'know!' I laughed.

The doorbell rang, and it was Theo, a customary ten minutes late. As I opened the door, I saw him wearing a crisp white shirt and a slim green tie, his hair trimmed razor-sharp. Anneli was pressed shyly to his side, holding his hand and smiling up at me. She looked like a doll in squeaky clean white shoes, her deep chestnut curls cascading down to a bright green party dress. It matched her dad's tie, of course it did. 'Hi guys, hi Anneli! You look beautiful, sweetheart! Oh wonderful, is that for Emmet?' She had jumped forward for a hug and then brandished a neatly wrapped present at me in delight. 'How kind of you. Oh, no, don't give it to me, he'd love it if it came from you!' She dashed off inside to find the birthday boy.

'Amy, love, how are you?' Theo leaned in to kiss my cheek; he smelled fresh.

'Honestly, I don't know how you do it, Theo. She looks like she's just spent hours in a salon! You could teach Julie and I a thing or two.' He laughed heartily, his perfect white teeth flashing. It was so good to see him happy. I'd wondered if we had lost his carefree side forever to grief, but slowly and more often now I caught glimpses of the gentle, light-hearted person he was before Laura's death. I placed my hand on his back and guided him to the living room, where Emmet was already gleefully shredding the wrapping paper on his present as Julie served everyone drinks. I looked around our small group of friends, as they hugged Theo and gathered around my son, and I felt a sense of deep contentment. These were my people. This small gathering was how it should be, together on a warm summer bank holiday.

Dinner was a success. The sun heard my prayers and stayed out, baking us all. Anneli loved Julie's hummus, which set a good example for Emmet, and between them they ate a tonne of veg. I was having more fun than I had expected, and yet there was something unsaid floating at the edges of the conversation. I kept waiting for Jodie to talk about her mysterious trip to Scotland, or for it to be mentioned, but we all tiptoed around any serious chat. Now and again, I caught myself looking at Jodie, who was smiling and nodding but seemed quieter than usual. She sat next to Ethan, holding his hand almost the entire time. I sipped the last of my sangria and chewed the fruit at the bottom of the glass thoughtfully.

Jodie finally locked eyes with me and cleared her throat. 'Anyone for a top-up?' Jodie asked, looking at me and waving her glass. The others waved the suggestion away and had become engrossed in a political conversation, Ethan ramping up passionately as Julie disagreed, calmer but determined to get her point across. I squeezed her shoulder and nodded at Jodie, rising with her rather than handing over my glass.

Inside the house it was cool and quiet. I could feel the heat radiating from my face and made a mental note to take out some sun cream for the kids. Jodie began to drop ice cubes into our glasses using the tongs, one cube at a time. She finally looked up and smiled at me.

I broke the silence. 'So? How are things? *Really?*'

'Good, thank you. You?'

I felt a flash of frustration. 'Jodie, I've been doing a lot of thinking about what happened–'

'This is yours.' She interrupted, passing the glass to me. 'I'm just going to use the bathroom real quick, okay?' Typical of her to avoid any sort of confrontation. I smiled and took the glass.

Julie came in, carrying some of the empty plates and glasses. Her fringe was plastered to her forehead with sweat, and she'd been running around all day playing host so I could spend time with everyone. I hurried to help her unload.

'Go on, I'll clean this up,' she said, smiling at me. 'You go and talk to your friends. I've got it.' *Your friends.* I really hope that one day Julie could see my guys as her friends too. But I accept that she doesn't want more friends - she has me, Emmet, her ex and her massive family. I'm already so grateful that she's here with us today, working so everyone has a good time.

On impulse, I wrapped my arms around her in a hug, breathing her in, this wonderful woman, my person. She smelled like fresh shampoo, summer days, and cake. I leaned back, still holding her tightly, and looked at her, so close that we were both nearly cross-eyed. I stared at her freckles, her slightly sweaty, earnest face. 'God,' I said. 'You are glorious.' She burst out laughing and kissed me.

'I'm a sweaty mess, and you know it!. I'll bring some ice water and maybe some sun cream for the kids. And you actually, you're going all rosy.' I kissed her again, longer, harder, and smoothed her fringe off her face.

'Thanks, Jules, yes, please. Listen, have a think about what you want for breakfast tomorrow. I'll bring you something lovely in bed, anything you want.' She smiled, kissing me on the forehead and I peeled away, walking back outside, squinting in the deep afternoon sunlight. Anneli and Emmet were sitting on the grass, her dress crumpled and his smart top rumpled in the heat, both of them gazing at the sky while she explained something with the authority of a child just a few years older than the other. The boys talked, close and quiet, and I moved forward to join them.

'Do you still believe she can time travel?' Theo asked.

'Forget it, she made a joke, and I took it the wrong way.' Ethan was dismissive, uncomfortable.

'Time travel? An interesting topic.' They were both a bit startled to see me. Too late, I realised there had been a serious undercurrent to their chat; maybe I should have let them finish. I tried to be casual. 'Can you imagine what it would like to be a time traveller?'

'Hardly.' Theo crossed his arms and looked up at the sky.

Maybe it was the sangria and the sun, but I thought about it seriously. Time-traveling sounded like a great idea. I thought about the good times I would want to revisit, and then I grinned and thought - I could re-live today again and again if I wanted to.

'If I could go back in time, I would do so many great things, you know? I would change the world! For the better.' I laughed, suddenly realising how enthusiastic I sounded. For a split second, I could see how different my life would be - all the things I would change. Then I thought about Julie. And Emmet.

Theo interrupted my daydream, 'What would you do?'

'To be honest, forget I said anything. I like my life as it is now. I'm lucky; I'm blessed, I've got Emmet and Julie.' I hesitated suddenly, keenly aware now that Theo had also had this happy life until Laura had been so cruelly taken from him. 'I guess, you know, it wouldn't hurt to win the lottery!' I chuckled, trying to change the direction this was going. 'You know, we could move to a bigger house or something. But that's just stuff.'

'You could make sure Emmet never hurts himself.' Theo added in a quiet voice. As I turned to look at the kids play, I could see in my mind's eye how good it would always be to be there to catch Emmet when he fell from the swing or knocked his head. To never see his tears or pain. I hesitated.

'As much as I love him, I don't know if I could do that, you know. Getting hurt, learning from your mistakes, growing to become a better version of yourself is part of life. If you're protected from all the bad things, the brighter days ... I guess they wouldn't seem so wonderful.' I thought about all the times I'd felt so alone, those nights looking for love and ending up at the bottom of a bottle instead. That feeling of being so empty, and then Julie walking into my life. It had been like I had spent my entire existence in the shade and I didn't know that there could be sun. Theo nodded. Ethan was watching something a thousand miles away. 'Why, what would you do?' I asked Theo, though I had an idea about the answer I would receive.

'Save Laura.' He said, simply. 'Along with all the other people who died that day.' Ethan shook his head absently, still not acknowledging the conversation. Theo continued after a pause. 'I'd try to prevent the worst kinds of disasters.' The sun had dipped behind a sudden cloud, and his eyes were dark. The sudden cold made me shiver.

'Like Brexit?' I gave a short false laugh, trying to alleviate a bit of the tension. Theo shook his head.

'Bigger, like 9/11 or whatever, warn people about that massive tsunami in India–'

'And how would you do that?' Jodie said. I hadn't even noticed she had come back outside. She fixed him with a cheerful smile and tilted her head slightly, as if she was evaluating something. 'I'm interested.' Theo seemed slightly taken aback, but Jodie continued. 'You'd be, what, calling up the police to tell them about a terrorist attack in America next week? I feel like they'd have a lot of questions for you, and you would have a very hard time getting anyone to listen.' She was the most animated I'd seen her all day, her cheeks slightly flushed. It felt like she was taking this personally, somehow. 'What are you going to do if you accidentally alter the course of history, and it doesn't happen. Someone could lock you up because they think you're crazy!'

'Maybe,' Theo said, wary of a fight. 'But a tsunami would happen no matter what. They wouldn't think I was crazy after it came true.' He shrugged.

'That's right,' Jodie nodded. The sun had come back out, and now she was squinting at him. 'And this time, because you still don't have a reason as to why you know, they're suddenly treating you like the messiah.'

'It might not be that bad.' He pulled his sunglasses down against the sudden glare, but the gesture was defensive.

'Do you really want a life where everyone knows who you are, knows what you're capable of doing? Where people are queuing down the street asking you to bring back their dead relatives, where paparazzi follow your every move?' Her voice had a definite edge to it now, and I needed to do something to diffuse this conversation before it went any further. 'Imagine you did all those great things, saved people, what do you think the first thing would be on any criminal's to-do list? Do you really think they're just going to ignore the fact that the famous and brilliant Theo Davies can see the future?' Jodie walked around the table and sat next to Ethan, still glaring at Theo. 'So, one day, you're walking along, and a bullet explodes out the front of your chest. You have a couple of seconds of awareness before you die - do you go back a few hours in time and save yourself, hide where they won't find you? What do you do after that? How long do you live in fear, just one step ahead, forever knowing you're a target? Or do you go back to the beginning, back to when you were anonymous, and let the terrorists and the criminals win, always living with the fact that you could have stopped them but didn't even try? And one day you give in to your conscience, Theo, and you do try to change history again, and the next bullet doesn't miss your skull, and that's it. You lived in agony and died like a rat.'

Theo said nothing. I realised I had been holding my breath and vaguely noticed that Julie was standing in the doorway, a jug of ice water in her hand. Emmet and Anneli had fallen silent, sensing the adults' tension. Jodie turned to me, her eyes flashing.

'You said you wouldn't protect Emmet, let him learn from his mistakes? So where would *you* draw the line?'

'What do you mean, where would I draw the line?'

'Would you save him if he was crippled in a car crash?'

'Yes, but–'

'Would you go back in time to stop him breaking his wrist skiing?

'Uh … I guess so, yes?'

'What if he accidentally crashes his new car, the one he worked for all summer. Or what if he cuts his hand, and then complains for the next two weeks that he can't work, or write, or go rock climbing. And you *know you have the power to change that.*'

'I don't know, Jodie,' I said quietly.

'People accept they can't change things. That's how they get through the week. But if you could genuinely turn back time, it would mean that you can prevent *anything* from happening. *Anything you choose.* Sounds great, but then - what kind of person are you if you don't help?'

I had to change the topic. 'I don't understand, and I don't know what's going on, but what Theo was talking about is impossible. It's not important, you know.' I smiled but Jodie didn't smile back.

'If you see your friend struggling with groceries, you can choose to help them, or not, right?' Jodie shrugged. 'But tell me, wouldn't you judge the person who doesn't?' She sighed, maybe noticing the frozen tableau, and continued more calmly. 'The truth is, good things rarely come without strings attached. Maybe you're a top brain surgeon, you drive a Porsche, and everything's great until you need to deliver bad news to a family who just lost their loved one. We often imagine how lucky we'd be if we could make it in life - if something good fell from the sky. No one ever really considers the other side of the coin. Nothing is ever simple.'

***

The heat of the day had mellowed to a soft and golden light; at the end of the garden, the thick oak tree swayed gently in the wind. Julie came out of the house with the rest of Emmet's gifts. Emmet was having so much fun, and it was infectious. He ran between us, bossing Anneli around and instructing her how to play with his new things. I looked around and felt a tugging at my heart, and realised I was missing Laura. I missed seeing how happy she made Theo. When he had looked at her, his smile had been different; he'd been utterly devoted. I couldn't help but admire him. If something happened to Julie or Emmet, I don't know how I'd go on. I shut my eyes and swallowed, trying to rid myself of the thought.

The sun sank towards the horizon, but I still hadn't had a chance to talk to Jodie. I glanced at her, but she seemed perfectly happy now. The image of her as white as a sheet and silent, wrapped up on my sofa - it seemed like a long time ago.

'Drinks, anyone?' Ethan asked, standing up and stretching with a lazy yawn.

'More red, please.' He took Jodie's glass and went to the kitchen. 'Love you,' she called after him, noticing I was watching her.

'Don't worry, Amy, I love you too.' She sent me an air kiss. Anneli laughed.

'Do you love me too, Aunt Jodie?' She asked

'Of course, I love you, angel, I love everybody!' she shouted happily. There was no trace of her earlier mood as she scooped up Anneli to cuddle.

Emmet ran over, shouting 'Whore!' and pointing a finger at Jodie, causing Anneli to squeal and giggle. Ethan walked out, handing me a fresh sangria and Jodie a large glass of red wine, and nearly dropping both as Emmet began chasing Anneli around the garden and into the house, yelling *whore!, whore!*

'Woah, kids, careful!' he smiled, looking quizzically at me.

'Jodie is a whore, apparently,' Theo said to Ethan.

'Oh, that's old news.'

Jodie playfully slapped Ethan on his thigh, then crossed her arms.

'Soo ... a person who loves everyone, hey?' I said, smirking at Julie as she grinned at me. She rolled her eyes at me as she went back inside. Just the four of us now; I looked at Jodie.

Before I even knew it, I'd started to speak. 'So...should we address the elephant in the room?' Jodie and Ethan looked at each other. 'It's a safe space, guys. I know Theo cares for your happiness as much as I do, and I thought we could talk it all out so it doesn't become a big thing.'

'Amy, Jesus. Everything's fine, don't worry,' Ethan looked irritated.

'Erm... no it's not, actually.' I steeled myself, but maybe the sangria was doing most of the talking. 'She came here a week ago looking like a bloody ghost, then left for

Edinburgh without telling anyone.'

'Amy, honestly ...' but I ignored Jodie.

'You chased her. Then you called me upset and angry ... I was worried, guys, even though I tried to stay calm!' I turned to Jodie. 'Did you hide your parents' home address from him? Why?' Theo nodded ever so slightly. 'He knows,' I pointed to Theo, getting caught up in the moment, 'I know. So how about you guys just tell us what the hell is going on. You can't behave like that and expect us not to ask any questions!'

'Amy, it's ...' Ethan began, but Jodie put her hand on his shoulder.

'It's okay, Ethan. I need to explain this.' I didn't move, having anticipated more of a fight. I could tell Theo was holding his breath.

'I went to see my parents in Edinburgh. I was ... seeking closure.'

'Closure?' I asked, 'Closure for what-'

'I told Ethan, and Theo already knows.' She stopped, and we all sat there. It felt as if Jodie was working out the right words, gripping her palms together so tightly the knuckles had gone white. She took a breath, and I suddenly felt bad that I'd been the one who asked, who had brought it up.

'I was abused as a kid.' She said it quickly and quietly, her lips barely moving. 'It was emotional and ... physical. And ... I never knew how to ... how to say ... to tell anyone.'

It was impossible to know how my face looked at that moment. Jodie wasn't someone who asked for help, but I hadn't expected that she would keep something like this a secret from us. God. Jodie. I shook my head as my eyes teared up and reached out my hand to hold hers, 'Jodie.' I couldn't comprehend it. How could she not have told me? Jodie didn't move, her perfect facade still in place, and she didn't even seem to notice my hand. I withdrew it.

'I needed to face my past, to move away from it.' She went on, determined, eyes fixed on her glass of wine. She had turned a little pale again. 'It started to affect my relationship with Ethan. I didn't tell anyone because it was my battle; I had to do it myself.' She looked at me, 'I'm sorry I lied about Stacey. You were the only person I wanted to see, and I know I needed help, but … I just couldn't get it out. I wasn't ready to tell. I'm so very sorry.'

I walked around the table and sat beside Jodie, wrapping my hands around her, trying to show how much I loved her by squeezing it into her. She yielded and went soft, head resting on my shoulder.

'Don't you dare apologise. I'm the one who should be sorry.' I whispered. Then I looked in the direction of the guys. 'And I owe you an apology too, don't I? Ethan, I was just so fucking furious with you! No wonder you were confused.' He gave me a pale smile, clearly relieved he was no longer on trial. 'Jesus, Jodie, I just can't believe it. What absolute dicks your parents are! I've always said it. Your real family is your chosen family, and that's us. Who needs those old farts anyway?' Jodie placed her hands in mine and smiled, her eyes glinting with tears, and thanked me. 'Well, except for the money.' I shrugged.

'Ah, yes. About that,' Theo looked at Jodie. 'Ethan said your parents don't actually ... have any money?'

I released my arm from around Jodie's neck and looked at her properly, and for a tiny instant, she looked genuinely scared. Then she closed her eyes, and I nudged her.

'Hey. What do you mean they have no money?'

Jodie squeezed her eyes shut. I looked at Ethan, who was suddenly lost in thought, and then to Theo. Emmet and Anneli wandered back out into the garden, whispering to each other as thick as thieves, both shining with sun cream.

'I never said Jodie's parents had no money,' said Ethan hesitantly.

Jodie opened her eyes suddenly and stared at him.

'Yes, you did,' Theo insisted. 'On the phone, when I told you where Jodie's parents lived, you said their house looked like,' he glanced at the kids and whispered '*shit.* You made out like they didn't have a penny to their name.'

'I was at the wrong address,' Ethan said. 'I'd typed the postcode wrong in my GPS.'

'Right.' Theo nodded, but kept staring at Ethan with a strange expression on his face.

'They stopped sending me an ... allowance. I'm done with them. It's over.' Jodie blurted out, forcing a half-smile. I felt a rush of affection for her. I could hardly imagine the pain she must have felt when she was there, alone, with those awful people. Especially as a parent, it made me feel physically sick. Ethan hugged Jodie, and she whispered thank you into his ear. Back to the happy, loving couple.

Amy

***

As dusk settled, we moved into the house to play games and began to wind down after the day. Everyone was full and sleepy; I saw how sun-kissed we all looked, Emmet's freckles showing on his cheeks. I caught myself thinking that he was starting to look like Julie, which was, of course, insane but made me absurdly happy. Halfway through a lazy turn of cards, Ethan's phone vibrated next to me and caught my eye. From an unknown number, it said: *Sounds lovely, can't wait till tomorrow x.* I looked away quickly, wondering about something.

Theo cleared his throat, a little awkwardly, and said as casually as he could,

'Does uh ... anyone remember Jordan from Leeds College? The pixie girl?' I was aware of who he was talking about, a petite dark brunette with a deep voice. She was prone to violently bright hair in various shades. Theo was right to identify her as a pixie; she was tinier than I was.

'Sure. She was incredibly hot,' I replied. Julie rolled her eyes at me.

'What about her?' Ethan asked, still looking at his cards. I'd heard the tone of Theo's voice and looked up, curiously. He looked a little shy.

'I ran into her a couple of months ago. We're taking things slow, but ... it's going well. Tomorrow is our seventh date, I think.' He had everyone's attention now, and he grinned, embarrassed but happy.

'You're seeing someone? That's so great!' I exclaimed as Julie gave a little cheer, and Jodie laughed while miming applause.

A voice drifted from the corner where kids were playing. 'Are you searching for a mummy?' Anneli's innocent question made everyone chuckle.

'Guys, guys. Calm down, it's only a seventh date? Who knows.' But he couldn't stop the grin. He waved his hands in the air revealing his cards, but I knew our hearts weren't really in the game anymore.

'Who is she again?' Ethan asked, lifting his slightly unfocussed eyes from his phone, coming back into the conversation from somewhere else.

'You remember her! Hot Jordan? She was in the gaming society, too. We talked about you. Apparently, she fancied you back in the day, glad it didn't work out!' He winked at Ethan.

'Yes, that's good news.' Julie said, still staring at her cards, trying so hard to win, although we'd all but given up.

'Jordan, huh?' Ethan asked again. 'I can't say I remember her.

'Shall we have a toast?' asked Jodie.

'To Theo,' everyone in the chorus yelled, lifting their glasses. Theo looked down at his cards, embarrassed as everyone sipped their drink.

'If we're doing toasts, I want to also say thank you to Jodie.' Everyone's attention was on me now. 'Jodie, even with everything that was going in your life. Despite everything, you moved heaven and earth to help Julie and I adopt, and start a family.' Julie was nodding fiercely. 'We are both so very grateful for everything you did to help bring Emmet into our lives. You were there every step of the way, preparing Julie and me for the interview questions, supporting us through the application process, always encouraging, always knowing the right answer, and always confident that we were making the right decision. Because of you, we couldn't be happier. Thank you. From the bottom of my heart.' I raised my almost empty glass. 'To Jodie!' Everyone joined me and cheered.

Ethan cautiously hugged Jodie around the waist as she smiled, through eyes bright with tears. 'I can't imagine better parents, better mothers. And ... seeing as you're all feeling so wonderful about me,' Jodie paused for a moment and laid down her cards, 'this won't matter at all!' She'd won the game. At the sight of Julie's face, I burst into laughter.

CHAPTER 14

Ethan

After the noise of Amy's party, the street seemed quiet, our thoughts accompanied only by the soft sound of Jodie's heels clicking on the pavement. The walk along the Thames was slow, meandering, full of opportunities to admire the view. Back when I was looking for a flat to buy, the proximity to the fresh breeze and the water was a strong draw, and we still enjoyed walking today. But it was getting colder now, and I put my leather jacket on Jodie's shoulders.

'Thank you,' she said, smiling at me, and I gently kissed her forehead.

'Anneli and Emmet are growing up fast. I still remember them as toddlers.' I murmured.

'I know; it feels like yesterday.'

We walked side by side, in a slightly uncomfortable silence. Clouds covered the moon, a dim, vague shape that was still visible in the sky.

'And thank you for lying for me.'

I hadn't wanted to lie to our friends, especially not to Theo, but in that moment at Amy's I had to choose: Jodie or them. I chose Jodie. I was still angry with what she had done, but I just wanted my old life back. I wanted all the drama to stop, to go back to us being the couple we once were. I wanted these peaceful walks along the river. I wanted our love. No secret powers, no more hiding, just us.

'Theo can never know about Laura. It will just hurt him too much.'

'I know. And I'm sorry you had to do this.'

I shivered a tiny bit, unsure if it was the wind against my bare skin or if it was the feeling that Jodie and I were covering up a murder. There was a leaden feeling in my stomach. In some ways, it was hard to believe that Jodie could fail to save anyone's life with the power she possessed. Couldn't she just prevent Laura from meeting her adulterous lover in that other reality, just as she had gone back to prevent me from meeting Stacey? The walk wasn't making me feel any better.

'I'm sorry about Stacey,' I said, feeling angry at that other me who had cheated on Jodie.

She was slightly ahead of me, and her steps slowed. 'You didn't do anything. There's nothing for you to apologise for.'

'I hurt you, even if I don't remember. We both know it.'

'We know only what could have happened. But those events didn't come to pass, in the end.'

'But they did, to you. You experienced it.'

'It doesn't matter. I'm used to experiencing things which never happen.'

We walked in silence, lost in our own thoughts.

'Can I ask you about your parents?'

'What about them?' Jodie looked at me curiously.

'When I was at your house, I noticed bruises on your mother's arms. Did David hit her too?'

Jodie looked away from me, into the river. 'Yes. Probably more once I wasn't there.'

'Then she wasn't the bad person I thought she was.'

'Watching your child scream as your husband hit them, doing nothing, that seems like a pretty shitty thing to do.'

'Why didn't you both just run away?'

'I asked her on the day I was leaving whether she wanted to come with me, I told her where I was going and about the money. I thought that I'd convinced her, but I was wrong. She told David everything. Maybe in her head she still believed he could change. They both tried to stop me.' Jodie let out a small, bitter laugh. 'I went back and left home without saying goodbye to her.'

'Why do you think she stayed with him?'

'I don't know. She chose her husband over her child and that's why I don't want anything to do with her. There will come a time when she will know she chose badly - and then she'll have nobody but herself to blame.'

A speedboat with pop music and people dancing flew past us, their laughter floating in the air even after their music faded. The apartments we walked past were occupied by families, largely: a good school and kindergarten were close, crime levels low, and tourists weren't drawn here. I noticed Jodie looking through the lit windows at their lives. Living rooms were filled with kids, toys, and overflowing laundry racks.

Jodie slowed down suddenly, causing me to stop and turn.

'I have to say something,' she said. 'I've been thinking about our lives and whether it was selfish of me not to ... try harder but ... maybe it's time to consider kids again?'

'Jodie,' I leaped towards her and took her hands into mine. 'Are you saying you're ready? For us to go ahead with adoption?'

'Yes, I think I'm ready now. Do you want to have a child?' She gazed at me, judging my reaction. This is what I wanted, what I truly needed. For us to be a team again, to make decisions again, to move forward like a normal couple. 'I do!' I shouted, grinning like an idiot now *because I would have a child.* A little person to love and do everything for. 'I do!' I shouted again, sounding like a crazy person.

Jodie hugged me tight and screamed into my neck, unable to contain her excitement and emotion. I picked her up and swung her around a couple of times, holding her tightly around her waist, her dress spilling out in the light evening breeze. Then she was on the ground, and I looked at her eyes; we both started to laugh at each other's tearful red faces.

'Well done to the young lady there,' a deep, stranger's

voice came from above and made us both lift our heads. A bald, middle-aged man was staring through the window. 'Even in these times, not many ladies dare to propose to their boyfriends.' We both laughed. I lifted my left hand into the air towards the man.

'Look at this ring!' I held my hand up, not sure if he could even see it. Jodie grabbed my hand, still giggling, and tried to pull it down but couldn't.

'Well done, mate!' The man clapped, and I kept on showing him my ring. Jodie finally pushed me down the path, around the corner and we burst out laughing, falling against each other. There was happiness and excitement in our future again, just as it had been on the day I proposed to Jodie.

CHAPTER 15

'Would you ever have a threesome?' Jodie asked me, eyeing me from behind her coffee cup as I dug in to breakfast. My mouth was full, and I had a chance to think about it. She read my face as I swallowed.

'Is this is some sort of test?' She barely shrugged. 'Are you thinking about another man or another woman?'

'I'm not thinking about anything, I'm asking you,' she replied, her smile still obscured by her cup.

'You can have a threesome with Amy and Julie if you want to.'

'Typical lesbian stereotyping, huh? Don't bring this up in front of Amy, or she'll be pissed.'

'Are you telling me she wouldn't sleep with you?'

'Maybe. She invited me to one of the orgies she organised back in university!'

'An all-female orgy?' I asked, a little rhetorically. I had

never heard *this* story.

'I didn't ask for an information leaflet.' Jodie rolled her eyes. She grabbed my empty plate and her cup and walked to the kitchen. Jodie's figure was lit by the sunlight coming through the kitchen window. For someone who wasn't exercising a lot, and in their 30s, she was very slim: *a great metabolism*, she would often tell me when I complimented her. She washed the dishes in the sink and hummed a song I didn't recognise. I was surprised how well she was coping, given that the power she had probably used every single day was suddenly missing from her life. I reflected that my life would also change a lot, now, knowing how much Jodie had protected me. But for the moment, everything felt exactly the way it had.

I stood, walking into the kitchen to lean against the wall, watching Jodie as she wiped the counter. She turned around, smiling, and I winked back at her.

Only a week earlier, she'd slapped me and raged through the flat. And the Jodie I saw in the forest was a completely different person again; sad, lost, and confused. But now the Jodie I had known and loved for so long was finally back.

That day in the forest, she had told me about my past. How things had changed, and how she had encouraged me - *moulded me* - to become the person I was today. But we hadn't really talked about her past, and we were about to start the process of adopting a child.

I wanted to sit down then and there and get to know the real Jodie. I wasn't sure how I should phrase it, but I had to start somewhere - we needed to talk about each other's feelings, and be honest.

But before I could start, Jodie walked up to me, kissed me on the lips, and left for the bathroom. I laughed at myself and went to get ready for work.

***

By 6:48 pm, I was already at the pub, the *Mayflower*. I'd come straight after work so I could get a table and have a beer before Dr Leigh arrived. Why was I nervous? Because of what happened with Stacey? No. I could control myself. It's just dinner.

The Mayflower was always busy. Even on a Tuesday, it wasn't uncommon to have to queue to get a table. It always smelt powerfully of beer and their homemade pies. The three busy bartenders were serving a fairly intoxicated crowd of post-work drinkers, some of whom were beginning to find the card machine a little challenging to operate. At the table next to mine, six lads were joking about how two of them shagged the same co-worker. The other four were shaking the first two's hands and shouting *"pussy brothers!"*. I wanted to find a better table, but the place was already overflowing into the street.

My phone buzzed. It was Dr Leigh asking me what I wanted to drink. Looking back towards the bar, I saw her waving her hand from amid the mass of people waiting to be served. I waved back with a smile and pointed to my phone.

My Wife Jodie

Guinness, if you don't mind :)

A few minutes later, Dr Leigh walked towards the table carrying my Guinness and a glass of red wine for herself. Her light blue dress moved gracefully as she walked.

'Here's your Guinness, sir. That will be nine pounds fifty from you.'

'Nine pounds fifty? What a rip off!' I gestured with my hand at the crowd, 'I'm never coming back here again!'

'Well … the beer was only a fiver,' she explained, 'but I added another four-fifty as table service and a tip - for the beautiful waitress.' She flicked her hair. We both laughed.

'I feel like I have to tell you that I don't normally ask my patients out,' she rubbed the back of her neck. 'Recently, my dog died, and I thought *fuck it.* If I don't put more effort into making new friends, I'll be forever lonely.' I tried not to show that her remark caught me off guard. 'Does that make sense?' She looked at me quizzically, narrowing her eyes.

'I think so, yes … ' and for the first time, I saw the real Dr Leigh, not someone who was trying to be funny, or wearing a mask. 'So if you normally don't ask your patients out, who *do* you ask?'

'Cute, funny, genuine guys,' she shrugged.

'Hmm … and which category am I?' She paused comically for a minute before she answered, pressing her index finger ostentatiously to her chin.

'Funny and genuine,' she said finally, with a smile. The pub was getting warm, and I took my jacket off.

'So I'm not cute then?'

'No,' she answered without hesitation, shaking her head.

'Why am I not cute?'

'I don't know! Ask your mother.' Maybe it was the beer but I found this incredibly funny, and she joined my laughter. When my eyes finally met hers again, she looked at me longingly, hungrily. Was she doing this on purpose? Why was I so drawn to her? Jodie. Fuck, this was not ok.

'Well, if you ever meet my mother, you can ask her yourself,' I said at last, and then I heard myself and my cheeks started to burn.

There was a pause. 'Awkward,' she said, finally breaking the silence and taking a long sip of her wine, looking past me. 'I guess I was right when I said you were genuine, though.'

An hour and three pints later, I felt I had gotten to know Dr Leigh. She had spent her school years being invisible, trying not to stand out, learning as much as she could without being called a nerd.

'You didn't want to stand out?' I asked.

'When we had nativity plays, I was perfectly happy to be the Christmas tree. Four years in a row.'

She chose to study medicine, and during her final years, she had pushed herself even harder to study. Dr Leigh's sister had finished a Masters in Biomedical Science, and so she was determined not to disappoint her family by achieving anything less. She'd tried dating for a while in university, but exam time always meant a new breakup.

'They were just boys, y'know? All they wanted was sex; they couldn't handle the fact that a woman had dreams, that a relationship is a commitment between two people. An equal commitment.'

By this point, I'd decided that telling her I was married would be too embarrassing for us both.

Dr Leigh got her dog when she was 27; she'd named it Ben. 'I thought it would make me happier,' she sighed, 'and as a bonus, he also kept me company when I went jogging.' She sounded a little sad. 'Everything was wonderful, until Ben got sick. The medication helped him, but I knew it was a losing battle. The vet told me Ben wasn't in much pain, but I knew it was a lie to make me feel better. Ben was in pain, I was able to tell that much. He'd lost his appetite; he stopped wagging his tail, and he could barely get up to say hello when I came home each night. About a month ago I put him to sleep. He was only eight.'

'I'm sorry.'

'Hey, but at least I had a dog and not a cat, right?' She suddenly brightened up, playing with her large, flashy earrings. 'Because otherwise, I'd just be this sad cat lady. Moaning about her dead cats. Can you imagine?'

I pretended to grimace, and we both ended up smiling. 'How do you feel now?' I asked.

'Well, all my life, I tried to please other people. First it was my sister because I wanted to be like her, studying hard to match her grades - I just wanted her to take me seriously. Then my friends. *Always be positive*, my mother used to say; *no one likes gloomy people*. Then all my professors at university, then my boyfriends. In the end, none of it matters because all those people moved away, out of my life, and I was alone.'

Dr Leigh lightly tapped her fingers on her glass, waiting for me to say something. I remained silent, watching her, and she continued. 'I tried to live by the rules: don't sleep with the man 'til the third date. Don't travel by yourself. Wear make-up but not too much. Be nice to everyone.' With every sentence, she was getting angrier. 'Make polite small talk at work. Ask your colleagues how their weekend went. Don't be weird. Be professional. Don't talk about your period. Fuck it all!' The bar was emptying and I signalled the bartender to get us another round. 'That's why sometimes I say inappropriate things at work, wear a Christmas hat in the summer, have a flask that's filled with water on my desk. I want to do whatever makes me happiest. I want to break those stupid rules. And I'm as good a doctor as anyone else in my practice, maybe better - because I try harder to prove that I'm not bonkers.' She sighed. 'That's why I asked you, my patient, to come for a meal. Because why not. Fuck the rules.'

'Fuck the rules, indeed!' I lifted my pint and lightly touched her empty wine glass, as it rested on the table.

* * *

The cold night air hit me as I stepped outside the pub, jolting me awake, and I held the door open as Dr Leigh walked past me brushing her fingers against my chest, telling me I was *such a gentleman*. Other couple's laughter faded into the distance, echoing down the cobbled street.

'This is me.' She pointed to a taxi.

'Where is your car? You're not driving?'

She laughed. 'Of course not, I'm drunk! I parked my car outside your flat. As far from your car as possible.' She winked.

'Why do you park your car in that residential parking lot, anyway?'

'Because the parking near my work is always full, and your parking lot is so well hidden that there's always spaces available for me. And you said you live there, right?'

'In the parking lot?' I smiled. It was a bad joke. 'But yes, I've got an apartment in one of those warehouse conversions on the river.'

'Oh, those? I lived there too.' She was excited, now. 'Maybe we were neighbours!' She clapped her hands. 'What was it, eight years ago?'

'Eight? I've lived there for nine! Reeds Wharf, Apartment 17.'

'No way! Apartment 9! We *were* neighbours! What a small world.'

'Why did you move out?'

'Oh, I got an amazing offer to sell up. It was so good I couldn't say no. I made a fortune.'

'Ha, I never thought of you as a businesswoman, Dr Leigh!' Another bad joke.

'Hmm ... I think after tonight we should be on a first-name basis, don't you think, Mr Page?' I took off an invisible top hat.

'As you wish, Charlotte. A pleasure to make your acquaintance.'

'Actually,' she lifted one long finger, 'my friends call me Charlie.'

'I see. Well in that case, thank you for the evening, Charlie.' I smiled awkwardly at her, and the taxi driver beeped impatiently, making us both jump and laugh together. Her hand touched my arm for a moment, just resting there lightly, then waving goodbye she got in the cab and it drove away in a cloud of diesel fumes and smoke. As I waved back, I remembered I still hadn't mentioned I was married, but then nothing happened, and nothing will.

What if I never kissed Stacey? Could Jodie have made it up so I'd be less angry with her for engineering my whole life? To make me apologise, and put me on the defensive? No, Jodie wasn't that kind of person.

It was just past ten, and I started to make my way home on foot. It was only a short walk; my open jacket flapped to the side, releasing the heat of the pub and the night. I walked the same path I had walked with Jodie the day before, and small waves lapped gently at the riverbank. Reaching for my phone, I found Dr Leigh's contact, smiling, and changed the name to *Charlie*.

Something in my mind clicked as I started to type, I wasn't sure what it was, but I opened the gallery app and scrolled down until I found the picture I'd taken of Jodie's green book. The list of names that I'd stared at for so long, trying to understand. Those names. Jordan, Camila, Kate, Taylor, Drew, Victoria, Jamie, Remy, Alex, Charlie, Laura, Riley, and Stacey.

Charlie   Neighbour   14-03-2008

Charlie's words just now - *We were neighbours! What was it, eight years ago?* Surely it was just a coincidence. *Oh, I got an amazing offer to sell up. It was so good I couldn't say no. I made a fortune!*

My hands were shaking. I had to call Theo.

'Hey mate I'm a little bus–'

'Theo, can you please do me a solid? Now, if possible.' I heard my own slurred, urgent speech.

'Sure … what's up?

'Can you please check who owns Flat 9, Reeds Wharf?'

'Now?' He whispered. 'Mate, I'm with Jordan.'

'Fine. Just send me a link to the site on my phone, or something? You told me it was simple to check the ownership. It's important.'

Theo sighed dramatically, and there was some murmured conversation in the background. A few seconds later, I was clicking on the link Theo had sent me.

'Right, what do I do?

'Just enter the address into the box, pay three pounds, and then they'll send you a copy of the title.'

'Right, let's see.' I typed *Mill Street, Reeds Wharf, Flat 9.* A payment screen. I don't know if I was sober enough to read the details of my bank card, but my phone just asked for a fingerprint. And then it was done.

'You all good there?' he checked.

'Yes,' I looked at the document I'd received, as I stood on the riverside path. 'It's owned by a Mr Lukas and Ms. Greta ... ' I struggled to pronounce their surname. Something Russian. Relief flooded through me. 'Thank you, Theo.'

'Cool. Stay safe, buddy. I'll call you tomorrow.'

I was about to close the browser when I noticed there were five more pages in the document. I clicked on page two. The previous owner was a Mr Michael Langley; he'd sold it to the Russians on the 20th of May, 2016. And on the 13th of July, 2012, he had purchased it from a Ms Jodie Page.

***

I threw up, then, on to the low wall by the path, not quite able to lean over and vomit into the river. I was wasted, and my head was spinning. I could barely walk in a straight line.

The list of all names in that book are of women. The first entry, Jordan. Jordan from the university, the cute girl who liked me? The one Theo is with right now? Stacey, the yoga teacher? Charlie.

It was a list of the affairs I'd had. That page in Jodie's book, thirteen women were on that list; I had cheated thirteen times. All these years, I'd believed that I had been a faithful husband, that every time was my first transgression. Could Jodie have made it all up? No. I'd seen Stacey, and I just went on a fucking date with Charlie.

I re-read the names, the screen of my phone blurry and bright in the darkness. Jordan, Camila, Kate, Taylor, Drew, Victoria, Jamie, Remy, Alex, Charlie, Laura, Riley, and Stacey. Jodie knew about all of these women, and she'd made them all just disappear from my life, as if we'd never met.

Laura, 17-09-2010. That date, two weeks before she died. My heart raced. It couldn't be right. It couldn't possibly be true. I could have never have done this to Laura, to Theo.

Laura's face flashed in front of my eyes as she sat next to me in a booth, in a gay bar in Leeds. Her brown hair had seemed even darker in the colourful lights of the dance floor. Her eyes showed that she'd had too much to drink, we all had; no one had dared say *no* to Amy on her birthday. Theo was off getting another round, Jodie and Amy were gone somewhere. That's when I kissed her. She was as confused as I was. It was so stupid, we were kids, and of course I blamed the alcohol. I promised it was a moment, nothing more, and that I'd learned my lesson. Jodie and Amy both stood up for me - trying to patch things up with Theo - and by some sort of miracle he forgave me after only a couple of months.

As I ran towards home, I cursed myself, that terrible part of me that Jodie had tried to erase so many times before. And I prayed that this was all an awful mistake.

CHAPTER 16

Jodie

If I were like everyone else, what would my life have been like? Would it have been simpler? Happier? Certainly shorter. Would my parents have loved me? Would Ethan have stopped cheating on me, if I had not changed anything, if I had faced the consequences together with him? Would Laura still be alive? I needed to stop thinking about it.

I was four years old the first time I realised I was different. It happened in kindergarten. One of the troubled girls went to another who just finished her drawing, paint still wet, and just ripped it right there in front of her. Viciously with no glimpse of remorse. The other girl cried, and I didn't blame her. The headteacher was busy dealing with the mean girl when I approached the victim and just told her to go back, to save her drawing. I remember her being confused, and as I kept explaining it to her, she started to smile. She thought I was trying to tell her a story.

That was the first clue that something was different, that I experienced my life in a way that no one else did. By the time I was six, I had realised just how alone and how special I really was.

When I was a teenager, I found the courage to talk to two of my best friends from school, Bridget and Lizzie. I told them to write the most random sentence they could think of on a piece of paper, and I'd guess what they wrote. They both lost their shit when I closed my eyes and read it back to them - one word at a time. The tests didn't stop there. I enjoyed it - showing them what I could do. After I passed every test they could think of, they both hugged me. *You're special*, Lizzie told me. *Don't tell this to anyone.*

Not even a week had passed before they started asking me to use my power to help them. At first, it was small things - like finding out whether their crushes liked them, or selecting the best dessert in the cafeteria. I liked it at first, sharing my gift with my friends, them knowing who I really was, but their demands grew over time. They wanted me to do more and more, to tell them the answers to the end-of-year exams, to go back and warn them every time they were about to be busted for smoking cigarettes, or sometimes just when they wanted to play tricks on other girls in class. I didn't want to go back in time more than I had to - all I wanted was to get to my sixteenth birthday, and get the hell away from my parents. Every time I went back, I had to live through more days at home, more time spent avoiding my parents, more time surviving their abuse. But when I finally said no to Bridget's and Lizzie's demands, they got upset.

They started to bully me, call me a selfish, evil witch. They hated me.

'*You're special, don't tell this to anyone.*' Lizzie was right.

Next time I saw them, they were gripping the piece of paper, excited, waiting for me to quote their sentences. We all laughed when I told them I was just messing with them. After that, our friendship gradually deteriorated, though it was mainly my doing. It was hard to keep seeing them as true friends.

Then finally, I turned sixteen. I moved to Leeds, to the new life I'd been waiting for, and to Gary. Gary was the first person I truly fell in love with. We met in a supermarket - he was blocking the aisle with his trolley. I tried to politely squeeze by, but he saw me, apologised a little too much, and we got talking. He was several years older than me and introduced himself as a part-time student, part-time musician, part-time artist. When I asked him where I could see him play, he invited me to his church. The people there were friendly, kind, and welcoming - even though I had learned a lot about religion at school and from friends, this was different. No fire and brimstone; simply being surrounded by people who shared similar goals, whose lives were dedicated to worshiping Jesus and learning the gospel. Every Sunday I spent in that cold auditorium listening to the pastor my heart got warmer, and the words of Luke and John slowly healed the wounds in my soul.

Gary was different from the others; religion was his truth, and he never questioned the sermon. He prayed more than anyone else, and he taught me just as much. I was so young then, and I fell in love with him almost overnight, but I waited patiently until he asked me out and when he did, I was the happiest I've ever been. He filled that void in my heart with his love.

Finally, I stopped being lonely after all these years of being punished by life. I loved him so much and I asked him to have sex with me - to take my virginity. But he didn't want it; he told me it wasn't the right thing to do before we got married and said that as a self-respecting Christian, I shouldn't ask him again. I didn't.

When I graduated from Leeds College, I went on to study project management. I thought my powers would mean it was something I could excel at, without appearing suspicious. My informal education was in Gary's apartment, watching him paint. He explained how his art reflected his belief and how he wanted to use it to inspire people. I would ask questions as he worked, and every night he would explain colour balance, tones, composition, how to mix different types of oils or how to thin them precisely, to achieve exactly the right shade. I never asked him to let me try, and he never offered. Painting was his thing.

He proposed to me the following year, when I was 19 and he was 25. There was a big announcement at church the next Sunday, and everyone hugged me. I was so happy I'd found him and found a church - a community that accepted me. That day the pastor gave a familiar sermon about one of Jesus' miracles, how he had calmed the storm while crossing the Sea of Galilee in a boat. Back then, I was spending a lot of time thinking about whether my power was, in fact, a gift from God. If Jesus had performed all these miracles, did that mean I was also blessed? Maybe Jesus did love me, and I wasn't an *evil witch*.

On Christmas Day that year, everything changed. It was the day I'd decided to share my secret with Gary - we were due to marry the following summer, and I wanted him to know the truth about me. After I told him, he laughed at first, said I was being silly, but I had ways to show him the truth and when I did, he recoiled in fear. He said that *indeed, God has given you this gift.* That he would be marrying God's messenger. He was vibrating with emotion, still afraid of me, but I cried with happiness.

That is, until he asked me what I had done with my powers. I told him about running away from my parents, passing my exams, and winning the lottery. He quietened, and asked that we pray together for a time. When we had finished, he was calmer - *we could make it work,* he had said. *Even the prophets were imperfect people.* He had plans. I was puzzled at first but then he started talking about helping others, about changing the world. He told me everything I would have to do, how we would lead a new church together and how the Word of God would ring from every corner of the earth: *this gospel of the kingdom will be proclaimed throughout the whole world as a testimony to all nations.*

I remembered Bridget and Lizzie - how it had ended, how they had wanted me to do more and more. I told Gary that I wasn't seeking power, that the world didn't need saving. I just wanted to live in love, with God and with him. His face dropped, and he told me I was no Christian because

I'd used my powers to cheat and gamble, to seek wealth. That it was the devil himself who was acting through me. He said I'd wanted to have sex outside of marriage, to drag him down with me, to serve evil. I didn't know what to say, how to calm him down. I was too young to understand.

After he stormed out I sat on the bed, his words cutting deeper every time I played them back in my head. In the end, in anger and sadness, I gave him what he wanted. I went back further than I had ever gone back before, erasing all those experiences and events and happiness, right back to the day I met him when he had stood there in front of me reading the back of a milk carton, blocking my way. I told him it was fine and left the shop without turning back.

Amy was the one who had pointed out Ethan, telling me he was the guy who'd stood up for her when a skinhead had pushed her, shouting *lesbo*. And when I approached Ethan sitting under that tree reading his magazine, I felt an attraction I hadn't felt with Gary. I wanted him to like me. I tried to talk to him, but he didn't seem to be interested, and it just got kind of awkward. I went back and tried again and asked him what he was reading. He said the magazine was about video games, his favourite game, *Resident Evil - to be precise*. I took the magazine, memorised it - ignoring his protests - and went back again, this time talking about the game as if I'd played it. He was well impressed, and asked me what other games I liked to play. Instead I asked him for his favourite game and he told me it was Mortal Kombat 3. I went back a final time and sealed the deal.

Ethan was very different from Gary - he lived in the

present. When I returned to the past, we could have the same conversation, but he would always say new things, have a different take on events. His actions were spontaneous, and he managed to surprise even *me* sometimes. He made me happy, and in return for his love, I gave him the best life. Gary had accused me of being selfish, and I was determined to prove him wrong; I wanted to be good, to do good things.

I made sure nothing bad ever happened to Ethan or his mother. If he tripped and hurt his ankle on the way to the mountain peak, I would be there to make sure to remind him to step carefully. If he was skiing and broke his leg, I would be there to remind him that the snow wasn't so great, and to be careful. If we crashed the car, I would ask him to drive slower, saying I wanted to sleep. If he caught the flu, I would go back two days and make sure he wore a scarf, washed his hands and ate enough vegetables. I wanted him to be at his best on important days at court. But I found that the more time passed, the more reckless he became; I would find myself going back and repeating the same days again and again, to prevent him making some new mistake. I knew that this was because he never got hurt, never learned, had never felt the pain of an injury - but I loved him, and I couldn't see him hurt. I'd created this reckless, irresponsible person, but for the first time I couldn't bear to fix the cause - me. All I could do was see it through.

When Ethan had kissed Laura in that dark, seedy nightclub, he was so ashamed. In the years that followed, Amy would remind him of his mistake at every opportunity, and I couldn't let him go through all of it again when he slept with Jordan. I wanted our marriage to be perfect, and I knew I was the one for him, because every time he cheated the story would go the same way. He would come back to me and beg for my love and understanding, crying, and I'd forgive him every single time. Because I knew what it was like to be blamed. To be called selfish, to be a bad person. Ethan's cheating hurt me, but at least I could take his pain away and bring back the happy days, our love.

And what was the point of my powers, anyway, if not to fix things? *To love, honour, and protect.* That's why I had always gone back, erased the embarrassment, the guilt, the shame. We would always love each other.

***

I closed the book I'd been trying to read, shivering as I stretched for the blanket. The living room was colder than usual, a sharp pain in my stomach as I stood up to get a glass of water. The kitchen was also cold, so I opened the window to let in some evening air. It was just past ten o'clock, but the night was still very warm. I put my empty glass in the sink, hearing a key fumbling in the lock. The apartment door swung open. I couldn't see anything, but I recognised the sound of Ethan's shoes.

'Jodie!' He yelled out. I kept silent, scared of his aggression. I heard him move through the apartment, searching for me. My heart started to pound as I tried to figure out what might have gone wrong. He checked the toilet, opened the bedroom door, shouting my name until suddenly he was standing right in front of me, blocking the kitchen exit. He was clenching his fists, eyes wide and angry. Smelling of beer and vomit. I wanted him to say something, but he just stared at me, his eyes not moving from mine. I waited.

'Did I have an affair with Laura?' He spat it out, like it was something disgusting in his mouth. My body went numb, sending cold chills down my spine. How did he know?

'What...what are you saying?' I was playing for time, but my throat was tight, now, and it was hard to speak.

'You know exactly what I'm asking you.'

'No... No, I don't. What are you talking about?'

'Don't you dare pretend, Jodie!' He shouted, poking his finger right in my face.

'Ethan! For the love of God, what are you talking about?'

'Laura Davies! Your fucking friend, Theo's wife. I was the *white guy* who stole her from Theo, wasn't I?'

How did he know? He couldn't. 'I ... I ... this is crazy. It's not true.'

'How dare you drop this bomb about ... time traveling, and then lie to me about my past?

'Ethan, I don't understand what you're saying.'

'Before all this, I was just Ethan, a good guy and a lawyer in the city, and now?' He turned, suddenly punching the kitchen wall. I jumped as something cracked. 'Who am I now? Who am I supposed to be? Some loser, working in a pub to pay the rent? No money, a crappy job, cheats on his wife - a man without any honour. Is this how you see me?'

I was still trying to figure out how he knew about Laura. Then it suddenly hit me ... my notes from the green book. He'd found my book.

'You have my notebook! How long have you been thinking about this?'

'Why the fuck does it matter? How can I trust you, when you said there was nothing more for me to know? I was already struggling to accept this new you and now this? We were going to adopt a child!'

'Ethan, I did all this - everything - for you!'

'Liar!' The slap came from nowhere, his hand against my cheek, throwing me back towards the kitchen sink. I leaned on the kitchen counter for support, staring up at him with tearful eyes, my face becoming hot. 'Tell me the truth!' My hands shook, holding the edge of the sink.

'You don't understand. I was trying to protect you.' I stood up, moving to the other side of the kitchen, manoeuvring around him.

'Was I the person that Laura left Theo for?'

'Ethan, please!' I shouted again, crying now. He was right in front of me. 'I did this for everyone.'

'Bullshit! You did this for yourself because you didn't want to let me go!'

'You weren't there!' I scream back at him, my face inches away from his. 'You go through my things, find something I kept hidden - hidden for your sake - and now you're blaming me, so you don't have to feel shit about fucking your best friend's wife!' He twisted his body; his hand stretched back.

I grabbed the knife off the counter before he could hit me again. 'No!' The knife was between us now, level and steady.

He lowered his hand. 'You're the one who kept secrets from me, Jodie, all my life. Don't blame me for being upset when I find out.' I didn't know what to say. 'Why did you keep everything from me? How can I ever trust you, knowing you are hiding the truth? What else have you changed that I don't know about?'

'Does it matter what I changed?' I was weeping silently now, tears rolling down my cheeks. 'I did those things for you!'

'Jodie, tell me what you changed.'

I was moving around him now, leaving the kitchen, backing deeper into the dining room but he kept a constant distance between us. I had to get out. I closed my eyes and inhaled deeply, trying to concentrate, but his hand suddenly grabbed mine and knocked the knife out of my grip. He shoved it away and it clattered on the wooden floor of the dining room.

'Tell me what you changed!' He repeated it again, louder this time. I tried to back away from him again, create some space, but he stayed close, in my face. 'Who is Jill?' It was the one name I wished he wouldn't ask about. The only name that had destroyed our marriage. 'Who is she?'

I had to get away from him so I could go back. I just needed space, a few seconds to focus.

'Fucking tell me who Jill is!' He kept screaming, irrational now. 'Who is she, Jodie?'

'She is...' it didn't matter. 'It's done. It doesn't matter.' I don't know how, maybe it was my body language, maybe it was my glance to the wall, but suddenly he understood. He knew everything.

His face changed, the horror dawning, the veins popping on his forehead. He didn't look like himself. He screamed in terror once then again. I covered my ears to stop hearing this agonizing cry. Ethan gave me one disgusted look before he pushed me so hard I fell across the room slamming into the edge of the dining room table. I felt something pop in my back, and a piercing pain shot through my body.

'You bitch!' He cried out, a plaintive note to his voice now. 'How dare you! How fucking dare you!' The pain I'd shielded him from for so long was washing over him now, all at once, and it was all my fault.

The adrenalin was making it so hard to focus. Ethan grabbed the painting of the two children holding hands, and he threw it at me. I shielded my face in my arms.

'You selfish bitch!' His look was murderous, now, and he started to stalk towards me, closing the distance.

'Please, Ethan, stop!' I cried, and turned around, grabbed the knife off the floor and ran towards the bedroom, the excruciating pain in my back making it hard to move but I did it anyway.

A thousand thoughts came and went in the space of a second, all at once. Passing the front door but there was no point trying; by the time I unlocked it, Ethan would be on me. I burst into the bedroom and locked the door behind me. Maybe there was enough time for me to escape and fix this, now. I lay there on the blood-stained carpet, trying to calm myself, to focus, to slow my breathing.

'Why, Jodie? Why did you do this?' Ethan yelled, kicking the door. It shook like it was cardboard.

I closed my eyes once more and tried to concentrate. The second time Ethan kicked the door, the cheap lock broke and it swung open. I held the knife up and out in front of me as my last line of defence, and he lunged into the room, tripping on the edge of the carpet, falling, falling on me holding the knife. The blade pierced his chest and disappeared into his heavy body. He recoiled and groaned, trying to say something, his eyes locked on mine, crushing me with his weight. All I could feel was his hot, sweaty body resting, pressing on to my lungs, my shirt wet with his blood, I couldn't breathe, the smell of vomit and beer and blood. My hand still holding the knife. I gathered strength and pushed him off me, onto his side. He still moved slightly; his eyes were fixed on mine. They didn't look angry any more. The pungent smell of iron filled the room; we were both covered in his blood.

I had done so much for him: I had cared for him, forgiven him after he cheated on me, given him money, friends, his health, his life, my love, but none of that mattered. I was always wrong. No matter how much I tried, no matter which path I took, the outcome was always the same. People ended up hating me. My body tensed, the anger coursing through me, as on the day he cut his finger. I was angry at myself for papering over the cracks, for hiding his lovers. Angry at myself for not being strong enough to go through with the drama. Angry at myself for not letting him learn.

I trembled and roared like the mad woman Ethan knew I was. I pulled the knife out of his chest, and he moved again, trying to save himself, but I shoved the knife hard, up under his rib cage and right through his heart, falling on his body, the blood covering my face. He spasmed one final time and fell still. I screamed, and screamed, and screamed.

***

I'd never asked that my life be this fucking soap opera. I just wanted to live quietly, to have a husband, to grow old together. I never wanted all this; the anger, pain, and death.

If I was still able to go all the way back in time, to when I was only sixteen, I would have. I would return and try again. Maybe I wouldn't lie this time around; maybe I would tell Ethan everything right from the start. Perhaps he would still love me, and if not, I would just try again, something different. But I was stuck here now, in this shitty timeline, unable to go back to before that awful day, our anniversary.

I have to accept this present timeline and I need to make it work, or the last 20 years would have been for nothing. Maybe Gary was right; maybe the devil did act through me and I was just one, big, supernatural joke. God messing with His universe.

I closed my eyes and concentrated, trying to focus.

CHAPTER 17

Ethan

Running just made me more tense, the anxiety rising with every stride. I feared that something had irreversibly changed, now, and my life would never be the same. Sweat poured down my face, my shirt stuck to my skin but the anger fuelled me, making me run faster. I opened the front door to our building, rushed up the stairs, skipping every other step. I almost kicked my way into our flat; the door flew open and hit the wall, leaving a small dent.

'Jodie!' I looked in the bathroom, in the bedroom, but she wasn't there. I moved into the kitchen, still shouting her name, no response. I peered around our dining room in the darkness, then my eyes caught her, sitting on the sofa where she usually read, staring ahead blankly. I half ran, half stumbled to her, seeing her more clearly now though my vision was still muddled by beer and anger and pain. She didn't turn to me, just stared straight ahead with no expression on her face.

'Did I have an affair with Laura?' I spat out, finding Jodie's calm demeanour irritating.

'Yes, you did.' She didn't even blink as she said it. No manipulation or denial. My knees went weak, and I wanted to shake her, to get some reaction. How could she have kept this away from me? Why was she keeping all these secrets? I stared at her as she clenched her fists. My jaw hurt from the continuous tension. I had to know everything she was keeping from me.

'Why haven't you told me this before?'

Jodie closed her eyes. 'Because I wanted us to remember Laura for who she was all these years, and not for why her life ended the way it did,' I was pacing around the room, and this stopped me dead. 'And I didn't want you to feel somehow responsible for what happened.'

'Why would I feel responsible for Laura's death?'

'Because it takes two people to have a relationship.' She hadn't raised her voice at all, nor showed any shock that I knew the truth or had asked her about it. 'You left me, Laura left Theo, and you helped Laura with the divorce and custody proceedings. The judge ruled Theo was unfit to take care of Anneli. Then you took her from him, too. If you had just said 'no' to Laura, it would have been the easiest solution. None of this would have happened. She wouldn't have left Theo, and he wouldn't have committed suicide, and I would have been able to save Laura's life the day of the accident.'

Was this how people with dementia felt? People telling

things you had done, even though you had no recollection of doing them? Jodie was describing this person that I didn't recognize. It was completely different from who I thought I was. It was absurd. I wasn't this person. I'd never imagined myself cheating on anyone, especially not Theo and Laura.

'You're lying! You have to be.' I just couldn't believe her words, but now I didn't know whether I was still angry at Jodie or if I was angry at myself.

'I can't prove anything to you,' she said calmly, 'but I think you know the truth, in yourself.' She finally lifted her head and looked straight into my eyes. There were deep red circles under her eyes, like she'd been crying, but her face was dry. 'Did you have any feelings for Laura before her death?'

I remember the months and weeks before the accident. After Anneli was born, I had spent more and more time with Laura. We would cook dinners, watch TV; we were doing things couples do. I had just wanted to be there for her, to help her raise Anneli, protect them both. Neither Theo nor Jodie ever said anything to us because we were all just friends; surely no one saw that Laura and I were forming a bond, one that was growing stronger every day. Our feelings were not romantic, but if Laura hadn't died that day, how could I be sure that nothing would have ever happened?

The day she died, my heart broke as I held her lifeless body in my arms. Her eyes wide open, staring blindly at the vast, dark sky above us. I held her close to my body, trying to warm her up, my tears falling onto her face.

Theo was destroyed, and I spent a lot of time with him after the accident. I told myself that I was there for him to give him the compassion he needed. But really, this wasn't true; I spent time mourning with him because it made me feel better. I needed someone to share my pain, and Theo was that person.

'Why did you lie to me? Why did you lie, for so long?' I asked, calmer now.

'I only told you half the truth because I didn't want you to experience what you're going through right now. The guilt and the shame.'

'You don't have the right to decide for me what I should and shouldn't feel!'

Jodie rose slowly from the sofa and took a step forward. She took a deep breath before she spoke.

'If you honestly believe that, then tell Theo everything. Let him know that you were seeing Laura before she died. Tell him about your feelings.' Her eyes were fixed on mine now. Neither of us moved, but we were both thinking the same thing. She was right, and I finally understood how she felt. If I'm to blame Jodie for all the time that she kept things away from me, how she disclosed only the partial truth, wanting to protect me, then I would have to tell Theo the truth. I couldn't have both.

'What do you think he would say to you if he knew the truth?'

'Just … shut up for a moment. Please.' It could have been my imagination, but was there a trace of a smile, of victory, on Jodie's face? I had held it against her that she hadn't told me the truth in Edinburgh; I thought she should have told me everything, about things that hadn't happened, that she had changed. I walked back to the dining room as everything started to spin.

***

My vision was blurry, but I recognised the smell of Jodie's sweet perfume before I opened my eyes, her hands pressing something cold against my forehead. I was lying next to the dining room table. Jodie's face looked relaxed now, the smallest of smiles.

'What's on my head?'

'Bag of peas,' Jodie shrugged.

'Why?'

'Because in the movies when people faint you put frozen shit on their head.' She shrugged again with another smile now, bigger this time. When I didn't smile back, hers faded. Slowly I sat up, my body feeling much heavier, less mobile. I was still drowsy from the beer I'd drunk.

'Would you like tea? I have a new Rooibos I got from Bermondsey market.'

'No,' I said, abruptly, ending her smile.

'I'm sorry yoi–' I raised my hand to make her stop talking.

'Please don't.' For the first time, my idea of who Jodie was had changed. She no longer was the person that I thought I'd loved. She might look the same, she might smile and laugh the way she used to, but the sweet Jodie I once knew was gone. She was my protector, my custodian, but she was no longer my lover.

She loved me and cared for me, but we had lived two separate lives. As I wondered what kind of restaurant we should go to for dinner, she was trying to figure out how she could prevent some *other* woman from crossing my path. As I blamed that truck driver for losing control at the T-junction, Jodie was in her world, trying to think of any other way she could have saved Laura without destroying Theo. Had we ever been a couple, or was everything we had, every happy memory and every spontaneous moment carefully planned, orchestrated by Jodie?

She must be happy with what she has, or she would have gone back to the time we met and not approached me. But I struggled to understand what she gained from this relationship. I wasn't a loving husband if I'd cheated on her all those times. I wasn't providing for her - she had millions in her bank account. Why was she here now, leaning over me with that frozen bag of peas? Why did she care?

I stood up to go to the kitchen for a glass of water, trying to sober up, find some solid ground. Jodie followed, quietly standing in the kitchen doorway. I needed a break from all of this.

Jodie stood patiently, watching me, waiting for me to say something. I didn't make eye contact with her, just made my way to the bedroom, stepping past Jodie as she stood leaning against the door frame.

'Where are you going?' Jodie finally broke the silence. I stopped, but I didn't turn to face her.

'To bed.'

'Should we talk about what happened?'

'When I wanted to talk to you, you didn't. You told me you were going to *fix this*.' I paused for a brief moment before I continued. 'Don't worry, Jodie. I'm going to fix it.' She didn't respond as I walked away.

I went to the bedroom to grab my pillow and an extra blanket from the wardrobe. When I was leaving the room, Jodie stopped me in a hall.

'You're not going to sleep with me?'

I lifted my pillow into the air. 'No.'

She took a deep breath, shaking her head. I turned towards the guest bedroom as she spoke again.

'Where's my notebook?'

'What notebook?' I turned around.

'The green book that you read, with the dates and names.'

I paused for a second. 'I'll get it for you.' I nodded, as Jodie's phone rang. She looked towards the living room.

'Get the phone.'

She turned and disappeared into the hall, and I went back to the bedroom, lifted the bed, taking the notebook from the box.

Stepping into the living room, I overheard Jodie saying goodnight to Amy. I passed her the small green book, labelled with her careful handwriting.

'I'm sorry I read it, but you disappeared, and I was trying to understand.' I said.

'It's fine.'

We stood there facing each other for a few seconds, neither of us knowing what to say.

'I asked you if there was anything more, and you said there wasn't.'

She dropped her chin to her chest, avoiding my look.

'I'm sorry,' she said. 'I just wa–'

'Is there anything else I should know?'

She kept her gaze low. 'No.' She shook her head. 'No.'

'Good night,' I said, and I turned away.

I closed the door to the guest bedroom and tucked myself under the duvet. When everything was silent apart from the cars outside, I could hear Jodie sob quietly through the wall. I didn't think she was a bad person. She might be one of the best people I knew. I could forgive her for keeping the truth from me, for wanting to protect my feelings. Hell, I could even forgive her for controlling my life the way she did, and in a way I already had. But I couldn't ever forgive her for lying to me about Laura. It meant I couldn't trust anything she said or anything she did, and where is a relationship without trust?

But something else, something even bigger was bothering me.

I couldn't fall asleep, and I kept replaying our conversations over the past week, all of them. Searching my memory, lying there, but I couldn't remember even hinting to her that I had read her green notebook. How on earth did she know about this? When I came back from Edinburgh I'd placed it back where I found it. I didn't want Jodie to know I had read it, but somehow - she knew.

CHAPTER 18

Jodie

Clutching my notebook, I closed and locked the door to the bedroom. My heart started to beat faster, remembering that only a few hours ago Ethan had kicked this door down and ... tripped. I stepped over the week-old bloodstain on the carpet, curled up in bed with my clothes on, watching the door. I was afraid because I didn't know what he was thinking, how much he knew. What if he tried to hurt me again? What if I couldn't go back, the next time? I dreaded the nightmares that would keep me awake.

The only thing I wanted more than anything was to go back to before the day my powers had disappeared, to make it so that I would have never run away, told Amy about Stacey or all the rest of this mess. Ethan and I could have continued living the beautiful life we'd created. Now we slept in separate beds, each afraid of the other.

My Wife Jodie

When my ability to travel in time had mysteriously returned, back at my parents' place in Scotland, I'd been so happy to finally make things normal again. And then I'd realised that there was some sort of wall. I couldn't go back beyond the moment my powers had returned, and panic overwhelmed me. I tried hundreds of times, returning to that moment over and over, months and months of practicing, pushing at the strange barrier in my mind, working until I became unconscious. The earliest I was able to go back to was August 27th, at 4:32 in the morning, and so there was no escaping the shit I'd left in London. I had to come back to face Ethan, to answer all of his questions, and to try and fix our marriage.

In the years I'd known him, each time I'd told him about my powers led to a downward spiral, to him not being able to cope with the knowledge. Edinburgh had been different, perhaps because he knew my abilities had disappeared and he didn't have to think about his future. He accepted me for who I was - and finally, I was able to talk with him, tell him about his past, about where I was getting money. It had been good to let it all out. I'd waited my entire life to share this with someone without feeling afraid of being used or rejected.

I didn't want to lose that, and so when my powers returned I did what I had been doing my entire life. I told him what he wanted to hear - that I was ordinary, like everybody else. I just wanted us to be happy.

CHAPTER 19

Ethan

'Do you want more coffee?' Jodie asked, raising the cafetiere. I shook my head and ate the last spoonful of my porridge.

I had woken up at 7 in the morning. My plan had been to leave early so I wouldn't cross paths with Jodie, but when I stepped out of the bathroom, breakfast had already been on the table. This gave me another reason to be suspicious. Was she using her powers to please me, make us talk, patch things up between us?

'Oh, cheers.' Forcing a smile on my face. Surely she knew I was still mad, and breakfast wasn't going to change that. I couldn't bear to talk to her, to discuss or confront her about her powers. I just wanted to go to work.

'Ethan, I'm sorry. I know this must be tough on you,' she was talking calmly as she filled the cup with coffee.

'Yes, we can talk later, but I need to go to work now.

Don't worry.' I stood up from the table and reached for my jacket, 'Let's talk about this tonight.' I would avoid that talk as much as I possibly could.

I wasn't totally sure that Jodie's powers were back, but I had a clue - just one small, precious clue. Jodie knew yesterday that I had read her green book. If I dared to complain, or if she detected a note of frustration, I was sure she wouldn't hesitate to wipe out this timeline and that precious piece of information. It felt so fragile, like carrying a butterfly in my palms. One wrong move, and the butterfly would be crushed.

'When are you back?'

'After work, the usual time.' I forced a smile. I just wanted to get the hell out of the house.

'Oh, and Ethan.' She walked closer, something in her hand. 'I found your ring - it had fallen down the back of the nightstand.' Her cold hands took mine and she gently twisted it on to my finger. The pain from the cut made me flinch. 'Sorry.' She pushed it all the way and gave me a kiss.

'I'm going to be late for work.'

'Ok, let's talk when you're back.'

I grabbed my backpack and headed out, waving what I hoped was a cheery goodbye. Outside, with the front door locked behind me, I took a deep breath.

I drove to work thinking about Jodie and her powers. Was it all in my head? Was there something I could do to test my theory? Could I set up some sort of trap at home? Maybe a bucket of paint falling over in the storage room, or breaking a vase she liked. Would she save it? It would have to look completely natural. If she figured out I was testing her, that'd be it. *Poof.*

There wasn't much traffic and I was at my desk about twenty minutes later. I closed the door to my office, pulling off my wedding ring. The tension I was keeping hidden inside finally began to dissipate. The plan was clear: I had to find out if she had her powers again, and more importantly, whatever I did, not give myself away. But I hadn't come up with many good ideas.

I was hoping work might distract me for a time, and maybe some stroke of genius would hit me when I least expected it. I opened my emails and saw there it was a new client, referred to me by Lucy, a criminal case. He was being held at a Kensington police station. I picked up my backpack again and went straight there.

When I arrived, they took me to a small, cold room, and a friendly looking policewoman brought my client, a Mr Amar Patel, into the room. She made sure we were settled and closed the door, telling me that she'd be outside if I needed her.

We introduced ourselves, and he nodded as I talked about our firm and explained my rates. According to his file, Amar was twenty-four, but he looked much younger. His mother, sister and himself had emigrated from Mumbai about twenty years ago. He had been raised in East London, and I was surprised he was able to afford to hire someone like me, working as a paramedic.

His whole body was shaking. I felt for him; he had

been charged with grievous bodily harm, and if convicted he wouldn't be getting less than five years in prison. The case wasn't looking good. He'd assaulted a young man at night with a hammer, right in front of an off-duty police officer; he had been arrested on the spot. I couldn't resist asking why.

'I tried to help him,' he paused. 'I have helped others before; they will be willing to testify.' His voice rose a pitch higher. 'I want to ask them to help my defence.' He kept blinking, his hands pressed tight under his armpits. I was accustomed to seeing people scared after being arrested, but he acted like his whole life depended on me.

'You wanted to help - and you attacked this man with a hammer?'

He jerked his head. 'Ethan. We live our lives believing we know what is right, and what is wrong. We judge other people's actions from the perspective of our own,' he sighed. I wanted him to elaborate, and waited. 'I know that it might sound like I am crazy when you don't see things as I do, and I'm not blaming you. Most people would say I'm crazy. But when I rescue people, I open their eyes; people can live their life more fully after a near-death experience.'

'But how can you tell if someone needs your help? Maybe they don't?'

'That's the problem with you people. Everyone has their own opinion; everyone *thinks* they know what's best. But the truth is, most of us don't. We get so involved in our lives that we refuse to take a step back and look at the bigger picture.'

'And you see that bigger picture?'

He nodded ever so slightly.

I nodded back out of politeness, biting my lower lip. This was what I was going to be dealing with for the next couple of months. Lucky me.

***

I left the police station, but Amar's words stayed with me. I played them over in my head as I made my way back to the office. He and Jodie would have a lot to talk about; they both seemed to feel like they were entitled to help others - without being asked. I didn't want to live my life knowing everything I did would be fixed by Jodie, just because she thought it best. I turned up the air conditioner, as high as it would go. I hoped it would cool me down and create enough noise to drown out my thoughts. It didn't work.

I just wanted all this madness to stop. I wanted to be in control of my destiny; for the first time in a long time, I felt lonely. Theo had messaged me to ask to meet him today, but I hadn't yet replied. Since Jodie told me that I'd taken Laura away from Theo, I couldn't bear to see him. I needed time to find the courage to face him.

And the pressure was rising the closer it got to the end of the working day. I had to face Jodie in about four hours, and I hadn't come up with any brilliant ideas. I grabbed a cheese and salmon baguette from the local cafe, sat in a shaded garden a few minutes from the office and breathed in deeply, meditating, telling myself I'd find the solution.

A few hours later, I was exhausted. The clock on my computer said it was three minutes past six, and I usually would've left the office half an hour earlier, but I didn't want to move from my chair. A few of my colleagues were still around working on their cases, but I'd done no real work since 3pm. I had to go.

I took my wedding ring out of my pocket, to put it back on before I returned home. That ring with its small engraved message was unsettling, now. *I will love you forever.*

I grabbed my backpack and headed to the parking lot. I couldn't deal with Jodie right now, so I typed a message - 'Sorry, dinner with my colleagues, back at 8pm. Don't worry about ordering food for me.' I kicked the metal door to the underground parking lot, and just before I could press send, I saw Jodie leaning against our car, waving at me. I gasped quietly and hit delete on my phone.

'Surprise!' She lifted both hands in the air. I smiled, forcing it a bit. 'I thought we could drive to the city and have dinner. What do you say?' She seemed much more enthusiastic than normal, and it irritated me.

'I'm not that hungry,' I said, still forcing my smile. My appetite had vanished as soon as I'd seen her.

'Ethan,' she took a few steps towards me, 'we need to talk. Yesterday must have been difficult for you.' She placed her hand on my shoulder; I shook it off and walked around the car.

'You mean it was difficult for me when you told me I was responsible for Laura's death?' I opened the door to the back seat, shoved my backpack in, and then got into the drivers' seat, closing the door. After a moment, Jodie walked around the car to the passenger side and joined me.

'I never said you were.' We were both buckling our seat belts on. 'I said that I *didn't* want you to feel responsible.'

I started the engine. 'Well, it's kinda hard for me to process this, when I have zero knowledge of any of it happening.' I was moving out of the parking lot, half listening, trying to avoid meeting Jodie's eyes. 'But you told me I cheated with Laura, and now Laura is dead becau–'

'Stop!' Jodie shouted, thrusting her hands in front of her; I stopped just inches from bumping into a red Golf. The driver beeped a few times and flicked me a rude gesture. 'Please be careful. I can drive if you feel unwell–'

'I'm fine.' Through gritted teeth, now. I accelerated and left the parking lot. Jodie lowered her window to let in some fresh air. I was watching the road in front of me; we hadn't discussed where we were going, and my autopilot was taking me back home.

'I told you back in the forest near my parent's place; everything that happens, all the timelines I explore, the decisions I make - these are my burden to carry. That is why it's so unfair on you. You don't need to feel any responsibility for Laura's death. It's not your fault.'

'But it still happened, didn't it? You have a memory of it.'

'No, it didn't!' she raised her voice for a moment, paused, and started again more calmly. 'Think about it as a dream, one where awful things happened. But you woke up, and it was just a dream.'

'But it wasn't just a dream, was it?'

'You can't take responsibility for something that ultimately didn't happen - or something you wanted to do, but never ended up doing. People don't go to jail because they have bad thoughts.'

'The church says your bad thoughts are sin.'

'Ethan, *please*.' She rolled her eyes.

'What I'm saying is - it wasn't just a thought, was it?'

'Look, hypothetically, if you had met a member of some gang when you were younger, and you'd fallen in with them, maybe you would have started dealing drugs, maybe you would have stabbed someone and killed them and gone to jail. It's one possible scenario.' She threw up her hands in frustration. 'Are you going to feel bad about that?'

'No, because it didn't happen.'

'Right. In that same way, you didn't have an affair with Laura becau–'

'But I would have had an affair with her, if she was alive today.'

'But she's dead, Ethan. I didn't save her.' She looked at the road ahead of her. 'I know this other version of our life *only because I happened to live through it*.' She sighed. 'We make thousands of decisions every single day, each of them leading in new directions. We can't feel guilty for something that might have happened but didn't,' she took a deep breath, 'and I don't think it is fair to punish me just because I have lived through more of those paths than you have.'

'Why did you stay with me?'

'What?'

'According to you, I've cheated on you thirteen times. Thirteen! Why did you stay? Why didn't you just leave me?'

She was angry, now. 'Because I fucking love you ok? And we were happy, not just us, but everyone! Amy, Julie, Theo. We are all so close, and friends like that don't just happen, we have such a strong bond, and I didn't want that friendship to change. You improved too, you cheated on me less over time.'

Our conversation was so casual. We were arguing about Jodie's time travel and the death of our friend. I gripped the steering wheel tighter, my hands numb.

'All of this is ridiculous.'

'What is?' She sounded surprised. It was like we'd had two completely different discussions.

'Everything!' I raised my voice. 'How can you expect me to live normally, knowing that everything in my life has been somehow altered?'

'It was,' she paused. 'Not any more.' She'd lied to me my whole life, and was still lying now. Fuck. She knew exactly what to say and how to say it. I remember how scared she was back in the flat when I cut my finger or the fear in her eyes in Edinburgh. But now, Jodie was back, fully confident in herself and her abilities. Normal service had resumed, and there was nothing I could do to escape.

'Who is Jill?'

'Jill?'

'Jill, from your book.'

'She's not important.'

'For fuck's sake, Jodie!'

Jodie sighed. 'She was a close family friend, we met her at boxing class, introduced her to Theo, Amy and Laura and Julie. In time she changed, and started to poison our friendship. She did so much damage that I had to go back.'

'We never went to boxing class.'

'Exactly.'

The engine rumbled, and for a while we both watched the road. 'Fuck, Jodie, why should I believe you?'

'Figure out how to go back in time and prove me wrong.' She crossed her arms. It was like I was talking to Amy. She knew how to push my buttons.

The car fell silent, and then suddenly, Jodie took a deep breath. She turned to me with a strange, confused expression and shifted in her seat uncomfortably.

'Ethan, I think I left my keys. Can you stop for a second?' I slowed down and parked on the side of the road. I didn't know if it was safe for me to drive when I felt like this; I was sure she could see that I was barely holding myself together. Jodie was digging inside her purse, and I was enjoying this small respite, just taking one deep breath at a time. She took her keys out of her bag and jingled them in front of me. 'False alarm.' Without saying anything I accelerated hard, merging back into the traffic.

'Wait, we haven't decided where we're going,' Jodie said.

'Home.' I just wanted to go home, to get out of this car and this conversation.

'I think we should go and get some food, talk it throu–'

Jodie stopped talking abruptly, halfway through the sentence, inhaling deeply again. She was nervous, looking around her, then back at me.

'Can you please slow down?' Her voice broke slightly.

'I'm sticking within the speed limit.' I hated her telling me what to do, knowing she could just go back in time whenever she liked. Jodie had always told me what to do; she was the reason I studied Law; she was the one who had told me to invest in Kodak. She manipulated my feelings, let me believe it was just a bad decision to invest, but it had been a carefully thought out plan to make me lose money. Nothing I had done was a bad decision. I wanted to do something she wasn't able to stop me from doing. I accelerated a little, just to annoy her.

'Ethan?'

'I know how to drive!' I said sharply, turning and looking directly at her, deliberately taking my eyes off the road.

The lights ahead of us turned green, and the cars started moving. Jodie gripped the car door. I looked at her and saw that she was scared. Was she going to stop me? The traffic light changed to yellow and the cars neatly one after the other stopped, and I joined them at the end of the queue. Jodie started to breathe more heavily. She touched the door handle, but I locked the doors. A click echoed in the silence. She looked at me, confused.

'For safety.' I smiled, but she didn't. She knew what I wanted to do. 'What's the matter?' I asked, tilting my head. Jodie didn't answer. The light in front of us changed to green, and the cars slowly started to move. Jodie checked her seatbelt and gripped the door, pressing her other hand against the airbag compartment. I kept glancing at her, but she didn't look back at me. She became paler as we drove closer to the crossing up ahead.

'Are you alright? You look tense.'

'I'm fine,' she turned to me, suddenly angry. 'Are you?'

'Yes.'

For the first time in my life, I felt that I was making a decision, a bad one perhaps, but a decision that was solely mine. I accelerated; there were only two cars in front of me when the light changed to yellow. I sped up to catch the vehicles ahead; Jodie was silent, her eyes closed. Both cars ahead turned to the left, leaving the crossing clear.

The red light blinked brightly at me, telling me to stop. Red for danger. I accelerated. The cross traffic shot through the intersection just as I passed the first traffic light. A pedestrian leapt out of the way, shouting. I loosened my grip on the steering wheel, and then with all my power, I braked. Jodie and I were slammed against our seatbelts as the car came to a stop a short way into the intersection.

A few cars trundled past in front of us, and Jodie slowly turned to me, and though I expected her to show fear, perhaps anger or frustration, I saw only surprise in her eyes. Surprise that we were ok, and it hadn't gone quite as she had expected.

Her actions, her visible display of fear and emotion had changed my mind in that moment, had made me decide to brake.

Was she aware I'd been testing her? Would she go back again to erase it all? I couldn't let her.

'I'm sorry,' I grabbed her arm roughly. 'Are you ok?' I looked deeply into her eyes as she nodded, still clearly shocked about what had happened. 'I don't know what got into me, this talk about Laura … I'm sorry. I'm so so sorry! This is a lot for me.' I shook my head, voice breaking.

'I understand.' She was nodding now slowly, watching me, evaluating the outcome.

I took a deep breath. 'I think I'm better now,' I pretended. 'It was like a brain fog or something; I'm so sorry.' She gave me a half-smile, and I smiled too. She placed her hand on mine, which was still holding the steering wheel. She moved her thumb up and down.

'I'm glad you feel better.' She looked a little happier, as if she was thinking *let's see how this goes.*

'I am.' I smiled, grabbing her hand with both of mine, and kissed it. Jodie's breathing was slowing now, her face relaxing.

'Thank you, Ethan.' She pulled back her hand.

'I love you so very much, and I'm sorry. I am sorry I've been such a dick and put you in danger.'

The car behind me honked. The light was green.

PART III

CHAPTER 20

Ethan

THURSDAY 01 SEPTEMBER 2016

Jodie's powers were back.

There was no point in trying to change her behaviour. She was a professional liar. I still loved her, those feelings might never go away, but I was locked in a marriage of lies and manipulation.

Divorce was the only option now.

I was trapped in a perfect prison. My heart ached as I imagined a future without her, but this was the only way.

***

It was 8:24am, and apart from a nervous intern I was the first person in the office. Luckily Jodie had still been asleep when I left home. The morning felt clean and fresh. The window overlooking the building's courtyard was slightly ajar, letting in the breeze. I skimmed through my email messages, hoping I'd missed something important, anything to take my mind off Jodie. My phone buzzed, and without even looking at it I knew it would be her.

Trying for Employee of the Month?

I didn't open the message, so she wouldn't know I'd read it. I had a few meetings on my agenda, but I guess I'd be spending most of the day browsing the internet. I got out of my chair and closed the door to my office, locking it. I sat down on the couch with a deep sigh, my body feeling a few pounds lighter. There were so many things in my head, maybe writing them down might help me see the bigger picture. I grabbed a notebook from the side table and wrote Jodie in the middle of the page. I looked at it, but nothing came to my mind. I circled it once. Twice. Three times. I kept circling it repeatedly, the pencil broke, and I threw the notebook across the room.

Since I had confronted Jodie in Edinburgh, I had been trying to suppress my thoughts. Somehow not thinking about her powers made me feel better; it was like going back to a normal life, leaving everything as it was. But now all I wanted was to tell her the truth, tell her that I knew what she was hiding from me. The pressure was intolerable.

It was like an itch - just one more scratch could help ease the irritation; but just one touch and the consequences would be severe. Jodie could go back as far as she wanted, destroying knowledge and memories in her path, making it *better*. Leaving me to live this life and carry on obliviously, tied to her forever, as if nothing had happened. And if I asked her, she would lie.

I went to the window and pulled up the blinds. I watched people walk on the pavement, heads down. Staring at their mobile phones. I had been like them only a week previously, going about my day, planning my next holiday, worrying about the small things I did. Now, I was losing my mind over things that hadn't happened. It was too much. It had to end.

How much did I truly know Jodie, considering everything I'd discovered in the last week? People always hide behind a facade, but Jodie was different; she didn't have to. Everyone else only had one shot at anything in their lives; they couldn't simply take it back and try something different. Jodie, on the other hand, had multiple, unlimited shots at anything.

Anything she ever said could be changed - she could try a different version, a different angle, a pitch that would produce the result she felt was "best for me." She had virtually unlimited latitude to do whatever the hell she wanted.

Who was she, truly? Did I even know this woman I had married? Was she the loving and caring wife I thought her to be, or the calculating, delusional, insane woman who had slapped me in the kitchen after I cut myself? She must be so proud of herself for *fixing things*.

The last meeting of the day was a write-off. I went through the motions, nodding when appropriate, and occasionally acknowledging the person speaking. When my boss asked me if I wanted to add anything, I said something generic about being proud of the team, and how I'd enjoyed working with everyone on the case. It went down well; I even got a few handshakes for my performance.

When I wasn't in a meeting, I barricaded myself in my office, away from everybody. I needed to talk to someone about this. Not Theo. Not Jodie. Not Amy.

I called my mother. She answered joyfully on the first ring. I tried to sound casual, but she picked up on my tone and she was worried. 'Is everything ok? Is Jodie ok?' My mother loved Jodie, and I couldn't bear to tell her what was going on. Even though part of me was convinced she would be ecstatic if she knew that Jodie was able to travel back in time to protect me, her son, and had saved her life. Of course, she would think that Jodie was an angel. Why would she believe otherwise?

I told her I was fine, and that I missed her. By the time I rang off, she was no longer worried. The conversation just made me more upset.

I kept scrolling, killing time, and it wasn't long before my finger stopped at the newest contact in my phone. Charlie. When we'd met for that meal, she had opened up about her life. It had made me feel comfortable, and I missed that feeling. Our conversation in the pub was genuine, and rare. It wasn't forced and proper, there had been a few awkward pauses between us, but it had all been real. I needed to open up too, and so I found myself typing —

Ethan

How are things, Doctor?

The little *tick* under the message changed immediately, to show it had been delivered. I waited a minute for it to change to *read.* It didn't. I placed my phone on the desk. When Charlie had told me she was lonely, I'd thought about how happy I was to not be in her shoes. Loneliness had sounded awful and sad, then. Now I was lonely, and somehow, she was the only one I could talk to.

I sat in my chair with my head in my hands. I wanted to scream. For just a few seconds, to let my feelings go. But the office certainly wasn't soundproof.

My phone buzzed.

A patient came in today, saying he had some pain when he was using the bathroom, so I told him I'd need to examine his anus. I spent much longer than usual trying to find the source of his pain because there were no abnormalities. So after several minutes it got really awkward, and I told him that he would need to come back in a few days if the pain was still present. Hope your day is going better...

I chuckled, and replied

Are you worried he never had any pain in his anus to begin with?

Her reply came almost instantly.

My Wife Jodie

NOW I AM!!!!! :o

I deliberately paused for a second, before replying again. I didn't want to seem too eager.

Any plans tonight?

***

People in London usually have their plans laid out two weeks in advance; life in the capital. When I had messaged Charlie and asked her if she wanted to hang out today, she'd seemed surprised, but we quickly arranged that I would pick her up at five, and we'd drive to Burgess Park to catch the dwindling sun.

I expected to feel guilt, meeting another woman - even if just for a walk! - but I didn't. With everything that had been happening in my life, this was somehow the least of my worries. I was excited to see her, excited for the novelty. There was also an irrational part of me that wanted to tell Jodie, so it would hurt her, as she had hurt me. She could never forget.

I slowed my car, stopping just outside the front entrance to the clinic. Charlie was already waiting for me on the bench nearby. She wore black sweatpants and a faded green t-shirt, her hair looking even more red in the sunlight. Before I could lower the window to get her attention, she'd already grabbed her handbag and was walking towards my car. She gave me a cheeky smile through the window.

'Look at us hanging out, being friends and shit,' she winked, sliding inside the car and putting her seat belt on. Her freckles were much more visible in the daylight; something I hadn't noticed the other night.

'So, Burgess Park?' I wiggled my eyebrows multiple times. Charlie nodded just as her eyes caught a yellow car driving on the opposite side of the road. Within half a second, she'd punched my shoulder, yelling.

'Yellow car!' I don't know if it was the punch or her scream that made me jump from my seat.

'What are you doing!'

'It's a yellow car game. Whoever sees a yellow car first hits the person they are with.'

'How old are you?' I frowned playfully.

'Thirty-two,' she paused briefly. 'And three-quarters.'

It wasn't the weekend yet, but Burgess Park was full of people and their pets. A group of dogs chased each other in circles around their owners, who were enjoying the sunshine, lying on picnic blankets. The afternoon was pleasant and warm and slow; the smell of grilled sausages was wafting from multiple directions; parents and their children played games on the grass. As we strolled around the pond, the sun became more intense, reminding me of all the times Jodie and I had been here together; her telling me to put on sunscreen. I asked Charlie if I should be worried. She didn't seem too concerned.

'Since Ben died, I stopped going to parks,' her voice was so quiet it was almost inaudible, as a group of joggers passed us, 'in a way, I had paused my life. I was just waiting to get a new dog, hoping it would stop me missing Ben.'

Charlie's love and pain for her dead dog still felt raw. Maybe, as she'd said in the pub, she didn't have a lot of people around her, so she sought comfort there. It was hard to be alone, now.

'I even stopped watching porn,' she said, unexpectedly.

'Do you sometimes worry that you might scare people with your honesty?'

'No,' she turned to face me. 'It's not about them. I don't want to please people anymore. I want to say what I want to say, because I've pretended long enough to be someone I'm not. Funnily, the only person who's harmed by pretence is me. What's the point? To be friends with people who wouldn't otherwise like you?'

'It might just be shocking at first. Perhaps you need to bring things up more gently?'

'No need,' she shook her head and waved her arms in front of her face, like a child refusing to eat vegetables. 'It's easier if everyone knows who they're dealing with at the beginning, and only the strongest survive.' She smiled, but it soon faded. 'That said, I don't have many friends. Maybe you're right, maybe this is a problem.' There was a hint of wonder in her voice.

'Well, for what it's worth, I'd be happy to be your friend.' Charlie didn't know that I needed her more than she needed me. I was surrounded by people, but not being able to talk honestly to anyone made me feel like I was slowly suffocating.

She looked at me, her eyebrows furrowed. Our eyes each held the other for just a second longer than they should have. I gave her a goofy half-smile because it was getting a little awkward, and she lunged suddenly at me, her soft lips on mine. I didn't do anything, but I didn't pull away either. My mouth was slightly open as she lightly moved over me. The park had been full of life, but all sound faded away, and I no longer heard the children's laughter or the cyclists passing by. Suddenly, it was just us, just two. I tasted sweet cherry and my hands finally grasped her arms and slowly slid upwards. I was keenly aware that - though the people around us didn't know who we were or that I was kissing someone who wasn't my wife - somehow I still felt their silent judgment, telling me I was doing something very wrong. Telling me that was why Jodie needed to fix every single shitty thing I had ever done. Charlie's tongue slid into my mouth for a second, before she slowly pulled back.

Not counting the time I'd drunkenly kissed Laura, or the one time I made out with Theo after Jodie had dared us, Charlie was the second person I'd ever properly kissed. It felt different, spontaneous, innocent with a hint of passion. Maybe it was a bit wet, perhaps a bit awkward, but I enjoyed it. Then I remembered my first kiss with Jodie. Had it been her first time? Or had she practiced on me time and time again before she finally felt it was good enough? *That one was a good take, I'll keep it.*

I swallowed, suddenly. There was a pain in my throat, and I blushed when I saw some pedestrians eyeing us. Did they realise I had a wife? I looked around instinctively, afraid to see Theo or Amy or Julie behind me, out for a stroll.

Charlie grinned. 'Wawaweewa!'

'Indeed,' I smiled more slowly, still looking around, guilt starting to creep in now like a cat approaching its prey, stepping so lightly you couldn't hear it, not until it was too late. I lowered my gaze to the grass.

'Are you ok?'

'I have a wife.'

Charlie jerked back as she heard the word. Her jaw dropped, and she covered her open mouth with a hand. Her eyes were piercing, waiting for me to tell her I was kidding. Waiting for me to say 'I got you,' or 'you're so gullible.' But I didn't, I just stood there.

Charlie shook her head, 'Well, it would have been better if you'd told me that about forty-five seconds ago.' She scratched her forehead, thoughtfully.

'I'm sorry.' She was right. I should have told her, right at the start, way back in her office when she'd first invited me for a drink. I should have just said I wasn't available.

'Damn... and you're hot too!'

I burst out laughing as she started walking again, back towards the car. I ran to catch up.

'You're doing this on purpose!' I accused her. 'You say things like that just for the reaction!'

'Sometimes,' she said. I lifted my finger to disagree. 'Fine, most of the time,' she winked, trying to lighten the conversation.

'Thank you.'

We continued walking, watching the ducks and the kids playing frisbee.

'Are you happy?' Charlie asked, absently stroking her hair. 'With your marriage, I mean.'

'I … I am,' I said it automatically, without even thinking, the default answer I'd always given. I corrected myself. 'I was.'

'Was?' Charlie repeated.

'There are a few things I discovered recently,' my voice tapering off, 'that changed everything. Everything I thought I knew about my wife was shattered. All this happened just a day after we'd finally agreed to adopt, something I'd wanted for a long time. And now … I don't know.' I heard my own voice, and I sounded defeated.

'I suspect you'd be a great father. Do you have kids already, or would this have been your first?'

'No, we don't … we tried a *long* time ago, but it turned out my wife couldn't have kids. Hence the adoption thing.'

'She's infertile?' Charlie spent a minute nodding, thinking about it. 'What happened?'

'Are you asking what caused the infertility?' Charlie nodded some more, as she waited for me to continue. 'She had a bad infection when she was younger, one that caused a blockage in her uterine tubes. We only found out about it when we were trying to conceive.'

'Oh, but that doesn't mean she's infertile. There are options; you can extract eggs!' She sounded excited, like she had found a solution to a problem that had clearly bothered me for years, until she saw my face.

251

'Jodie didn't want that, and … adoption seemed like the best alternative. It just took a while for her to come around to the idea.'

'And now you're not sure you want to go ahead with it?'

'I'm going to divorce her.'

'Oh, Ethan … because of these things you just learned about her?' Charlie's hand gripped my arm, hard - 'am I being too nosey?' I shrugged, but before I could answer, she waved me off. 'Hey, you didn't mention your wife, and so you owe me big time. Continue.' She prodded me with her elbow.

I sighed, trapped. 'Well … As I was saying, I learned things …'

'Things that she was hiding from you?'

'Sort of … yes.'

'Why was she keeping them a secret?'

'She said that she was protecting me.'

'And did she protect you?'

'Kind of … until I learned the truth.'

'I see. I think. I'm sorry.'

We had continued walking around the pond, and now we were back at the same spot we'd started from. 'Well.' she said. 'If we are not going to kiss anymore, should we get back?' She used a playful tone, and though it was clearly a question, I chose to take it as a statement.

By the time we reached the parking lot, the sun had almost set and it was the golden hour that Jodie loved so much. She'd always insist on a selfie if we were outside.

Charlie and I walked towards the car in silence, but it was a comfortable silence, the kind where words are unnecessary, the kind that shows support and understanding. She knew me. Lost, angry, and sad.

I unlocked the car, and we got in, sitting for a few moments, both of us staring just through the front window. I had no idea what would happen now, between Jodie and me, how long a divorce might take. I couldn't simply tell her we were done; she would want to know why. She would want to fix everything. I sat in that comfortable silence for a few more moments, anticipating the future; then, I started the engine.

'Do you think Jodie acted from a place of selfishness or love and kindness?' Charlie's question was direct, straight to the point. I wished I knew the answer.

'Is there a difference?'

'Hell yeah!' she raised her voice, not giving me a second to question her response. 'We make plans, good and bad. Sometimes, those plans don't work out as we hoped - but the only thing that really matters is intent.'

'What do you mean?'

She clenched her fist in front of her, tensed as if ready to punch someone. 'Intention is everything, Ethan.' She took a deep breath and then suddenly melted into her seat, still looking at the sunset through her window. 'Can you be angry with your wife, when she only tried to do what she thought was best?'

'Yes, of course I can be angry - she made a mistake!'

Charlie continued talking, so withdrawn now, it was

like she was about to fall asleep. 'Then be angry at the mistake, or at the circumstances - but it seems like your wife might deserve some forgiveness.'

We drove in silence, Charlie watching the darkness settle over the city. The sun was barely visible, only a sliver of it visible, glimpsed through buildings. I stopped the car outside Charlie's home, and we sat there in silence a bit longer.

'I am sorry. I wish I could do something for you.' Charlie gently placed her hand on mine and squeezed it. This minute connection, this passion, it jolted me like electricity.

'Thank you. It was good to talk to someone today.'

'If you want to come inside, I–'

'Okay.' I nodded, interrupting her. She seemed surprised.

I locked the car, and a minute later, I was standing in her old fashioned kitchen. There was still a strong scent of dog. She poured us tea in monochromatic mugs and offered me fruit from the basket resting on the windowsill. I refused; my eyes locked on hers. She didn't look away.

CHAPTER 21

WEDNESDAY 07 SEPTEMBER 2016

I stepped into the running shoes Jodie had given me for our anniversary. The fit was still uncannily perfect. Had I chosen them myself? Had she erased my memory just so they could be the perfect present? Our entire life had been a game to her. Now, I was pulling the strings.

I struggled into a tight vest and looked at myself in the mirror, seeing those low cut running shorts, and I hoped Charlie was into sportswear.

Cheating had proven to be a bit of a challenge. Since Jodie and I shared our locations with each other, she always knew where I was. I had told her I was with a client when she asked me about my whereabouts when I was at Charlie's. I had rented a hotel room so it wouldn't look like I spend a lot of time in one place. And now, for the second time in five days, I was going on a half marathon run; it was the safest bet - leaving my phone at home meant she couldn't track me.

My phone buzzed with another message from Theo, asking what the hell was wrong with me. It had been more than a week since we'd properly talked, since I'd discovered why Laura was dead. Fuck. I put the phone back in my pocket.

I stepped into the hall, setting my watch. Jodie came in from the terrace, soil smeared over her forehead, bucket and tools hanging off her wrist.

'You're going for a run?'

'Yes, a long one today.'

'What about dinner?'

'Well, if you're willing to wait for a couple of hours.' I spoke harshly.

I had to make her stop loving me - my only option was to phase it out, do it gradually. In time I would become an unbearable husband, someone *she* wanted to leave. In reality - it didn't matter what I wanted. She had to be the one to divorce me, to let me go free, because if I try to leave, ... well, maybe I'd already tried. Ignorance is bliss.

Jodie seemed a little disappointed. 'I see. I'll wait for you to come back, then. Can I give you a kiss before you go?'

'Sure.' I forced a smile as she awkwardly leaned over, but before she got a chance to kiss me, she flinched slightly, letting out a soft moan, her hand pressing on her stomach.

'You ok?' I asked.

'I've been having these pains, here,' she indicated with her hand, her face still contorted, 'and some days are worse than others.'

'You should get it checked.'

'I am.' She lifted her head, like that was a stupid thing for me to say. 'I've had an ultrasound and I'll get the results soon.

'Great. I'll be off then.' I turned to the door, 'the sooner I leave, the sooner we can have dinner.'

'Ethan!' She raised her voice. 'What's the matter with you?'

I turned back to her. 'What do you mean?'

'I mean you. Yesterday you came back with your head bleeding and refused to let me help you, you wouldn't even tell me where you fell. Now you're talking with me like you're mad.'

I took a few steps forward. 'I'm still a bit irritated about what you told me about Laura. I just need some time to process it.' Jodie stared at me without blinking. Was she thinking of going back? Did I say too much? 'But I love you, and I want us to work on this together.' I smiled as her face relaxed.

I was so happy with Charlie, but the sneaking around was adding a layer of anxiety. I wished I could just break it off with Jodie, right this minute. I wasn't worried about her discovering my relationship with Charlie, and being angry; it was more about fearing that the discovery would make her erase it all. How can you run away from someone who can turn back time whenever she wants? Who would keep trying to fix things, stuck in her own loop until everything was made perfect.

'You're overthinking it, Jodie, honestly don't. I'll be fine.'

'I guess it's all in my head,' she sighed. She wrapped her hands around my waist and kissed me. I responded to her kiss, but only barely.

She took a step back and turned her head to the side, looking at me quizzically. 'I made some enquiries about adoption, and started the process. Amy's going to give us an excellent recommendation.'

'That sounds great.' I was glad she was only capable of going back in time and not able to read my mind. Adoption was the last thing on my mind right now. 'I'll head out.' Jodie waved goodbye and blew me another kiss.

The evening was warm as I set out running. My heart filled with joy at the thought of Charlie's smile. Despite all the uncomfortable conversations with Jodie, despite the constant anxiety that she would find out about Charlie and me, I was happy. Despite everything.

CHAPTER 22

Charlie

My hands gripped his. Our bodies moved in sync. Sweat rolled off Ethan's back and on to my body as he tightened his buttocks. I moved one hand to caress his neck, the other pressed against his cheek. The last time I'd been with a man was sometime in the previous year; Ethan had made that wait worthwhile. I wanted him to keep going, to fuck me so hard for all those missed opportunities, for all the times I'd said *no*.

He was looking straight at me, and I stared back into his eyes. I bit my lower lip to prevent myself from moaning. The bed rattled and banged, reminding me of the cheap porn I used to watch. The tension in his muscles was slowly dissipating. I wasn't sure if he had come; he was still moving his penis in and out of me, gradually slowing down. Ethan kissed me, his lips moving down to my neck as he melted against me. It was hard to take a breath with him on top of me, but I still liked the feeling of his body on mine.

'I love this,' he whispered in my ear.

'I'm not complaining either,' I said, laughing. 'I wonder if Mrs Freeman will complain about all the noise.' I grinned at Ethan as he tensed again.

'Well, if she hasn't before, she will now.' He placed his hand over my mouth and went all in.

***

Ethan watched me from the bed as I fiddled with my bra.

'Here, let me help you.' He grabbed a couple of loose straps and snapped them together. I didn't need his help, but I enjoyed his cool fingers softly touching my skin. He leaned forward, kissing my neck, and I could feel his semi-erect penis against my back. I'd had a wonderful week with him, the best week in a long time, but it was wrong. He was still married. These thoughts only crept in after we'd had sex. Each time we had slept together I'd told myself it would be the last, but another day made me want him again.

'I'll take you to work, ok?' he whispered in my ear.

'I can't. I have to collect the car *you scratched* from the mechanic.'

His hands wrapped around my stomach, mock-pleading now. 'But I want to spend more time with you.'

'Honestly, Ethan, I can't. There's a huge storm forecast for tonight, and it would be a pain to have to catch taxis.'

'That's even better then; you shouldn't drive during a

storm. It's unsafe!' He was grinning at me, happy to find another reason.

'I don't think it's a good idea. I need my car.'

'Please,' he said, as his lips kissed my neck again. I exhaled deeply.

I thought of the previous Thursday and how miserable he'd looked. It had been difficult to see him that way, confused and lost, but now he was happy, smiling, playful, *knowing* he was happy because of me. I'd helped him. Wasn't that the most important thing?

'Fine...' I said, instantly regretting it. What had happened to the Charlie who'd stopped pleasing other people, on principle? Why, after working so hard on setting boundaries for myself, did I still feel the need to do this?

I looked at Ethan in that moment, my heart beating faster, and I felt embarrassed, knowing he could probably feel it too. I liked him a lot, but we couldn't keep doing this while he was still married. This had to stop.

***

The road was cleared of the morning rush. Ethan was driving slowly and in silence, occasionally glancing over and smiling at me. I smiled back, hiding the frustration I felt at not insisting on collecting my car from the service station this morning.

'Are you not afraid your wife may find out?'

'I told Jodie I was going to meet a client first thing in the morning, which means - if she were tracking me via our location sharing - she shouldn't be alarmed.'

I didn't know much about Ethan's job or how long a client meeting might take, but maybe discussing courtroom tactics could take about the same time as passionate sex.

He extended his arm and turned on the radio to break the silence. The weather forecaster, with his robotic voice, was announcing a strong gale tonight.

'We expect wind speeds up to 90 kilometres per hour, and we advise people to stay home.'

'I love storms.' I said out loud while looking out the side window.

'As in?'

'When you're cocooned somewhere safe as nature goes completely wild. Storm, rain, snow, you name it. Those are the times when you really get to appreciate life, a reminder that the world doesn't simply revolve around you, that nature is ultimately much more powerful than any of us.'

Ethan nodded.

Silence again accompanied the gentle sound of the engine. Neither of us knew what to say. I was happy and conflicted about being with Ethan; even though we were breaking the rules, I'd found a connection I really wanted. Even if it was bound to fail. I couldn't stop thinking about his wife. Would I be the tipping point, cause them to break up? Was that ok? It wasn't, I decided. The sex might be great but today had to be the last time.

'So, what time are you finishing work?' he asked.

'...and small talk has finally erupted!' I announced, with joy that I didn't really feel.

'I'm just caring for a *friend*. Because of the storm,' he leaned towards me, raising his eyebrows for a moment before fixing his sight back on the road. I wasn't sure if he really did care, or if he just wanted to see if we could have sex again tonight.

'At 5pm, but I have training straight after, so I won't be home before 7pm,' I went back to staring out the window.

Ethan stopped around the corner from the clinic, near a construction site. They'd been renovating a block of flats there for what seemed like forever. He looked around before unlocking his car doors, wished me a lovely day, and I stepped outside. He reversed away almost instantly. I waved, imitating the queen; he laughed, the roar of the engine drowning him out. A few seconds later, he was out of sight.

As I walked through reception, Emily was more jolly than usual; I bet she was back with her boyfriend now. She gave me a big hug; her breasts pressed tightly against mine.

'Emily, your breasts are just–'

'I know,' she smiled, squeezing them together with her shoulders, pouting. 'God's gift,' she winked.

***

My first patient was Mr Crocket, back to check on his anal pain. After what happened last time and Ethan's observation - *are you worried he never had any pain in his anus to begin with* - I referred him straight to a proctologist I knew. A male proctologist. Mr Crocket seemed slightly disappointed to hear that I wasn't going to examine him.

Then, Mrs Weston. I would say, on average, that she comes in every two weeks to complain about her knee pain, her arthritis, or the effects of high blood pressure. She was always fine - after a chat, which she clearly needed more than anything else.

I told her I would listen to her chest, just to be safe. Once she was facing away from me, I pressed the stethoscope to her back and listened to her deep breathing. Those long deep breaths reminded me of Ethan. His trim, spiky chest hair against my palm, his broad shoulders, the veins straining on his arm when he gripped me.

On a break between appointments, I placed a small plastic Christmas tree on the side of my desk and put on a Santa hat. Even though it was Friday, the weather was bad and people seemed miserable, and I was hoping for a few smiles from my regular patients. *They* seemed to enjoy my sense of humour.

Ms White was so nervous sitting in the chair, looking down at her mobile that she didn't even notice my props. Like Ms Weston, she had arrived with a shopping list of the health issues she knew she had; the difference was that she also liked to do her own research on the internet. That led her to believe that the pain in her neck was a sign of cancer.

I stood up and examined her, not because I needed to, but to calm her down. I already had an idea about what was causing her neck problems.

'Neck pain can also come from spending too much

time looking down.'

'What do you mean?' She said, while swiping something on her phone, trying to bring up the cancer information she had found.

'Like if you're reading when you're sitting on a chair,' I let her process what I was saying, 'or using a mobile.' I smiled, studying her face. It lit up, as if she'd won an Oscar.

Nearing lunchtime, I popped out for five minutes to buy myself a sandwich. While I waited for my next patient, I sent Ethan an aubergine emoji for no reason, regretting it slightly but craving his attention. I googled some dog pictures to think about something else and a knock on the office door made me jump. Emily stuck her head in and asked if I wouldn't mind taking Dr Yeoman's patient, who had been waiting for a while. I told Emily to send them in.

Taking off my Christmas hat, I quickly closed the browser and opened the patient's file, which Emily had sent through. A slight noise at the open door made me look up from my computer before I could read it properly, and a young woman wearing a beautiful blue summer dress walked in. As soon as she saw me, she stopped, and I smiled, hoping to get the same from her, but she just stared at me.

'Would you like to take a seat?' I indicated to the free chair next to my desk. But she was still frozen. Then I followed her stare to the side of my desk, to my old Christmas tree. I was sure she must think I was some sort of a fool with Christmas decorations out in September. I slowly grabbed it and placed it under my desk. 'Sorry about that. Only 107 sleeps until Christmas!' It was getting hot in here now.

The lady nodded and sat down, clearly feeling uncomfortable.

'Dr Yeoman wasn't available today,' I said, hoping to reassure. 'She asked me to take her appointment with you. I hope that's ok.'

'Of course, it's absolutely fine.' She smiled, but it was still wrong, somehow.

'Well, Ms. Page, how...' as soon as I said it, a chill went up my spine, 'how can I help you today?' Even before glancing back at my computer screen, I had the worst feeling.

The patient's details said she was Ms Jodie Page, 17 Reeds Wharf, 33 Mill St. That was Ethan's home address. This was Ethan's wife. The air in the room suddenly became heavy and very hot. Ms Page was talking to me, but I didn't hear a word. All I wanted was for a pit to open up under my chair and swallow me whole.

I'd slept with Ethan yesterday and this morning and here was his wife in front of me, here in my office. I stood up, interrupting Ms Page, telling her I was going to open the window. In the three steps to the window, I stumbled over nothing but managed to right myself without falling. I pulled the window handle to the side and let in some fresh air.

Of course I'd known about Ethan's situation and what I was getting myself into, but meeting his wife like this was something I hadn't been prepared for. I should have ended things right when it started. I took a deep breath, turned around, and went back to my seat.

I lowered my gaze, just hoping she wouldn't recognize me, which was silly because we'd never met and I was sitting right in front of her. Then another wave of chills swept through me. What if she'd seen me get out of Ethan's car? I shook my head slightly again, Ms Page was again saying something to me, but I hadn't heard her.

'Doctor?' Ms Page leaned forward. 'Do you?'

'I'm so sorry, I haven't heard a single word you said,' I admitted. Ms Page straightened herself in her chair, abruptly. 'Brain fog,' I explained unconvincingly, and after a long pause she finally gave me an uncomfortable smile.

'What I was saying, *Doctor* - I had some abdominal pain, and Dr Yeoman sent me for an ultrasound at Guy's Hospital.' It was hard to concentrate when the only thing I wanted to know was why she was here. 'I received a message yesterday that the test results were ready.'

It was quiet for a few seconds, then I realised that the silence in the room meant Ms Page was waiting for a response from me.

'Yes, of course... let's see the results.' I looked at the picture and followed the notes from the doctor from St Guys. 'I can see here, Ms Page, that you have nothing to worry about; the test shows you're perfectly healthy and you have no abnormalities.' Ms Page smiled and looked down at her lap.

'What about my belly pains?'

'Stress is a common factor in abdominal pain. Have you

been under a lot of stress lately?' I could guess the answer.

'Yes, I believe I have been,' I saw her lip tremble for a split second, but then she squeezed her fist and got up from the chair. 'Thank you, Doctor. I'll try to look after myself more.' Ms Page turned around quickly and left the room, without saying goodbye. When I sank back into my chair, the tension dissipated, but not the shame. I wanted to help people, not hurt them. I was one of the reasons she was in pain. This thing with Ethan had to stop now. I turned back to look again at her file, and her perfect ultrasound picture.

And for the third time in five minutes, a chill ran down my spine. I remember Ethan talking about the *things* that he said had come to light, the secrets that had destroyed their marriage. Staring at the ultrasound, I realised there was one more secret that Ms Page was keeping from Ethan.

***

The wind began to howl outside, dark thick clouds covering the sky. A light rain started to patter against the windows. Even though I preferred the fresh air, I went to close the window in the office kitchen; it wouldn't be wise to leave it open during the storm. Silence. I sat on the cheap IKEA couch, waiting for my training to start. Whoever thought to book training on Friday evening must really hate doctors. A cup of hot tea was warming my hands, and I sipped it slowly, thinking. Thinking about Ethan and Ms. Page and her ultrasound. Maybe there was something I didn't know about them, about her, perhaps I saw only part of the image, but I was almost certain Ethan didn't know what was going on with his wife.

I went to the sink to wash my cup. Although we had a dishwasher in the kitchen, I wanted an excuse to warm my hands. Would it be wrong to tell Ethan the truth? It wasn't my business - and she was a patient! - but at the same time, surely he deserved to know. Walking out of the kitchen, I switched the light off, grabbing my phone off the table in the half-darkness, contemplating my decision.

If I tell Ethan what I know, would he think I was creating an excuse for his divorce, that I was trying to bring him and me together? And if I didn't tell him, it would mean lying to him too, at least by omission.

The wind was viciously shaking the trees, now. Even through the well-insulated windows, some sounds from outside were creeping in. Standing at the window in my office, I stared out into the street. The construction workers from the building site across the street had disappeared, now. Empty plastic bags were getting caught on the thin tree branches. A poor cyclist was sheltering in the bus stop. It looked bad out there.

I grabbed my phone and found Ethan's contact. My hands were shaking. I knew what I was going to do was so, so wrong - but I couldn't stop. I had to let him know. He deserved to know the truth.

> *Ethan, your wife visited my clinic today.*
> *There is something you need to know about her.*

I pressed send and instantly regretted my decision. 'Shit!' I shouted into the empty room. What had I done? I'm a doctor; it's my job to help people, not to break them apart. I had no right to be interfering in their marriage.

I was typing another message to Ethan, telling him it wasn't anything serious when Emily peered into the room.

'Hey Charlie, that guy can't make it anymore for training; he said a few roads are closed. He'll reschedule for next week.'

I looked at the mess outside and back to Emily.

'This is what you get for ignoring global warming,' I said, shooting at her with hands like pistols.

Emily laughed. 'Do you mind giving me a lift back home? There is no way I can cycle in this weather.'

'My car's at the mechanics. But we could split an Uber?'

'Or you could do me a solid because I'm an underpaid receptionist?' She winked and I couldn't help but smile.

'Of course, Em. Give me a couple of minutes and we'll get out here.' Emily closed the door to my office. Hiding the message I'd been writing to Ethan, I ordered an Uber. Eight minutes away. Excellent. I grabbed my handbag and locked my office without changing into my casual wear. There was no point, I'd be soaked in ten seconds just running to the taxi. There was no point even trying to use an umbrella.

I opened the outside door, and a gust of wind ripped it out of my hand and slammed it against the wall. The glass almost shattered from the impact.

'Shit, fuck!' Grabbing at the handle, I pulled it back closed. I looked around to see if anyone saw me, Emily wasn't at reception. She had to have heard the slam, though. Better to stay inside. I checked my Uber and it was 14 minutes away, now. Driving backwards on the map. Bullshit. I shouldn't have let Ethan drive me to work this morning. I opened his messages again.

Before I could type anything, a heart-wrenching scream echoed from the street. I was still for a full second trying to figure out if it had been the TV in the reception area, but no, it was too clear. The heavy rain hitting the patterned windows reduced the street outside to indistinct blobs. With the door open a small crack - firmly held this time - I could see nothing unusual, except the storm itself.

The cyclist was gone, probably into one of the buildings. Another scream and louder this time. Tossing my handbag into the reception area, I stepped outside. There was a woman down the cross-street, in front of the surgery, kneeling in the middle of the road. The distance between us was no more than 50 meters, close to the construction site where Ethan had dropped me earlier that morning. She wore a bright orange raincoat, and her backpack lay beside her. I wasn't sure what had happened. I watched from the shelter of the small porch.

Why did no one from the construction site help her? She tried to stand up, but the wind blew her back. I didn't think anymore, just ran towards her. As soon as I stepped onto the street, the wind pushed me to one side, but I was able to regain my balance. The wind made it almost impossible to go straight ahead. Still, though slower than expected, I managed to move forward. Everything I was wearing was already drenched. Bins from the nearby apartment building slammed onto the ground, releasing their contents into the street. Plastic bags broke free, like doves from a cage.

'Hold on,' I shouted. But there was absolutely no chance that she would hear me. The wind was howling through the scaffolding of the building side, still blowing me sideways. She was facing away from me, and I couldn't even tell how old she was; my guess was she was quite frail, just from how disoriented she seemed. I was completely soaked, but I didn't care. In my whole life, I could not remember a time I had ever heard such a desperate scream. I wanted to tell her to hold on, that I was on my way, but I was afraid to shout. She was now maybe twenty meters away, just past the construction site. She was on her knees now trying to get up, hands on the pavement.

'Are you ok?' A man shouted from somewhere behind me. The words wouldn't come, so I waved and pointed towards the woman. He struggled closer to me. I wondered where all the construction workers had gone, why was there no one here?

'Miss,' I shouted. 'Are you ok?' I couldn't tell if she heard me, but she slowly moved towards her backpack, still on her hands and knees, still facing away. Her raincoat hood was covering her head, so that I couldn't make out her facial expression. Was she hurt? Maybe she was just scared. 'I'm coming!'

A sharp metal screech echoed down the street. I glanced behind me, but the man was still making his way towards us. I turned back to the kneeling shape, and the woman was by her backpack now, moving faster and crawling away down the street.

'Look out!' The man behind me yelled. I looked back at him, seeing he was pointing to something over my head. There was another scream from the woman with the raincoat, louder than before, ripping through the air. She was almost standing now, running away from me.

'Run!' The man behind me yelled again. Time had stopped. I didn't know what was happening, but my brain analysed the situation, where I was, what I could see, in which direction the man was pointing, which way the woman was running. Something was badly wrong. As I looked towards the construction site, it looked different. It was much closer now than before. And it was moving towards me. The scaffolding.

CHAPTER 23

Ethan

I burst into the apartment, the wind slamming the door into the wall. My clothing was soaked, water dripping everywhere as I undressed. I wiped my face on my wet elbow and left everything to dry in the hall, walking into the living room in my underwear.

'Jodie?' No answer. A few lights were on; her slippers were by the front door. She'd probably popped out to the shop. The strong scent of turpentine assaulted me, she must have been painting. As I stepped into the dining room, it was clear that she had finished for the day. Her work station was clean; the easel wiped with no traces of paint. Wet brushes were drying on the windowsill, and a canvas was facing the window to dry.

One of the things I had loved about Jodie was this hobby. Coming home and seeing her art and hearing her talk about it was inspiring. 'I saw this boy outside playing with rocks. He was so happy. I envied him,' she'd said after she'd completed a piece of a man with his hands raised like Jesus Christ on the cross, screaming at the sky as it rained rocks. That painting was hanging in the study.

I walked around the easel to see the other side; this canvas was one of the bigger ones. Right in the middle, there was a large, beautiful, brightly lit, gilded cage with a pig inside. It looked happy, with floppy ears, healthy skin, a curly tail. But shadowy figures, painted in black and dark blue seemed to be moving in from the darkness at the periphery. Half-seen faces jeered and hands pointed at the pig with twisted fingers, though he seemed unaware of what was happening. I felt a little sad, but I couldn't really explain why. It was strange.

A distant sound echoed outside, almost as if something nearby had been torn apart by the wind. I looked out the window instinctively, but couldn't see anything more than water flooding our street. The storm was wild, now. Dark clouds loomed across London and the street lights swayed from side to side like a metronome, their crazed light adding to the sense of unreality.

I watched a few people battling through the storm and I wondered what I was doing with my life. It had been a week since I'd started with Charlie. I had felt great initially, but as the novelty had worn off, that feeling was turning into disgust. I was a cheat, and she was a liar; maybe we did deserve one another.

According to Jodie, I'd done it many times before. I couldn't decide if that made it better or worse. Was it easier to know it wasn't the first time - and that Jodie expected it to happen again? I no longer wanted to hurt Jodie, but sex with Charlie made me happy. It was a bit like I'd discovered a new flavour of ice cream.

I took my phone out of my damp backpack. A message from Charlie was waiting for me.

> *Ethan, your wife visited my clinic today.*
> *There is something you need to know about her.*

I read her message again. What did she mean, Jodie had visited the clinic? Did Jodie know about my affair? Surely Charlie would have phrased it differently if there had been a big confrontation. Jodie had complained about having pains in her stomach earlier, and maybe that's why she'd gone to the clinic. As the initial panic subsided, I wondered at how Charlie must have felt meeting the wife of the man she was sleeping with. *Awkward as fuck,* I imagined her saying.

I was sure Jodie would have called me if there was anything badly wrong with her.

> *Can we meet tomorrow?*

I waited for Charlie to reply. It was just before seven, and she'd be finishing up her training. After another minute of no answer, I set the phone down.

***

The chaos in the street was getting worse. I was just leaving the bathroom when the outside door swung open again, Jodie almost falling inside. She was even wetter than I had been. Though she'd taken a raincoat, it seemed it hadn't helped.

'For the love of God!' she exclaimed, shutting the door behind her.

'Got caught off guard?' I asked, amused by the sight of her.

'I've survived!' She clenched her fist and thrust it towards the ceiling. I smiled, and she continued talking without looking at me, taking off her wet clothes. 'I took my raincoat expecting rain, not a hurricane!' That almost rhymed. 'Look, look!' she made sure I was looking, and then started to swing her hair from one side to the other like a shaggy dog, whipping water droplets on everything within range.

'Thanks,' I said sarcastically.

'You're welcome,' she smiled. I smiled too, feeling nostalgic for what we'd had.

She passed me her raincoat to hold, still dripping on the carpet.

'This is a nice colour.'

'Cheap from Primark, I got it as an emergency, but I ended up liking it.' She pulled off her hodie and passed that over too.

'Wait. Didn't you tell me you knew about the coming storm - that two people had died in London? Why did you go out?' I asked.

'We were out of London this weekend, in that timeline. We went to stay with your mother. Brighton wasn't hit as hard, and I figured I could make it to the supermarket ok. Boy, was I wrong.' It was jarring hearing her talk so casually about things that had never happened.

Strangely, when I looked at Jodie in the muted daylight, she reminded me a little of Charlie. Both were beautiful, incredibly smart, and caring. They both made me laugh. Jodie was stripped to her underwear now, and she hung her bright raincoat on a hook, carrying her wet clothes to the bathroom.

'I've got some wine if you want to watch a movie tonight,' she said, closing the door. 'It's in my backpack.' Her voice was muffled slightly by the bathroom door.

Jodie seemed happy, happier than usual. Maybe it was the weather; in some sense, I was happier too. Charlie had said this morning that big storms were an impressive demonstration of nature's power, a spectacle to admire, and she was right. Thinking about her made my mind drift back to the strange message she had sent me, so unlike her jokey style. There was something I should know about Jodie, something she was hiding from me.

I checked the status of my reply to Charlie. Delivered. But she hadn't read it yet.

CHAPTER 24

Ethan

MONDAY 12 SEPTEMBER 2016

*Fucking hell, Ethan! I can't believe you
don't have the courage to tell me what's going on.
Anneli misses you! Talk to me!*

I hadn't spoken to Theo for almost two weeks. He'd called a few times, but I just ignored him. He probably wanted to know why I'd asked him to investigate the neighbours flat. Why, since that evening, I'd become so distant. I couldn't give him any answers without talking about Jodie, and if he found out about what I had done to Laura, then that would have been the end of us.

I couldn't do that to him. I needed to face him at some point, but avoiding him was the best I could do right now.

I hadn't heard from Charlie in two days, and I needed to see her. Since her cryptic message about Jodie's, it seemed she had completely vanished. I'd messaged her multiple times and even sneaked out of the house to call, but her phone went straight to voicemail. It felt as if she'd cut me off, blocked me. Which made no sense after she'd been the one to say we needed to talk. My message still sat there, unread. It felt more and more likely that she'd blocked me.

As we didn't have friends in common, there wasn't really an easy way for me to find out anything casually. I took my lunch early, telling my boss I had an urgent meeting. That's how I found myself at the clinic. Stepping out of my car into the tree-lined street, I saw the destruction caused by Friday's storm. I made my way to the clinic entrance, picking a path through tangled fencing and steel bars. The scaffolding had fallen away from the construction site and was covering the road. Police tape was flapping in the gentle breeze.

I pulled open the door to the clinic and was greeted by the same receptionist. The place was cold and damp, and three people were sitting silently in the waiting area.

'Good morning, do you have an appointment?' The receptionist asked, quietly. She looked tired.

'Hey there, I wondered if I could talk to Dr Leigh.' I placed both hands on her desk. 'It's not an appointment.' I smiled, but the receptionist didn't smile back. Her eyes were sad, and I noticed she was squeezing a tissue in her hand. She didn't reply to my inquiry but stood up and walked around the desk closer to me. Then she took my hand; it was obvious something wasn't right.

'I'm very sorry, but Dr Leigh was in an accident,' she pressed her lips tightly together, to stop them trembling.

'What kind of accident?'

'It happened on Friday, during the storm. All we know is that she tried to help someone who was struggling on the road and–' her voice tapered off.

'And?' I waited, but she just raised her hand and pointed behind me. When I turned around I saw the scaffolding again, this time in a different, more horrifying light - that flapping police tape was sinister, now. The bottom dropped out of my stomach.

'Is she?' My eyes were still fixed on the street; I was completely still, as if any movement might change the answer the receptionist was about to give me.

'I'm so sorry.' Her hand touched my shoulder and squeezed, and my heart collapsed with the pressure. I closed my eyes, hoping to see Charlie's face in the darkness. To tell her I was sorry, to say she hadn't deserved it. I took a deep breath to try to stay calm, trying not to show any emotion.

'The family is going to have a memorial service today and tomorrow at Borough.' Without acknowledging her words, I left the clinic, stepping back into the street.

***

I pushed open the door to the funeral home. It was quiet. The hall was empty, and there was no one at reception. I wanted to call out, but remembering where I was, I didn't. My eyes followed the wall ahead until I was struck by the photograph of a beautiful young woman. It took me a few seconds to recognize that beautiful smile and high cheekbones. Charlie's hair looked much lighter than it had been when I'd last seen her. I walked up to the photo and took a few deep breaths to calm myself. I wasn't going to let myself cry. The plaque read,

Charlotte Leigh
1984 - 2016
Beloved daughter, sister, and friend

The small plaque indicated the memorial would be held in Room 2. I followed the signs upstairs, keeping my breathing steady. The rumble of voices grew louder as I went up the stairs, and at the top, I saw several people gathered in a small group. They glanced at me, and I nodded slightly, acknowledging them. On my left, the double door was open to a bright room with the coffin in the centre.

I stepped inside a small atrium, and despite the sunlight shining through a wide skylight, it was cold. The room was full of people who sat quietly whispering amongst themselves, some sobbing silently. I took a few more steps towards the casket. As I got closer, a woman wearing a muted black dress turned away and towards me. For a moment, my heart stopped. Charlie? Then minor differences became noticeable. It must be her sister.

'I'm sorry for your loss,' I said to her, and she nodded, squeezing a handkerchief in her hand. The dark circles under her eyes told of sleepless nights.

'Thank you,' she crossed her arms like hugging herself. 'I'm sorry, I don't … Did you know Charlie well?'

'Enough to know she had a wonderful spirit.'

Her face brightened.

'Yes,' she smiled sadly, 'a lot of people would agree on that.' I looked around the room filled with people who had gathered to pay their respects. Charlie had told me she was lonely and that she didn't have many friends, but that didn't seem to be true. She had touched more people than she'd thought. It was sad that she'd never know just how many people did care about her.

'Such a tragedy,' I said, wanting to touch Charlie's sister's arm. I saw Charlie in her, and somehow, part of her was here.

'That construction company,' she was hugging herself hard, now, her knuckles white against her skin. 'They will pay for what they did. We'll sue them.' She spat it out.

'I'll do that for you,' I said, feeling her anger. 'I'm a lawyer with VA Thompson. I'll make sure they pay for what happened.'

She took my hands tightly in hers, now, tears threatening to fall; her lips trembled. I took a deep breath and hugged her. It could have been my imagination, but she used the same perfume as Charlie.

'Thank you.' Her body relaxed as I held her close. This scent, this almost familiar touch; it felt as if this moment would be the last time I'd be close to Charlie again.

Her sister pulled back, wiping her tears, thanking me again.

'Do you know what happened?' I asked. She shook her head.

'Most of what we know is just what's been written in the newspaper - there are some by the entrance.'

'Thank you; I'll take one if that's ok.' She nodded, and I asked her for her phone number.

Before I left, I grabbed one of the newspapers, reading as I walked to my car.

Martin Simpson, 47, was at the scene and saw the accident. "It was just after 6, and the doctor rushed into the street to help someone who'd fallen on the road," Mr Simpson told this paper. "Before she could reach them, scaffolding fell from that construction site. It was awful. That site was clearly dangerous, but the government has ignored my requests for an inspection." Paramedics were quick to respond; however, Dr Charlotte Leigh was pronounced dead at the scene. Police ask that a person who was also present and wearing a high-visibility jacket to come forward to give a statement. Dr Charlotte Leigh was the third victim within the M25 whose death was caused by the storm, said to be the worst in the last 27 years.

When Jodie had returned from Edinburgh, when we were talking about her powers, she had mentioned that there would be a huge storm. But I was sure I remembered her saying that there would only be two casualties.

***

On the way home, I stopped by the clinic to take another look at the wreckage. I stepped out of the car and walked towards the scaffolding, which still blocked the street. If not for Charlie dying, this would have been cleared the following day, but there were still a couple of police officers taking photos.

I walked around the wreckage, metal pipes and broken planks stuck out in various directions. I was afraid I might see a bloodstain, but then remembered the rain would have washed everything away. There were no builders around; all construction would undoubtedly have been stopped while the investigation was pending. I wished I could have asked them a few questions.

While looking around, I discovered that the street had some CCTV cameras seemingly pointed in the right direction. One of the houses near the wreckage also had a camera attached to the entrance. I walked over. There was a red Volvo parked outside with a scaffolding pipe sticking half out of the smashed side window.

Answering my knock was a kind-looking middle-aged man. I introduced myself as Dr Charlotte Leigh's family lawyer, here to collect any evidence. He was accommodating, telling me what he'd witnessed that day.

'There were maybe six or seven of us who ran into the street to help the poor girl, but by the time we pulled her out, she'd stopped breathing.' I nodded, clenching my fist in the pocket of my coat, containing the anger by pressing my nails deep into my palm. I needed to stay professional.

'Would you mind if I view your video footage from the day of the accident?' I indicated the camera above us, pointing mutely at the wreckage on the street.

'Of course,' he pressed his hands together. 'It is a bit old, not the best quality, but it is clear enough. It *is* a good angle,' he added.

I thanked him, and we exchanged email addresses. He said he'd try to forward it some time tomorrow.

***

I wasn't sure how long I sat in the car before I found the strength to walk into my apartment. Once through the front door, I'd have to pretend I was back from work, just a typical Monday. To tell Jodie that a *friend* she'd never heard of was killed Friday might raise more questions. It was almost 7 o'clock, and if I didn't go soon, Jodie would wonder why. Since I'd started working for VA Thompson, the unwritten rule between us was that if I wasn't going to be home by seven, I should let her know so she wouldn't wait to get dinner. I wiped the cold sweat off my forehead, stepped out of the car, and went upstairs.

The aroma of curry inundated me as soon as I opened the door.

'Excellent timing!' Jodie announced. 'I ordered curry. It just arrived!' She wasn't visible, but I could hear her in the dining room.

'Excellent timing indeed,' I said, rolling my eyes. Before finding out that my wife had the ability to change time and reshape reality, I'd admired how she managed to time everything so perfectly. She'd never been late; she'd never overcooked a single egg - and dinner was always just out the oven when I walked through the door.

I walked into the dining room, to find a table nicely set with the fancy wine glasses and a casserole dish in the middle. Every time Jodie ordered food, she would serve it like it was made at home. She was opening a wine bottle as I stepped closer.

'What's all this?'

'Cauliflower and potato curry.' She raised her hand. After a moment of hesitation, I returned her high-five. 'Come on, let's eat!' The cork popped out of the bottle with a satisfying sound, and Jodie poured a rich, plum-coloured wine into our glasses. 'Mm-mm!' she hummed, slightly comically.

The curry from the little Indian place just outside our apartment was always excellent, and the cauliflower melted in my mouth. I ate in silence, looking at my plate.

'Is everything ok?'

'Everything is perfect,' I forced a smile.

'Buuuut,' she waited for me to continue. As hard as I wanted to pretend that everything was ok, I couldn't.

I turned around and reached over to retrieve my backpack from behind me. I unzipped it and took out the newspaper, placing it in front of Jodie. 'Have you seen this?'

'Of course. Very sad.'

'There were three casualties on Friday, not two.'

'Oh, really?' She stopped eating and placed her cutlery on her plate, taking the paper from me. Her eyes skimmed the front page, and when she got to the end, she flipped to page three to continue reading. I waited patiently, wondering what she might say.

'Damn…' she said, exhaling.

'Damn?' I clenched my fists under the table. 'What do you mean … damn?' Jodie looked up from the newspaper.

'What do you want me to say?'

'You said there would be only two casualties.'

'Yes, but something must have changed.' She gazed down at the newspaper.

'Well, isn't it strange that you were wrong?'

Jodie looked back up, angry now. 'You don't believe that I used to go back in time?

'No, that's not what I was saying. Dr Leigh from the clinic we go to was crushed under scaffolding. It fell from the building site outside the practice.' I hoped my voice was steady.

'Oh … I saw her only a few days ago, when I went to get my results.' I was taken aback that she admitted seeing her so openly. I'd expected her to lie about it.

'And?'

'My test came back ok, it was just stress.' She shrugged. 'Dr Leigh was covering for my doctor, Dr Yeoman.'

Jodie was so calm, reading the newspaper, talking with me like she had no ability to go back and save Charlie. I lost my appetite; I was disgusted to be sitting here discussing this when Jodie could have ended it so easily. She could save a life, but was choosing not to. Surely I only needed to ask - but if I did, she would know that I knew, and I'd give her my only card. Did it matter who knew what, though - who was winning between us - if Charlie could be saved?

'Jodie?' She looked at me. But if I asked her to save Charlie, she might also suspect that there was something between Charlie and me. I didn't speak, my mouth dry.

'Yes?' she sensed there was a big question coming up.

'If you had your powers back, would you go and save those people?'

'No, I wouldn't. Unless, of course, I knew them personally.' Her answer was simple, offhand; she hadn't needed to give it any thought.

'And are you ok with it? Seeing all that pain and suffering without intervening?' She swallowed her food before answering.

'I told you before, I'm not a superhero; I don't go around saving people. I do my share for the world.'

'Your share? How?'

'Look, it doesn't matter.' She placed her cutlery back on the table.

'But all these people ... they were alive. They have families. You could have saved them.'

'People are dying everywhere, every minute, every second – even if I save a handful, I can't prevent every single disaster. And if I chose to save some, I'd then carry the responsibility for those I didn't save. I can't decide who should live and who should die.'

'But you chose to save Theo instead of Laura.'

She suddenly smacked her fists on the table, knocking her fork and splattering curry over the tablecloth.

'Damn it, Ethan! I told you, it was the hardest decision I had ever had to make. It fucking destroyed me; every single day I ask myself if I did the right thing. Fucking hell - all those nightmares I have, they might never go away. All because Laura cheated and I decided to intervene.' She stopped, and exhaled. 'Anyway. That time, I made the decision because I knew the outcome; I lived long enough to see how my decision would unfold; in the end, I chose the lesser evil.'

'But this woman, this doctor, you could have saved her? It happened just around the corner, on Friday.' We were both playing the game, pretending that it wasn't possible.

'If I saved her, where would I draw the line? The guy who died in Richmond park, drowned in the lake - why should I save the doctor and not him?

'Because her accident happened just around the corner.'

'So I should save people who are more convenient for me to save, based on my proximity to the accident?' Jodie frowned, her expression comical and incredulous.

'But she was a doctor. She was a good person.'

'The guy who drowned was only 23 years old. He had just joined the police force.' She pushed the newspaper back to me, and her eyes were fixed on mine. 'If I choose one of them and leave the other to die then I'm responsible for that choice, in the same way that I'm responsible for Laura's death. I'd have to live with the decision for the rest of my life, and I can't have more people on my conscience. I don't want to decide who lives and who dies. I don't want to play God any more.'

We ate the rest of the meal in silence.

CHAPTER 25

Just as Richard showed the last slide - it had been the most boring presentation I had ever sat through - my phone vibrated. I missed Charlie and her silly jokes. I missed playing games with Theo, and Anneli's tight hugs.

Work no longer interested me with everything going on. My wife could change the course of the future, but somehow I was required to spend eight hours planning a defence for Amar, who believed he helped people by fucking their heads with a steel hammer.

I surreptitiously checked my phone, and it was from the man I'd spoken to the day before, the one who lived across the road from the medical practice where Charlie had worked. The subject line read: 'CCTV Foota...' and the already boring slideshow suddenly became even more agonising. I counted the seconds till it was done, and as soon as Richard asked if anyone had any questions, I was first out of the door, excusing myself, saying I had another meeting.

I made it back to my office, closing the door behind me. Opening my email on the work computer, my impatience grew with how slow it was. I desperately wanted to see this footage, but at the same time, I knew there was a risk that I wouldn't be able to cope with seeing it, that it would haunt me. But it had to be done if I was going to be able to sue the construction company responsible for Charlie's death. I hovered the mouse over the subject of the email, still conflicted for just a moment, and opened it.

The video was eighty-seven seconds long and in colour, though the cloudy weather and the rain that day made everything look almost monochromatic. It showed the street, but there was no one there.

The top part of the screen was filled with scaffolding, and you could see how heavy the rain was even in the low-resolution video. Six seconds in, there was still no one on the street, and the thought that this might have been the wrong angle crossed my mind, but at about eleven seconds a person wearing a high-vis jacket came into view.

They were wearing a backpack and carrying a plastic bag. They were walking in the middle of the road, clearly struggling, when the plastic bag was pulled out of their hand and flung across the road, disappearing from view. That same gust of wind knocked them to their knees.

Grabbing their backpack, they unzipped it and took out what seemed like another plastic bag, which was also blown away as soon as it emerged. They were crawling towards the side of the road clutching their backpack when Charlie appeared. Her hands were in front of her face and she was walking towards the person in the middle of the road. Her body was pushing against the force of the wind.

She seemed to wave at the person crawling in the street, but there was no reaction. It was impossible to tell if they were speaking. After several more seconds of struggle, Charlie stopped slightly, turned to look back, and pointed to the person kneeling in front of her.

Then the bottom of the scaffolding started to move, and the kneeling person suddenly leapt up and ran away. The whole scaffolding structure *fluttered* slowly in the wind, from left to right, breaking at the bottom. Charlie turned to face it, too late, noticing it just seconds before it fell on her.

The camera shook and for a few seconds, nothing moved in the frame, and if it hadn't been for the rain, it would have seemed a still image. I wasn't able to see Charlie. The video ended just as another figure, possibly a man, ran into view from the other side of the frame.

I released the breath I'd been holding, and blinked my tears away. Poor Charlie, she'd just tried to help someone. The company had to pay for what they'd done. It was basic health and safety; the scaffolding they'd made had been unsafe. The person Charlie had been trying to help just ran away. I remembered from the news article that the police were asking this person to come forward to give additional information.

It had been only four days, but I missed her so much. When I was with her, the world stood still. What if I do ask

Jodie to go back and save her. Would she? The choice was tearing me apart. Charlie's life against my freedom.

Moments later, I found myself scrolling through our messages, the evidence of our connection with each other. They were the only things I had left of her, these five little conversations.

Ethan, your wife visited my clinic today. There is something you need to know about her.

I'd never had the chance to talk to her about that last message. There was something strange there; those words, *something you need to know,* so urgent and different to her usual jokey tone. Something I needed to know. Was it serious? Maybe Jodie was dying, and hadn't told me? Knowing how Jodie hid bad news from me, it wouldn't be surprising if she'd hidden this too, but surely she could have gone back to save herself?

Charlie was dead; I couldn't somehow go to the clinic and ask for Jodie's records. But maybe the receptionist could be convinced to help me. No, that was a dead end - what if she told Jodie I'd tried to access her records?

Something crossed my mind. While Jodie and I had been traveling in Asia, Theo had been scammed. He'd described the sense of urgency he'd felt when someone called telling him there'd been a breach in his bank account. Luckily he'd only lost around £700 - but he hadn't told us until after we'd come back to London. I guess Jodie didn't warn him about it because we were away, and he'd waited too long to tell us.

I created a fake email address online, something I thought I might need if I was going to pull this off; after a quick google search, I found a phone number for the clinic and called. The receptionist picked up on the first tone.

'Bermondsey Health Clinic, Emily speaking how can I hel–,' I interrupted.

'This is a physician assistant at St Thomas hospital,' I deepened my voice. 'Ms Jodie Page is about to undergo critical surgery. Our records show she is a patient at your surgery?' I kept talking, keeping my voice stable. I heard some rattling sounds on the other end.

'Sorry, who?' I wasn't sure if she wanted to know who I was or repeat Jodie's name. I didn't want her to question me.

'Ms Jodie Page!' I lifted my voice. 'This is urgent.'

'Yes ... yes, sorry one minute,' I was quiet and my heart pounding; I only had one shot at making this work. 'Jodie Page, right?' I heard the keyboard typing fast. 'Yes! She is a patient here!' She sounded like she had guessed the correct answer on a game show. This was going well.

'I need her medical history–' an intern walked into my office.

'Mr Page, Richa–' My eyes widened; I pressed the palm into my phone microphone and gestured to the intern to be quiet. He stood there staring at me, and if I hadn't been talking to the clinic, I would have shouted at him to get out. I gestured angrily that he should leave the office; he blushed, raised his hand in apology, and closed the door.

'I need those medical files now.'

'Normally doctor–'

'She's dying; we need to operate on her now. Fax or email? Which is the quickest?'

'But–'

'Fax or email?' I repeated, showing my annoyance. She hesitated for a second.

'Email'

'Do you have the files ready?'

'What?'

'Are you ready for my email address?' I said louder.

'Yes, sorry.'

'D - R DavidBrown. One word. Got it?'

'DrDavidBrown. Yes, I got it.'

'@gmail.com' As I said it, I realised how ridiculous it sounded. I tensed, waiting for her to challenge me.

'Ok, sent.' She sent it? Just like that? Damn, I was good. I saw the email come through on my computer.

'Thank you,' I said and hung up without waiting for her reply.

I studied Jodie's file for several minutes, hoping to understand what was wrong, what it was that Charlie had wanted me to know. It wasn't long; there were entries for prescriptions, her contraceptive pills. Even though she couldn't get pregnant, she had used them to stop her acne and make her periods less harsh; this much I knew. Then she had visited a doctor once for tonsillitis, and there was a prescription for antibiotics. I remember how annoyed she was about this, not wanting to talk about it, the pain when she swallowed. Jodie *never* got sick.

Then there were a few general check-ups, checks for breast, ovarian, and skin cancers. There was nothing particularly odd about her medical history. The last page was the ultrasound picture of Jodie's belly, and Charlie's notes attached saying that nothing was abnormal; any pain was likely due to stress. Was this what she'd wanted me to know? That Jodie was under a lot of stress? Surely that wasn't a secret.

I leaned back in my chair.

'There has to be more,' I whispered. This report didn't justify Charlie's urgent message; she wouldn't have said *you need to know.* I was almost ready to give up, but there was one last avenue to try. I picked up my phone and found Dr Alice Do-Hee. She was our consulting doctor on many of the cases we had at VA Thompson. On the third ring, she picked up her phone.

'Hello, Ethan, how are you?' Her Korean accent was almost completely gone after almost two decades in the UK.

'Hey, Alice, I have a small favour to ask; it's not work-related, more like a personal favour, a question.' I was overexplaining.

'Any time, Ethan. It's my pleasure to help you.' I imagined her sitting at the cluttered desk in her home office. I'd visited once, when she had been ill and we'd needed some files.

'I sent you the medical history of my...' I hesitated, not sure how Alice would react, knowing she was my wife. She could probably guess when she saw the name, but I had to at least pretend, 'of one of my clients.'

'Ok, let's see what we have here.' I sat in silence. 'So...' she paused for a moment, 'we are dealing with a female, 36 years old. By reviewing the first and last page, I can tell she is healthier than the average individual.' Yes. 'Nothing unusual about her contraceptive pills or her tonsillitis. Every time she was checked for cancer, the results were negative. Her ultrasound is fine too; the doctor said this person has been experiencing abdominal pain because of stress.'

'Is it common?' I asked.

'Yes, quite common.' Alice muttered slightly as she read, and I could hear her clicking through the file. 'Everything seems completely normal, at least as far as the records held by this clinic. Are you looking for something in particular?'

'What do you mean, this clinic?'

'Yes, the NHS and private practices are very poor at sharing information, and this report likely isn't the full story for this individual. Often you do need separate permission to access a patient's data from another hospital.'

Of course, there were no signs of Jodie's uterine tube infection. She had said she'd visited a different, specialist infertility clinic.

Dr Lee gently prompted me, breaking the silence. I guess she was busy. 'Are there any other files you would like me to review?'

'No, I don't have anything else. I do know however that this woman had an infertility problem. Uterine tubes blocked by an infection in her teens. But I don't have those files with me.' Alice didn't say anything, so I continued. 'I might be able to get them at some point if you think they are necessary.'

'Hmm...' There was an uncomfortable silence on the over end. 'Are you sure that this report is for the same individual who had an infection as a teenager?'

'Yes, absolutely.'

'Because I can see from the ultrasound picture attached that, unless the picture was taken before infection, even though I can see that the time stamp on it is very recent, there is nothing wrong with this woman's uterine tubes. They look as healthy as any I've seen.'

CHAPTER 26

Theo

The rich sound of a violin sang out, vibrant and filling the whole flat. Listening to Anneli play, watching her grow and improve was one of the things which reminded me just how beautiful life could be. God knew, some dark days, I needed the reminder to pull me back to the light. The days of wearing earplugs when she practiced were thankfully all but gone. My daughter may have been an angel, but when your child tells you she wants to learn the violin, be warned that you will be living with the sounds of a fatally wounded cat through the first year. And you'll have to pretend to like it.

Around six months ago, however, her dedication had begun to pay off. Anneli started to connect the notes, then found her sense of tempo, flowing through the piece. She heard the melody as she played rather than reading notes and playing them one by one. Her hand gestures were growing smoother; there was a hint of elegance when she moved from one side to another, her head floating with the music. There were glimpses of the woman she would become, and I saw her growing to look more and more like her mother, which hurt and healed my heart in equal measure.

Laura's violin was locked away safely in a storage room, waiting for Anneli to be old enough to play it. When I'd spoken to Anneli's teacher, she'd told me that she might be able to use a full-size violin when she was about twelve, I couldn't wait.

On her final note, she extended her bow arm with a flourish and gave a theatrical bow. I clapped hard, and in a brave imitation of an Italian accent, called out, 'Oh brava, ma darling!' I threw imaginary roses into the air, Anneli giggled and pretended to catch them.

'Was I good, Daddy?'

'You were excellent!' After placing her instrument on the table, she ran to hug me. I kissed her on the cheek, holding her tight, 'Hungry yet? Think my mini musician would be up to some pizza stuffed peppers?' I asked, and she grinned at me with two thumbs up. 'I'll nip to the shops. Maybe you can set the table?' Asking Anneli to help me around the house had varied success, but she loved to be the other half of our small team.

Ethan, Jodie, and Amy had been there for me every step of the way since I'd lost my Laura. I'd come to rely on them all so much, needing them every day. But things had been changing, and although I knew it was inevitable, I did occasionally feel panic. How could the world move on so fast when I would never be ready? Amy and Julie finally adopted, and although I knew they would both be incredible mothers, I found it so hard that they had each other. Amy's focus had begun to pull away from me and more towards her own family. I couldn't begrudge her happiness, and Julie was, admittedly, wonderful. It just made me feel a little lost.

Jodie and Ethan would come over fairly regularly under the pretence that they were 'just walking by' and I was quietly grateful - especially in those dark early days when the pain was still fresh and bright. Jodie would come and spend time with little Anneli, who was too small to understand fully but was still filled with sadness. She knew there was something wrong with her father.

I was grateful she'd had love and company on the days I could barely have a shower or even make it out of bed. I'd find batch cooked Tupperware meals in the fridge, and the fruit bowl stocked, so at least we ate well. Occasionally Jodie would play some music loud and dance around being goofy, dragging Anneli around with her until she got a giggle for her efforts. Some days, when I was really bad, she'd bundle Anneli into the car and take her swimming or for a picnic, so I could just fall apart with Ethan by my side.

Ethan would usually attempt to help out around the house, insisting I sit on the sofa and running the hoover vaguely about, but mostly he would put on some garbage TV and try to draw me out of my numbed existence. He was quite literally the friend who made sure I survived Laura's death. Over ancient cartoons and terrible car shows, I slowly opened up and shared everything with him, my deepest desires, my wishes, the silly dreams. I was closer to him than my brother. Ethan understood, without demanding anything from me. He had been there my whole life; they both had.

Now, something was going on in his life, but he refused to tell me anything, and this feeling of being shut out had made me see red. I wanted to be there for him as he had for me - but also with Amy focusing on her family and Jodie going through her share troubles, Ethan shutting me out was pushing me over the edge. I'd gone beyond being confused to being genuinely angry.

It broke my heart knowing he didn't trust me to share whatever was bothering him, and now after a few weeks, I had given up; I stopped messaging and calling him.

My jaw was clenched hard, now, and I took a second to breathe and relax - something from a bereavement counselling session that had stuck. Wrenching my thoughts away from Ethan, I tried to clear my head. I thought about Jordan and felt my heart lift a little. It had felt so odd trying to date again, almost like the first time, but she was kind and sweet, and Anneli liked her, which was my main concern. I was happy to see them together, and after Anneli had told her how much she loved her changing hairstyles, I caught Jordan on YouTube watching a lesson on creative hairstyles for girls with tightly curled hair, which had touched my heart and filled my eyes with tears. I cried a lot more easily these days.

I put on my shoes to leave the house, hoping to clear my head.

As I opened the door, I was startled to find Jodie standing

in front of me. She smiled, holding a colourful gift bag.

'Theo! I was hoping you'd be at home.' She leaned in for a hug.

'I was just heading out.'

'Well, good timing indeed then,' she shrugged.

'What are you doing here?' I asked in surprise.

'Just walking by,' she waved her hand. 'I have something for Anneli.' She stretched her hand for me to take the bag.

'Oh?'

She whispered, unaware Anneli was upstairs, 'it is an *amazing* Halloween costume I got from one of the mothers in my kindergarten class. It's a fox.' I took the bag from her. 'Trust me, she'll love it.' Jodie winked. 'Anyway, have you been doing well? How's Jordan?'

'She is great. I love her.' Jodie's eyes twinkled as she heard the word love slip out of my mouth. I waved my hands to dismiss it, smiling, but she seemed to be getting emotional now. 'Jodie, come on. It's nothing.'

'No, no,' she held herself strong. 'I'm so very happy for you. I …' she pressed her fingers to her nose to stop herself from getting even more emotional. 'I'm just so happy for you two. You deserve to be loved.'

Warmth flooded me. The feeling I'd been craving for a couple of weeks finally lifted my spirit. I knew Jodie had been through a lot, and I appreciated her being here, thinking of me and caring for Anneli despite everything in her life.

'Thank you, Jodie. I appreciate it. I hope you and Ethan are doing better.'

She frowned ever so slightly. 'Why would you say that?'

I didn't really want to bring Jodie into mine and Ethan's business, but she was like my sister.

I sighed. 'Because he doesn't want to talk to me. Ever since Amy's party, he's become distant. Was it because I asked you about your money? Or that silly argument about time travel?'

'That was silly,' Jodie pressed her hand into her forehead, shaking her head slightly. 'No, I don't think it was any of those things. Give him time; he'll get better. He's been distant with me too.'

'Why with you?'

She took a deep breath. 'Because I did some things, hoping they would be an investment in our future. But Ethan's angry because I didn't involve him in those decisions. In retrospect, maybe he's right to be angry. I don't know.' She paused for a moment, looking into the playground at the kids playing touch and go. 'I often think these days that if I could go back and change it all, I believe I would. I wouldn't make the same decision again.' Her last remark was odd, I was curious what decision she was talking about, but she already seemed saddened that I'd asked about their relationship. I didn't want to push further.

'I'm sorry.' I put my hand on Jodie's shoulder, and she placed her hand on top of mine.

'It's fine.' She bit her lower lip. 'We'll be ok.' She squeezed my hand and let it fall. I said thank you again for the costume she'd brought, but I could see her mind was somewhere else. She gave me a cheery wave as she walked away, up the street.

I glanced at the costume Jodie brought for Anneli. I wouldn't have picked this for Anneli, but Jodie usually had pretty good instincts. I hid it in the walk-in wardrobe and went back outside, calling to Anneli to say that I'd be back in ten minutes. The sun was setting as the fresh, cold breeze played on my skin.

The grey streets were full of litter after the storm on Friday - covered in shopping bags, torn cardboard boxes, and plastic packaging. I only needed a pack of peppers, and I didn't want to leave Anneli alone for too long, so I dashed around the store, heading to the self-checkout, nearly slipping on a puddle of water by the freezer section. And I ran pretty much headlong into Ethan. The awkwardness was palpable. He straightened his jacket as if he didn't know what else to do.

'Theo hey! How's things?' Ethan's excitement was fake and forced. I tried to smile but I could barely look at him, not when it felt like he was doing me a favour by talking to me. He seemed scruffy and exhausted.

'Anneli's been asking when you guys are coming for dinner next,' I said, trying to act like this wasn't excruciating.

'Oh yes, have to do something soon!' he said, in a falsely cheerful voice, 'I'm just swamped at the moment.' He had visited Anneli and me at least twice a week since Laura's passing, and now the only thing he was able to say was *soon*.

'Right. Well, then, I'll let you be.' I pushed past him and continued on my way out.

'Theo?' He said behind me, but I didn't stop. 'Theo!' He raised his voice, too much, and a few people stared. I hurried out, not looking back. I walked straight through the checkout area and out into the street, increasing my pace almost to a run. My jaw ached, and I was about to cross the road when a hand grabbed my elbow.

'Theo, please. I know we haven't spoken much lately, but–'

I yanked my arm out of his grip and took a step back. 'Well, whatever you think is going on, you should've just told me. Instead, I'm here wondering what the hell happened to you.' I raised my voice.

'Yes, I know... It was a mistake.' Ethan was trying to say something, but I carried on.

'I've been worried, Ethan! I still am, blaming myself for whatever it was I must have done. And Jodie's in the same boat, you've just totally dropped everyone. Everyone who cares about you.' I still cared about him. 'After everything, we've been through, why would you do this?' He was just staring at something in the distance, as if I wasn't even there. 'Mate, I don't need this. Forget I said anything; I need to get back to Anneli.' I moved away, towards the bench we had placed as a memorial for Laura, and I suddenly realised that sat on it, wearing a black t-shirt, jeans, and a perplexed look, was Amy. Ethan and I rarely fought.

'Trouble in bro paradise?' Amy asked us, having eyed us both warily and decided to go with humour. She liked drama but really hated when anyone was fighting. When the silence stretched too long, her face fell a little. 'Do you want me to leave?'

'It's fine,' I said, feeling myself soften a bit.

'I was just telling Theo off for stealing a pack of mixed peppers,' Ethan said, and I lifted my hand, which still held the plastic bag of colourful vegetables. I stared at them in horror.

'Fuck!' I shouted in surprise. 'Should I–' but Amy started to laugh.

'You dirty thief, Theo!' Amy pointed at me accusingly, still laughing.

'No, I'll go back and pay for this.' I kept looking between Amy, Ethan, and the shop, waiting for security to come running out and arrest me.

'Theo, don't. Not a good look to get a criminal record at your age,' Ethan said, placing his hand on my shoulder. I felt my mouth go dry, but then he started to laugh too. They were teasing me.

Amy stood up from the bench and hugged me tightly.

'You lovely, strange man. Today has blessed you with a small package of free groceries. You must accept your fate.' Then she pulled away and looked at me. She must have seen something in my face, my jaw still felt tight, and I hadn't smiled. 'It's ok, Theo. You know? Breathe.' I stared at her.

'What are you doing here, sitting by yourself?' I asked.

Amy sighed and sat back down, gazing at the trees that lined the small square. 'I know it sounds crazy. I've been feeling weird all day. It dawned on me that I'd been thinking abou ... well ...'

No words came. I was pretty sure that we all knew who she was thinking of. I walked around her and sat on the other side of the bench. A breeze rustled through the damp leaves of the sycamore tree above us. It was peaceful, here, the sound of a few passing cars and some kids running around the raised garden.

We sat together in silence for a moment, paying our respects. I turned to look at the plaque dedicated to Laura and felt a lump rise in my throat, the sting of hot tears. It sometimes felt that it would never get easier. I shut my eyes, put my head in my hands, and tried to relax my clenched teeth.

'I miss her,' Amy said softly, 'so much.' her voice cracked a little, and she released a deep sigh, trying to ward off tears. She placed her hands on mine. 'Sorry, I know this isn't about me. I just–'.

'Don't say that. Please.' I took another deep breath and swallowed, trying to keep my voice steady. 'She was your friend. You loved her too.'

'It's her kindness I miss the most. She was so fucking kind.' She clenched her fist. Then another moment passed, and the tension slowly receded from her face. 'I never saw her walk past someone begging in the street. She always had something to give them - a sandwich, some coins. A blanket, once.'

She laughed. 'But she never preached about how we all just walk past, did she? She gave us and everyone else credit, believing that we just did the best we could. *Isn't this what we all do?* She once said to me. *Just trying to be the best version of ourselves.*'

'We all miss her.' I said quietly.

'I was here with her two days before the … you know.' she said quietly. 'Right here. Jodie, too. We'd had such a lovely day.' I looked at her but saw straight through her, instead seeing Laura in my thoughts, her smile, her laugh, and felt a stabbing in my chest. Ethan and I used to call the three of them *our girls*. We hadn't used the phrase since Laura's accident.

'What did you three do?' Ethan asked gently, and I jumped. I'd been so lost in thought I'd forgotten he was there, forgotten all my anger at him. I guiltily remembered Anneli, patiently waiting at home for dinner, and my fingers closed over the stolen peppers, but I wanted to ask the same question. I loved hearing new stories about Laura; it made her feel a tiny bit closer, somehow.

'It was a simple thing, you know?' Amy shrugged. 'We went to Tesco and bought a couple of tinnies and some sweets like we used to do in college. We just sat there. And, you know. Hung out.' Amy turned around and pointed at a raised garden bed, which was in between us and a shop. 'It was great. We talked about jobs, us, sex lives. Ethan's fetishes.' I turned to Ethan, who seemed taken back. Amy turned around slowly to look at him, with a cheeky smile, biting her lower lip. Ethan turned red, and I burst out laughing, the memory of the fight forgotten.

'Oh, you think that's funny? How *is* your mother's greenhouse, Theo?'

My mouth fell open, and I felt the heat rise in my cheeks. I couldn't believe Laura had talked about it to Amy, but in a weird way, it made me happy. I shut my eyes and remembered how she was, the good times.

Slightly tipsy, eyes sparkling when she giggled. When

she used to look at me, deep in my eyes, like she could see all the way to my soul. I thought about that night in the greenhouse and felt something change, deep in my stomach. My eyes snapped open.

'Look at The Shard,' Ethan said, quietly. We gazed up. It really was beautiful, the very tip lit up like a rainbow in the darkening sky, just visible above the buildings.

'Did you know it's covered in 11,000 glass panels? I prepared a case study on it once.'

'Tallest building in western Europe,' added Ethan. 'Shame having those council buildings blocking the view.'

'Come on, I'll show you something!' Amy jumped up, grabbing my hand, Ethan following behind. 'Come here, no, right here. In front of the street light,' she pointed to the ground. Ethan and I craned our heads together, 'Do you see?' I exhaled and heard Ethan give a low whistle. The view was amazing. The Shard stood razor-sharp and glittering with lights, perfectly framed in a small gap in the deep black buildings on either side, elegant white limbed trees softly reaching up and rustling at its base. You had to stand in this exact spot, or the buildings would block the view. It looked like something alien and fantastical, the light at its peak beaming up into the mist, calling to the mothership. Ethan was busy taking a picture with his phone, but I couldn't stop staring.

'This is amazing. How did you even discover this spot?' I murmured to Amy.

'It was Jodie!' she said happily. 'When we had our picnic. We were here so long that the sun was starting to go down ...'

'What?' Ethan raised his voice, I stepped away slightly to better see his face, and he grabbed Amy's shoulder. It felt unnecessarily aggressive. His eyes were boring into her.

'It was Jodie,' Amy said, trying to turn away. He held fast.

'She told you about this, two days before the accident, about the Shard?' He demanded it, as if something had shocked him. I couldn't see the big deal, but it was like he was on another planet. Amy glanced at me uncertainly, and then back to him.

'What's the matter?' I asked, but he didn't respond. He staggered a few steps away from us, breathing hard. He was looking around wildly, at The Shard, at us, and I could see tears welling up in his eyes. His face was ragged and pale, and I knew again that there was something he wasn't telling us. I wanted to be angry at him, tell him he was unreasonable, that he'd ruined a lovely moment, but I couldn't; I was suddenly more worried for him than I had ever been. I took a step towards him, but he raised his hand, stopping me.

'Don't.' His voice was final, resolute, dangerous. I froze.

'Ethan, what the hell? What is going on with you?' Amy said.

He turned without answering, walking away quickly, almost running.

'Ethan, for God's sake!' Amy shouted and grabbed my elbow, turning me to face her. 'What on earth did I do, did I say something?'

'No. No, you didn't.'

CHAPTER 27

Ethan

Much as I tried to breathe, it felt like I was drowning in air. Streets and houses spun around me as I tried to walk straight. I wasn't sure where I was. Everything I knew about my life - about what it had been, about the person I had once loved, everything was crumbling around me. I stopped walking and closed my eyes, but all I could see was Jodie showing Laura the beautifully lit Shard. I imagined Laura clapping her hands, admiring the view. She'd lain there in that same spot Amy had shown us today - I'd lifted her broken body from the ground and carried her away from the ambulance sirens, to a bench where I'd said my goodbyes.

No, no, no. It couldn't be true; it must have been some sort of awful coincidence. Jodie had said that night was just an accident, and it was. Destiny, Jodie had called it, and it was unavoidable. Darkness.

My Wife Jodie

***

I had no memory of walking home. I took one step towards the entrance, then stopped. My hands were shaking; my sweaty palm stuck on the railing as I climbed the stairs, trying to delay going in, in case she was home.

As soon as I closed the front door, the air inside became heavy, cold. I crept around the house, afraid she would hear me though I'd checked her location, she was at the gym. I sank into the living room couch.

I saw her laptop resting on the dining room table, and almost without thinking, I found myself typing *LadyBird*. Her laptop opened up with a beautiful picture of us, smiling at Emmet's birthday. We'd been so happy then - though it had been after I'd found out about her powers, I had accepted what she had done. Now I was searching for the evidence that I hoped not to find.

I went to the messages app, which was synced to her phone. I clicked on the search bar and typed in *Laura*. Even after six years, she hadn't deleted the contact, but then, neither had I.

Scrolling through their message history.

27 SEPTEMBER 2010

Jodie: *Just a reminder about this Friday, us celebrating Theo's promotion. FYI: Amy is going to babysit Anneli.*

Laura: *Awesome! That would be amazing; I wanted to see Wicked ages ago. Thank you for buying tickets!*

314

Jodie: *It was Ethan and me :)*

Laura: *But it was your idea. <3*

Laura: *I'm soooo excited!!!!!!!!!!!!! Xxxx*

Jodie: *Let's meet tomorrow with Amy. Have a girls night out, ok?*

Laura: *That's good. Theo and Ethan can look after Anneli; I'll have a small break from all the screaming ...*

29 September 2010

Laura: *:DDDDDDDDD*

(There was a picture of me attached trying to balance five books on my head and reading to Anneli)

Laura: *Anneli loves it!*

Jodie: *:D*

Jodie: *FYI, tomorrow let's meet at Tesco. I need to get something before we go to see Theo, ok? 6:25 sharp.*

Laura: *To get what? More gummy bears?? My stomach is still upset after yesterday : (((*

Jodie: *Haha no.*

30 September 2010

Laura: *Jodie Page is late??? :oooooo*

Jodie: *OTW.*

Jodie: *Remember that spot we found yesterday? The sky is amazing now! Take a picture of the shard for me :)*

Laura: *OMG, you are so right.*

Jodie: *Laura?*

Jodie: *I'm sorry.*

My Wife Jodie

My hands were numb. I sat in silence, afraid to move, afraid to return to reality. Laura had been murdered; there had been no accident, no anguished choice by Jodie. She had calmly murdered Laura in a way that no one would ever suspect. I'd never questioned Jodie when she'd said that this was Laura's destiny, that when she tried to save her, it had all gone to hell; I'd trusted her. But it hadn't been destiny. It had all been Jodie.

Jodie had proposed the day, to celebrate Theo's promotion. Jodie had set the meeting place near the shop and asked Laura to take a picture of the *magical* view she'd pointed out just two days before.

Jodie possessed the power to know everything that was going to happen, and she could make anything look like an accident. Anything - like luring a person into a particular street, knowing four storeys' worth of scaffolding would fall on them.

Without even thinking, I signed in to my email address on Jodie's computer and found the CCTV footage of the street outside Charlie's clinic. I watched it again, not watching Charlie but instead the other person with the shopping bags. I closed my eyes, trying to remember that Friday when Jodie had come in, soaked. She'd told me she took a raincoat with her, but it hadn't been enough to keep her dry.

Jodie only had one raincoat, a bright fluorescent colour that could look a bit like a high visibility jacket. I grabbed it from the wardrobe, squeezing the material thoughtfully as I walked back to the living room. Though the colour in the video was washed out, it looked like the jackets matched.

'Jodie, no,' I whispered, my voice trembling. I collapsed into the chair, letting Jodie's jacket slip from my fingers to the floor. 'But why?' shaking my head because I already knew the answer; when she died, Charlie was moments from telling me about Jodie's medical history. There had been no teenage infection; no reason we could not have had a family. I clenched my fists; my heart was racing. 'No,' I whispered, digging my nails into my palm. 'No!' I stood up and kicked at the table, Jodie's laptop clattering to the floor. The table hit the wall in front of me, dislodging the canvas of the two children holding hands. It landed on the floor on its edge and stood still for a few seconds, as if looking at me then, like a domino, gently flopped face down.

My eyes caught the brown leather book tucked behind the canvas, resting inside the frame. I'd seen Jodie drawing in it many times before - it was her sketch book. I reached for it just as I noticed the writing on the back of the canvas. I could make out the words, but I refused to believe them. Shaking uncontrollably, I walked around the table so I could read them more clearly.

Jill and Adam
2009

Jill and Adam? Jill? No, this cannot be what I think it is. It can't be. I grabbed the brown leather notebook and opened it.

My Wife Jodie

There was a pencil drawing of a baby, coloured carefully, with bright blue eyes. There was a sketch on almost every page, scenes from the life of a beautiful girl. Here, she was playing with dolls, or building sandcastles on a beach. My hands started to shake uncontrollably as I turned the pages, somehow guessing where this was leading. And on the last page, she was having a picnic with her parents - the surroundings roughly sketched even while the girl was drawn in uncanny detail, her pointy cheeks, her missing front tooth.

I placed the notebook back on the canvas and scrolled through my phone until I found the photo of the page from Jodie's green book. There it was, in black and white.

Jill   *11-05-2009   02-05-07*

It was sometime in mid-2009 when Jodie had told me her test results, that we would never have a child together. I believed her, but this was another lie. She went back seven years, five months and two days in her life to forget, to erase someone called Jill. I looked at the painting again, of the kids holding hands. That little girl in Jodie's painting, wearing a summer dress and a straw hat, standing in the high grass, holding the hand of a boy, was the only thing remaining of the daughter I had never met.

Jodie erased her own daughter from existence. The life of a precious little girl, vanished before it even started. Why, Jodie? Her own daughter. Who was this heartless woman I had been living with all my life? Someone who was capable of murdering an innocent child and not shedding a single tear.

'Oh, Jill! Jill! No, no, no!' Half screaming, half crying in fear and pain. 'That selfish bitch! How dare she? How fucking dare she!' I was hitting the wall, where the painting had hung, again and again, the skin breaking around my knuckles and the wedding ring. The burning sensation in my hands was the only good thing left in my life. 'Why, Jodie? Why did you do this?' I wanted everyone to hear. 'No!' My eyes filled with tears as I kept hitting the wall, wanting nothing more than to die here, surrounded by all these cryptic paintings of the lives I had lost. The family at their picnic, the man about to leap from the building, Jill and Adam, the pig in the cage, they all mocked me. I wanted to die - but not before I strangled that woman.

The keys rattled in the lock, and the front door opened.

'Ethan?'

I stayed quiet. I had to clean this up before she saw. I heard her walking into the study, then the bedroom. She called out a few more times, as I quickly pushed the table back into the middle of the room, placing her laptop - with a surprisingly small dent - neatly into place.

'Ethan!' She shouted again, and I finally answered.

Her steps approached as I was trying to place the canvas back on its hook with one hand.

'What happened here?' I turned to face her, and she pointed to her artwork.

'It fell; I was just putting it back,' I said, holding my right hand up and against my chest to hide the small trickle of blood now running down my arm.

'Is it damaged?' She started to approach me, but I managed to put the canvas back up, now covering the dent in the plaster and a small smear of my blood, and turned towards her.

'No, no damage.' I put my hand in my back pocket.

'Amy called me and said you'd been acting weird.'

'I think I ate something bad.'

'What did you eat? You look so pale.' She was so close now that I could smell her subtle, sweet perfume. I nodded, not sure what she wanted. She lifted her hand and placed it on my forehead as if checking my temperature. Her hand was warm, I held my breath and wanted her to step away, but she came closer. She placed her second hand on my cheek. 'Ethan, you're so cold.' I nodded, still holding my breath. All I wanted was to grab her by the neck and squeeze until she stopped struggling. She started leaning in for a kiss. Oh no, I can't do this. I pushed her roughly to the side, and she staggered against the table as I rushed past.

'Ethan!' Her words chased me into the bathroom. I barely managed to open the toilet lid before I threw up my lunch. Then she was there, next to me, holding a pint of water.

'Here you go,' as she held the glass out, but I didn't take it from her. The drink was placed next to my knee as she crouched beside me for a moment, then jumped up to open the window.

'What did you eat?' I ignored her question, afraid of any interaction. 'Ethan, what did you eat and when?'

I closed my eyes and gathered strength.

'Can you please leave me alone and close the door?' Her eyes widened, but she nodded and stood up, keeping her eyes locked on me warily. The light scent of her perfume reached my nose, and I threw up again. The door closed, and I collapsed on to the floor, feeling like something poisonous had left me. I didn't want to leave that spot; the fresh air coming from the window tickled my nose. Unexpected tears started to fall, rolling down my face. I sat thinking about how my life had changed in just a few weeks, about how I would never meet my beautiful baby girl. I covered my face with my arm and sobbed silently, my shoulders shaking.

***

The knock on the bathroom door startled me.

'Ethan, you've been in there for a long time,' she said.

'Please ... give me another moment.' I wasn't sure if the same weak excuse would work, but relief flooded through me as I heard her walking away.

I wish I could confront her with everything - her planning Laura's death, erasing the memory of my daughter, pushing Charlie under that scaffolding. But I can't even hint that I know.

Why had she done it, murdered these innocent people? Because these women had been too close to me, that they somehow took my attention away from her? Was she jealous? Could it have been jealousy even of her own daughter? I cried out again, for the daughter I had never met.

No one was safe while she was around. If I couldn't report her to the police, if I couldn't leave her, if I couldn't even tell her that I know everything, then there was nothing I could do.

I studied the painting that hung in the bathroom, the man standing high up on a narrow spire amidst swirling storm clouds, his arms black wings. She called it freedom. Was it me she painted? Trying to flee from her, as far away as possible, even if it meant my death? Was the painting a warning to me, to be understood at the right moment? Had I tried before, in another version of these events?

How could I possibly hope to escape? She was too powerful. I was no match for her. I had only a handful of options. Confront her, tell her everything I know and hope she would feel sorry for me and let me go. I let out a silent, painful laugh. If she was murdering people just for the sake of having me next to her, then there was no way she would just let me go.

I could try and pretend to love her, to live this life she created for us. Isn't that what she wanted? No, I'd rather kill myself before I did anything for that woman. But even death wasn't an option for me, if she saved my mother and Theo. Without a doubt she would grant me an unlimited number of lives.

I drank the water she'd left me. It cleaned out my mouth, the same way I needed to empty out my emotions if I wanted to survive this. I gathered my strength and pulled myself away from the toilet. I had to be strong; I straightened my back and stood up. Taking a deep breath, I stuck my head out the bathroom door listening to hear where she was, but there was no sound. She wasn't in the bedroom, but I found her in the dining room sitting at our table, her hands in front of her, fingers intertwined. As soon as she noticed me her face brightened.

'Ethan, how are you feeling?' I nodded, stopping in the doorway, keeping my distance. 'What and when did you eat?' She'd asked this a few times already, insistent.

'I don't know what I ate; I don't think I had anything today except porridge this morning.'

'Strange,' she said, 'you eat porridge all the time, you wouldn't have had food poisoning from that.'

'Yes. But it's fine; I feel much better now. Thank you for looking out for me,' I tried to look happy.

'I'm sorry ... your colour is getting back to normal, though,' she smiled. Without acknowledging her, I asked the question that was the only way I could see to escape this.

'Should we take a holiday?'

'What?' She was taken by surprise at the sudden shift in direction.

'A holiday ... we haven't been on one for a while.'

'Of course! Let's do it!' She leapt up from her chair and came around and hugged me tightly. I held my breath while she held me. After a few seconds, she pulled back and looked into my eyes. 'Where?' she asked, her face full of hope and innocent anticipation.

'Somewhere, just the two of us. Far away from here.'

CHAPTER 28

I'm going to murder my wife.

My days had started to merge into one continuous blur of half-waking existence, a dreamscape. Instead of my usual seven hours of sleep, I was barely getting an hour at a time. I napped and tried to make it through. If I was lucky, my dreams were not violent. Those moments gave me joy; I cherished each of them and held their memory for as long as possible.

I would often wake up from a nightmare to find that reality was worse; the biggest nightmare was here in the real world, lying inches away from me, her hand occasionally resting on my bare chest, and then it would be impossible for me to fall asleep. I'd stopped going to bed naked, explaining it away by telling her it was more comfortable as the weather cooled in September.

When she slept, it was my chance to plan. I'd been in a courtroom many times, as a husband was being accused of his wife's murder - maybe he pushed her down the stairs, or strangled her with a pillow while she slept. Or a wife, on trial for killing her husband; a little more poison every day. More often than not they ended up in jail, because there was usually proof that the couple had been fighting before the murder. That was all the prosecution needed to convince a jury.

I knew I wouldn't be able to pull anything off myself - not successfully. My road trip around the country after she'd fled, with Amy testifying I'd cheated; it didn't look good. I'd always be the main suspect, no matter what.

If poison wasn't an option, maybe I could hire a hitman. But in this day and age, you have no way of knowing who you're talking to, and most of the advertisements online are law enforcement, out to catch people stupid enough to hand over their bank details. I was still willing to consider it, but I needed to be smarter if I wanted any chance of getting away with it.

No body, no crime. If I could make her disappear, I could never be tried for murder. Acid bath? Pushed deep into a ditch, fed to pigs? They were all easy solutions in Hollywood, but this was real life. One mistake could mean the end of my freedom. Was that worse than living in this hell?

Now, the third night after learning the truth, I snuck out of the bedroom and lay on the living room sofa. A street light shone outside, harsh white light through the windows. The venetian blinds cast striped shadows across the ceiling, like prison bars. Maybe I could get a few hours of sleep here, and return to bed before she awoke.

Today was Saturday and the perfect time to tell her I needed to work. I was exhausted from lack of sleep and the constant tension of being around her, pretending to be a loving husband. It was like being on stage, in the spotlight, observed by hundreds of people and the scene never ends.

I opened my eyes to find her in front of me.

'Did you sleep on the couch?'

'I… I…' I stretched, giving myself a few seconds to gather my thoughts and come up with a good excuse, 'I woke up early, but I must have drifted back to sleep.'

She looked concerned. 'I'm leaving to meet Amy for the hairdressers, back in a few hours.'

I stood there staring into space long after she'd left the apartment. I didn't know if I had enough strength to keep this up, to go through with my plan to kill my wife. Even after everything she'd done, part of me still questioned if it was the right solution; to risk my freedom just to be free of this woman. To become someone who made his own decisions and lived by their consequences.

I ran through my plan again. Acapulco, Mexico, was notorious for a large number of homicides every year. Most of those were drug-related; still, a couple of naive tourists attacked by an intoxicated gang member could work. It was only necessary to create reasonable doubt.

I would book an AirBnB for a couple of weeks, something with large windows and access to the first floor. Spending two weeks there meant I would have a lot of time to prepare the crime scene. Collecting enough samples from some used clothing shops to plant scraps of fabric in a few careful locations. A visit to a barber would give me an excuse to collect a pinch of hair, to be scattered around the rooms and on her. To minimise risk with the forensics, I would stab her and then try to save her life.

The forensics would be able to tell I tried to keep her alive while waiting for the ambulance. Maybe I could give myself a hammer wound on the back of my head, or something like that. *Someone was inside the house. Knocked me unconscious while I tried to save her life.* I didn't need a perfect crime, just enough for it to be believable, and that was doable.

Her birthday in two weeks gave us the perfect reason to be going away. She'd already said yes, and even though Acapulco was a dangerous city, I doubted she'd have too many concerns - she knew she could always use her powers at any point. That is why I'd have to kill her instantly.

I walked to the kitchen, filled a glass with water, grabbed my notebook, and sat down at the dining room table to make a list of everything I'd need.

Firstly, no one could know there were any issues between us before we left. Theo knew something was happening, but luckily he didn't know anything real. I would tell him that the adoption process had been a lot of hard work. Amy already knew about that, and it tied up the loose ends neatly - that there were no issues between me and Jodie; we were happy as always.

Then, in Mexico, we'd have the most expensive, ostentatious holiday imaginable. That meant uploading as many memories to Instagram as possible, making sure she talked to her friends about how happy she was, and sending postcards home to Amy and Theo.

Third, book an expensive AirBnB in a dodgy part of town. I should pick the moment to coincide with any event that might be happening.

Fourth, plant the evidence. Pick up the hair at the barbers, leave that tiny but easy-to-notice shred of fabric from a charity shop dangling over the open window. I knew better than most about how even a small piece of evidence could turn an innocent person into the prime suspect. *All I need is reasonable doubt,* I reminded myself.

Fifth, when everything is ready, execute the plan. Don't hesitate.

Sixth, get back to England as soon as possible. The UK and Mexico had an extradition treaty, but it would make life much harder for the Mexican authorities to prosecute me if I had left the county, and arresting some local dealers would sweep it all under the carpet, something they would be eager to do in peak tourist season. It might be difficult to explain my abrupt departure, but not impossible. I could play on emotional distress to help me get out.

Seventh, be sad, and not let my happiness show once I've returned to London. Remorse is a huge factor for both the judge and the prosecutor. At least I'd had a lot of practice pretending recently.

I knew the possibility of success was slim, but that was enough for me to try. It was about doing the right thing. If I let her live, more people would die; and I'd always know I could have done something, but didn't.

I ran over the list again, repeating each of the points several times to memorise them before ripping the page out of the notebook and grabbing the matches. I watched the flames swallow my scribbles. Number eight: destroy the evidence.

***

We usually fly business, but I booked first-class tickets to Acapulco so it'd be easier to avoid her.

Closing my laptop, I took a deep breath, again seeing the paintings in front of me. The portrait of *my daughter*, now also conveniently covering the hole I'd punched in the wall.

'Damn it!' I banged my fists on the table again, and again, trying to find that cleansing pain, but my heart wasn't really in it and then the tears finally came. The pain in my chest grew until it was hard to breathe.

'Fuck it,' I whispered, 'this needs to be done.' I opened my work account and sent my boss an email, booking a holiday in two weeks' time. I pressed send, knowing it brought me one step closer to doing what was necessary. What was *right*.

I heard the keys in the door again, and went quickly

to change into my running gear. One of the only ways I could get any respite was a long run, even though I'd been spending most of that time sitting on a bench in the park, running the plan over and over in my mind.

***

'Jodie, I want to apologise for how I've been these past few weeks.' She looked up from the canvas she was working on, her eyes wide. The new, red highlights in her blond hair shone in the strong morning sunlight. I held the bouquet of white lilies in front of me; a peace offering. Of all the lies I had ever told in my life, this was amongst the hardest, telling the person who was responsible for my daughter's death that I was sorry. 'It was work, and coming to terms with what you *did for me*, I ...' I paused, focused, got back to the apology. 'I just want you to know that I appreciate everything you have done for me, I see it now, and I'm sorry for the way I hurt you.'

'Oh, Ethan,' she stood up from the stool. 'I don't know what to say.' She was coming closer, and I instinctively took a step back. Placing her arms on my shoulder, she pressed her cheek to mine, squishing the flowers slightly. They had been expensive. 'Thank you,' she whispered, and nibbled my ear gently. When she stepped back, she smiled sincerely, and for a brief moment, I lived in two worlds at once; for that second, I wished that our lives were as they had been when we were both deeply happy.

'I'm sorry too, Ethan. I should have handled myself

better, these last few weeks. It's been challenging to navigate, and I was hard on you. I am as much at fault. And I understand, work can be stressful,' she said, 'but I'm always here if you ever need me. You can trust me.'

I could never trust her. I pretended to smile and held out the flowers, slightly crushed.

'And I'm sorry for not telling you everything about Laura. I wish there had been a better ending to that story, that I had been able to do something, *anything*, to save her and Theo.'

I shook my head, held the smile, wanting to scream that I knew that she had planted Laura right in that spot, had murdered her in cold blood in a way that only Jodie could. There was no chance, no destiny that day.

'The holiday I mentioned to you earlier, I wasn't joking. I really think it's time for us to forget about all this and start afresh.'

'Yes,' she said, her eyes watering, she was so happy, 'I want that more than anything, now.'

'I bought us tickets to Mexico.'

'You did what?'

'Mexico, in two weeks.'

She laughed with genuine, uncontrolled joy, throwing her hands in the air, dropping the flowers.

'This is amazing!' She jumped at me, and I instinctively caught her, her fingers in my hair. 'Thank you,' she said. 'I really needed this.' I lowered her gently back on to her feet and placed my hand on her shoulder.

'We leave next week, in time for your birthday.'

My Wife Jodie

***

She didn't stop smiling that whole afternoon; she placed what was left of the lilies in her favourite bright yellow vase on the dining room table. While I made dinner, she spent her time looking between her canvas, the flowers, and me. Each time our eyes met, I made sure to smile.

As I watched the romesco sauce bubble, I thought again about how difficult it would be to poison her. The main problem was that an autopsy would show the cause of death, and if they found anything even slightly suggesting poison, I would be the suspect - and any slow death would give Jodie time to go back and save herself. Who knows, maybe I'd already tried it, on some other, forgotten timeline - and she was just toying with me now, pretending to be happy, waiting for my next move.

The tension was killing me.

'The sauce smells great!'

I thanked her. It was almost burnt, and I turned off the stove.

While setting the table, I heard her humming songs we both liked. I couldn't believe that this seemingly innocent person was capable of doing what she'd done. Capable of cold calculation, and killing the people she loved.

'Dinner!' I announced it without looking at her. She jumped from her stool and walked around the table to where she usually sits, her back to Jill. 'Slow-cooked salmon with *home-made* romesco sauce.'

'This looks wonderful,' she said, and again the thought of poisoning went through my mind. It would be so simple; just add something to her food and watch as the life left her.

She kept the small talk going all evening, still happy about the trip, and I tried my best but the pretence proved more difficult the more wine I drank. I had thought the wine would help me get through the evening, but the more I had, the more afraid I was of saying something that might give me away. She was quiet for a while, thoughtfully chewing on her last bite.

'So, what's happening with our adoption then?'

I choked on a tomato. I'd already had a family, until she had killed them all. Now all I wanted was for her to choke on a fish bone and suffocate in front of my eyes. Wouldn't it be perfect? I wouldn't have to lift a fucking finger.

'I'm excited about it. Has Amy written her recommendation letter yet?' I said while my mouth was full; it was easier to hide my emotions.

'Yes, she sent it yesterday. Should we meet the agent next week or wait till we're back?' she said.

'Let's do it next week.' More evidence that we were happy, planning a future together. She reached out across the table, her hand resting on mine. Very lightly, she squeezed my knuckles and smiled. I pulled my hand away, holding the knife, and took another bite. She didn't move her hand, as if giving me time to take her hand back, but I continued eating.

We sat in silence for the remainder of the meal, sipping

wine and avoiding eye contact. Jodie wasn't stupid; she knew something was going on. I caught her eyes several times as she was staring out the living room window. I didn't know what she was thinking but I prayed that she wouldn't try to undo this, that I would be able to hold the pretence until we were in Mexico. That I would have the strength for another week or so of this.

I cleared the table and went back to collect her plate; as I reached for it, she placed her hand on top of mine again. This time I didn't move away. I waited for her to remove it, but she didn't.

'Thank you, Ethan. I had a great evening.' Her hand was still on top of mine. She started to stroke mine lightly. I took slow, deep breaths. Then she stood up and wrapped her arms around my neck. Our bodies touched, she kissed me. I held my breath. Moments later, her hand slid to my cheek, then down my chest. Grabbing the hem of my t-shirt, she raised it to remove it, but I stopped her before she could.

'I ... am ...' She didn't say anything, but I could guess what she was thinking. She was testing me; she knew something was up; it was her way of seeing if there was a big problem. I couldn't keep blaming imaginary food poisoning for not wanting to have sex with her. We had always enjoyed it, and now I had no real reason to say no. She waited for me to finish the sentence. 'I–' I stuttered. The silence was uncomfortable. 'I–' I felt my body radiating heat. If I didn't do this, my entire plan would fall apart. If there was to be a solid chance of getting away with murder, she could in no way mention to Amy that something was up with me, that I hadn't wanted to have sex with her. If I was not going to have sex with her, I might as well give up and live the rest of my life pleasing the woman who had killed my daughter. I grabbed her suddenly and returned her kiss, with passion.

***

My naked torso was rubbing against her breasts, and she was kissing my neck with her lips and her tongue. She unbuttoned my pants, and roughly pushed them down to my knees with her legs. Charlie's soft hands slid down my body, while our moans filled the room. My tongue explored her ear. Her hands pulled down my boxers, and my penis bounced out. She exhaled and arched her back, wanting me to touch her, to feel her. Her face was completely covered by her fire-red hair. I pressed my palm on to her torso, slowly sliding it up her sweaty body, and she moved her head to reveal her perfectly symmetrical lips.

My hands slid gently around her throat. She inhaled, and moaned. Charlie was one of a kind, a bit zany but smart and brave. Looking at her body, seeing her enjoying me was everything I wanted. But then she lifted her head to meet my eyes, and the illusion was swallowed by Jodie's gaze.

I squeezed her neck tighter, and her hands suddenly gripped my wrists, hard. Her eyes widened. She'd hurt so many people; it was time for her to be punished. My buttocks were working even harder now. Pushing myself into her faster. She was trying hard to pull my hands away, now, but I held them in place. If I just kept going, held the course, then all my problems would just disappear. All I had to do was make her lose consciousness. My hair was wet now with the exertion, droplets of sweat running down my body onto hers. I went for a final push with both my hips and my hands.

She shuddered, and so did I, exhaling as my body collapsed onto hers, releasing her neck, and she took a deep breath, followed quickly by another. Neither of us moved for a while. Her chest was heaving.

'That was–' she didn't know how to finish the sentence.

'Something different,' I pulled myself away from her slightly. 'I just wanted to spice things up a bit.'

CHAPTER 29

Ethan, stay safe and hurry back home, okay?
I just read an article about the crime levels in Bermondsey.
Apparently there's gangs.

I ignored her message and I put my phone back into my pocket, with no intention of responding. I wasn't afraid of getting robbed or attacked. Standing alone on this dark pedestrian street, Theo was the only person I was afraid of now. Through his kitchen window, I could see lights were on; he was at home.

I had delayed this for as long as I could, but the time had come to face Theo, and to tell him that I had cheated on him with the woman that he loved more than anything in the world. This was the only way I could make peace with myself before I left for Mexico.

When I'd confronted Jodie about Laura a few weeks

ago, she had told me that if I truly believed she was a bad person, I should tell Theo about my feelings for Laura. For far too long, the secret had been eating me alive.

For the third time, I took a step forward and then another back. I lacked the simple courage to knock on the front door. The night made it easy to see through his kitchen window, but I hadn't seen him or Anneli.

Theo had been my best friend for so many years; we'd been through hell together. He wasn't just my friend, he was my brother, and I was about to tell him that I had been prepared to have an affair with his wife. But the truth was - if I chose not to tell him anything, if I kept hiding it from him, then I would be just like her.

I took a step forward, and with it, a deep breath. Suddenly, Theo's door swung open, and the sound of Annali's laughter filled the quiet street; I stood still. She saw me first. Her eyes widened, and she ran towards me, screaming, *Ethan*. Then a moment later, Theo saw me. The surprise on his face was unmistakable. Anneli slammed to my chest, wrapping her arms around my neck. I stood up and swung her around; she grabbed my neck tighter as her legs lifted into the air. She giggled, almost screaming with joy. *Ethan, it's uncle Ethan,* she repeated. I carefully placed her onto the ground and kissed her cheek. She wiggled as I did it.

'Uncle Ethan! Are you coming with us?'

'Depends… where are you going?'

'We are going to the top of the Shard with Jordan!' She waved her hands into the air, and I couldn't help but copy her gesture. She took so much joy from simple things.

'Oh, I'm sorry, sunshine, I can't go, but you, Jordan, and your dad will *love it*,' I said, making her excited and sad at the same time.

'But Ethan, I missed you.'

'I missed you too, bunny.' Would Anneli and Jill have been friends?

'It's been so long since you came to visit us.'

It was true, and I was ashamed of letting down a girl who loved me so much because I was simply afraid to tell Theo the truth.

'I promise I'll come again, soon.' An empty promise, I had no idea when I would see her again. I feared that this might be one of the last times I was able to talk to her.

'Anneli? Would you mind getting your jacket? I'll keep uncle Ethan company.' Theo gestured Anneli towards the house.

'But I don't want to!' She cried out.

'It's cold.'

'But–'

'Don't be a potato, Anneli.'

She crossed her hands and frowned theatrically, stomping back into the house.

The muttered words *I'm a grown-up, too!* drifted back to where we stood.

Theo closed the door behind her and took a few steps towards me.

'Are you finally going to tell me what the hell is going on with you?' He crossed his hands, and I couldn't help thinking about how alike he and Anneli were.

'Yes,' it was hard for me to look straight into his eyes. 'I will,' He was angry and impatient for me to start talking. 'Theo, you're my best friend–'

'Great. Let's get straight to what you need to say to me.' He was firm, annoyed at the interruption to his evening. I needed to be honest, to tell him the truth. I hid my shaking hands in my jacket pockets.

'I'm so sorry for disappearing from your life the last few weeks.'

'Good to know.'

I don't remember Theo ever being like this to me, ever. 'The reason for that was ... shame. For what I'd done to you.' Theo frowned, untangling his arms. 'There was something I did a long time ago, something so bad I hid it deep inside and never had the courage to face it, or tell you.' I watched his face muscles relax; it was the person I knew and loved, now.

'Ethan, you can tell me anything.' He placed his hand on my shoulder, and I gripped his hand. Suddenly, I was sobbing. Really sobbing. Theo pulled away in shock. I don't know if he'd ever seen me cry before, even after the death of Laura. Now he was the only person left that I genuinely cared about, the only person I could trust and fall back on, and I was about to destroy everything.

'Ethan, just tell me what you're talking about.'

I shook my head. I was trying desperately to delay the inevitable, but there was no way out now. I could do what Jodie had done and tell a half-truth: just tell Theo how sorry I was, that I'd not been a good friend recently, apologise for making a move on Laura back in university. He would forgive me, confused, and we would move on. But I couldn't. I wasn't going to be like her. The lies and the deceit had to stop. Theo deserved honesty just as much as I deserved mine. He had to know.

'I had feelings for Laura before the accident.' He pulled back. I couldn't look at him.

'Okay..?' he said slowly, confused.

'And I would have left Jodie to be with her.'

'What?' I lifted my eyes up from my shoes, and as soon as he saw my face he took another step back. My chest tightened, like an icy hand was gripping my heart.

'I don't understand.'

'Laura and I would have run away together.'

'Did you sleep with her?'

'No.'

'Did you kiss her?'

'No.'

'Then what happened between you two?'

'Nothing, but I was planning to–'

'Why?'

'Because we were developing feelings.'

'No!' He yelled, 'why are you telling me this now?'

'What do you mean?'

'What the fuck are you trying to achieve with this conversation?'

'I wanted to confess!' Desperately, hopelessly. This was not how I expected it to go.

'Confess what?'

'Wanting to cheat with Laura.'

'But you didn't. She passed away.'

'I just want you to know the truth.'

'What truth?' He yelled, turning away from me.

'That I would have taken Laura from you.'

He turned back to face me, but I only managed to register his punch a millisecond before his knuckles hit the side of my face.

'No!' Anneli screamed, coming from the house.

'Stay in the house!' Theo yelled back at her. I tried to look around, but my vision was blurred. Footsteps got louder, and then a hand grabbed my collar and pulled me up. I was on my knees. Theo's face was inches from mine.

'What right do you have to come and tell me things about *my wife?* To tell me what she would have done, that she would have left me? Because you think you're better than me? *Who do you think you are?'*

'Jodie... she...' I couldn't finish it. He would confront her. But he wasn't even listening now.

'I could understand you telling me you slept with her, that you were sorry, but telling me that she would have left me for you?' His warm breath was on my face, 'you can keep all those sick fantasies for yourself, you absolute scumbag. It's almost like you didn't know what to say, so you tell me this shit, just to play me - to make me feel bad without actually telling me anything. Because you can't stand me moving ahead in life, you can't stand me sorting my life out while yours is going to hell. It's like you cannot accept that for once, just once, maybe *you're not the lucky one.'*

'I just–'

'Stop talking!' He yelled, raising his fist at me again.

'Daddy no!' Anneli cried out. I wasn't sure where she was.

'You disgust me.' Theo spat out, letting go of my collar, letting me drop to the ground and all I saw was the black sky above me.

***

I walked towards home along the Canada Water canal, nursing the bruise on my face, swans splashing in the water. Thinking. She texted me again, and I told her I was talking to my mother.

I strolled up and down those same paths, delaying going home. She'd see my eye; she'd ask questions. I could only hope she would believe that I was attacked by the gangs she believed were roaming Bermondsey.

After hours of walking, my knees were tired, and I sat on a bench looking out at the still water. There were no more swans or ducks, now. I was alone.

I couldn't stop thinking about Theo and how he must be feeling right now. Had I made a mistake? Was it wrong to tell him that I'd been planning to take Laura away? I'd told myself that he had to know, because he deserved the truth. But the more I thought about it, the more I believed I'd done this only for myself. I was the only one who gained from a confession. I wanted forgiveness, and demanded this of Theo.

I wanted to think I wasn't like her; that I was better; that I did the right thing and faced the consequences, and that I deserved to be punished.

'Ethan?' The gentle voice startled me, and as soon as I looked up, I felt silly not to have recognised Amy on the river path. 'Mother of God, what the hell happened to you?' She placed her shopping bag down on the bench and leaned over to look at me. Her soft hands gripped my head as she turned it towards the light to see the damage. 'Are you ok?' she was looking straight at me, now, staring at me, worried, and a single tear fell from my eye. I didn't deserve to be cared for, especially not by Amy.

'I'm ok,' I tried to smile, but she pulled me up and wouldn't let go.

'Let's go.'

***

Moments later, I was sitting in Amy's bright kitchen as she tried to patch me up. Her hands shook every time she touched the bruise; she wasn't sure what to do, and it was a mix of googling and reading the labels of medication she had at home. Julie held Emmet in her arms. His eyes were red, he wanted to go to bed, but everyone was worried about me.

'Please tell me what happened?' Amy asked.

'This gang–' I stopped. 'I don't want to talk about it.' Everyone was quiet, and with the floor lamp turned to light my face, it was like I was under interrogation.

'Hold still, this is going to sting.' Amy poured something on my wound, and it was cold and refreshing.

'It doesn't sting,' I said.

'Oh, really? That's strange,' she grabbed the bottle and looked closely at the label again. I missed Charlie.

'Does Jodie know you're here?' Julie asked.

'No, but I–'

'Don't worry, I'll call her,' Amy grabbed her phone on the counter, and I quickly put my hand on top of hers.

'Please don't.'

Amy's eyebrows went up, but when she looked at me again, she must have seen my eyes pleading with her.

'Julie, could you take Emmet to bed, please? He's tired.'

'Not tired!' Emmet shouted, but Julie was already marching him out of the kitchen. He yelled a few more times before the sound of the bedroom door closing muffled the noise.

Amy didn't say anything but sat quietly, waiting for me to start talking; she sensed something wasn't right. I swallowed hard, opened my mouth and then immediately shut it again.

'Ethan,' she placed her hand on my lap and tried to catch my eyes, but I avoided her. 'Ethan, I'm worried about you. You were all weird the other day - and now this.'

'It was Theo who hit me,' I blurted out, instantly regretting it.

'What?'

'I'm sorry I shouldn't have…' I stood up to walk away, but she grabbed my shoulders and forced me back.

'No, Ethan, when Jodie came here a month ago she didn't feel like she could trust me; she wouldn't let me help, and it was my mistake to let her go. Now I can see in your eyes that you're the one I should help. I won't let you leave, you will stay here, and we will talk. I know you haven't been well these last couple of weeks. Jodie told me you fought with her.'

I wiped my sweaty palms on my t-shirt. To say something to Amy would be like saying it to Jodie.

'Amy, I really have to go,' I tried to leave again, but she grabbed my hand and pulled me back.

'No!' Her eyes were fixed on me; her hands grabbed my wrist and squeezed hard. 'Do you remember Emmet's birthday, how happy we were? We're meant to be here for each other. When Laura died, everyone rallied around Theo; the same for me and Julie with our adoption. When Jodie told us about her abusive parents, we supported her. Maybe it took more for her to open up, but aren't we supposed to accept each other's differences? Theo's competitiveness, me being a complete bitch most of the time. But nevertheless we care about each other. Don't break the wonderful thing we have here. Let us help you now.'

I bit my lower lip.

'Ethan, I know you think I'm Jodie's friend - and if not for her, you and me wouldn't be friends,' her eyes still fixed on mine. 'But you're wrong. You're my friend equally as much as Jodie or Theo is.'

'Amy, I–' she raised her hand to stop me.

'Ever since you stood up for me back in college, I've

respected you more than you believe. There were so few people who would find the courage to do what was right, but you were one of them. And yes, maybe Jodie and I are close because we have more in common, but that doesn't mean I like you less than her. I would like you to hear what I'm saying to you right now.' We both stood quietly for a few moments, Amy releasing her grip on my wrist. 'I'm your friend too … you're my best friend, and it breaks my heart knowing you don't trust me.'

She took one step back and sat down on a chair. It was a sign that I could leave if I wanted to, but I didn't, now. I was saddened that after being friends with Amy for twenty years, she still felt the need to say this, that I had never let her get close.

'Theo hit me because I told him I'd had feelings for Laura.'

'Holy shit, fuck!' The words sounded like they had popped out. 'I'm … so sorry.'

'The fight Jodie and I had was about this, and I haven't been myself since.'

Amy stood, opening her arms to me. She hugged me so tightly, and I felt my body relaxing. My tears were dripping on her t-shirt. 'I'm so sorry, Ethan, so very very sorry,' she rocked me gently. 'But you will get through this; we all will, including Theo.' I pushed myself back, still avoiding eye contact.

'That is why we are going on this holiday, just two of us, to escape this, to relax.' Amy's face brightened.

'This is great! You will have a good time!'

'But…' I hesitated. 'I don't want Jodie to find out I spoke to Theo about Laura. I don't want her to see me like this.' I pointed to my eye.

'Why?'

'Because she'll want to talk to Theo, to try to make … amends, and the holiday will be ruined because she'll be worried. I need her to be happy now.' Amy nodded, thoughtfully, and was quiet for a few moments before her face brightened. She disappeared from the kitchen and ran upstairs, and I wondered if coming here had been a huge mistake. Amy came back with a smile, carrying a large black box.

'What's this?'

'My make-up kit.'

***

There were about twenty bewildering products in Amy's make-up kit, but she only used maybe three of them. All these words like primer, bronzer, concealer, shimmer, and setting powder made no sense to me.

'This will be good enough.' Amy handed me a mirror. I looked older, with puffy eyes and skin a few shades darker but the bruising like magic was gone. The redness had disappeared completely.

'Amy, this is–'

'Good, I know. But you'll need to be careful because this will wash off. The bruising might take four days to disappear, so you should use this concealer every morning as well as when you go to bed. If you can, change your sheets to a dark colour, so if you do smudge it through the night, it won't show. You wake up before Jodie, so you shouldn't have too much problem hiding this from her. Also, try not to stand in the light; keep your distance where possible. Jodie will see that you're wearing make-up if you are not careful. If she does, tell her you have been using a tinted moisturiser I gave you. It's a solid excuse and should stop her from asking too many questions.'

'Thank you,' this was all I could say, still fascinated by myself in the mirror. She handed me a small bottle.

'I mixed the colour for your skin shade. Remember, to apply it in small quantities and build it gradually, tapping, not rubbing.' I smiled at the enthusiastic and comprehensive *solving* of my problem. 'And don't worry, I won't say anything to Jodie … mainly because I want to see just how good I am at giving you make-up lessons.' I shook my head. 'Take this tinted moisturiser, don't use it; it's just a prop if she asks. Make the most of your holiday. I'll talk to Theo and try to calm him down, and maybe when you're back, we can all go back to normal.' I smiled again, more broadly this time.

'I love you, Amy.'

'I love you too.'

CHAPTER 30

I dabbed the cream Amy gave me around my eye and watched the dark skin underneath vanishing, as if by magic. Amy had done a great job. Yesterday, at home with Jodie, I'd been able to fly under the radar; there were no questions at all about what had happened to me. I had tried to keep the lights dimmed as much as possible and had changed the sheets to our black bedding set. Jodie accepted it without digging too deeply.

When I arrived from work that evening, she had both of our suitcases laid out in our bedroom; she'd started to pack even though there were still two days before our departure. She was so excited. I was sad for Amy and Theo; they would lose a friend they cared about, but they just didn't know the truth of who she was. Maybe one day I would tell them everything.

Her dresses were all neatly folded next to her suitcase,

waiting to be packed. I didn't have much to add to my bag other than what she'd already packed. It didn't matter. Nothing mattered anymore.

I'd become calmer the past couple of days. My past, who I was, who Jodie was, had slowly sunk in, making more sense. I was less angry at Jodie, knowing what was in store now. There was little point in being angry any longer.

After dinner, she did some painting; she'd wanted to finish the piece before we left, leaving it to dry while we were in Mexico.

I sat in the dining room, watching her, listening to music. A soft, soothing melody filled the space between us. We were both silent, simply existing in each other's presence.

I closed my eyes and imagined just how much simpler life would be if I was like her. I could go back to being a teenager, start my early years all over. I would never fall in love with her, never betray Theo. Everything would be good again, no drama, no heartbreaks, no loss.

She hummed with the music, full of joy as she painted. I looked again in disbelief at the art hanging around the room. If Jill was my daughter, who was Adam, the boy holding her hand? Who were the twin ladies at the picnic, one watching the happy family?

I was sad to know that we could never go back to how things were; how everything had already changed. Theo and I would never be as close. I had no idea if Amy would be able to patch things up between us, but perhaps he'd feel sympathy for me once I returned from Mexico a widower.

I walked across to the kitchen with the empty beer can. Placing it on the counter I watched as she smiled and turned to me; she looked so innocent.

In an instant, right in front of my eyes she changed, horror striking her face, like someone had changed the channel on a TV. She gasped loudly and fell from her chair, her brush clattering to the floor from nerveless fingers. A loud bang echoed through the apartment as she spasmed, hitting the wall behind her, her legs kicking the stand out from under the easel, knocking it to the floor. Paint splattered, turpentine spilled, and I watched, frozen in a mix of fear and confused helplessness. It looked as if she was being attacked by an invisible assailant. I instinctively moved closer but another half-scream, louder and with the hint of an incoherent cry for help, stopped me. I was standing between the kitchen and the dining room, aware of every detail, trying to understand what was happening.

Tears fell from her eyes as she kept gasping again and again and finally pushed herself from the wall, rising to her hands and knees. One hand was still pressing hard against her throat, as if she was trying to strangle herself. Slowly she crawled towards me, and I stood there, just watching her struggle. Was she dying? She dragged herself forward along the floor; her face was inches from it. She was coughing, still gasping for air. When the coughing stopped, she sat back on her legs, lifting her head, brushing away the hair that covered her face. Our eyes met and for a moment were locked together, then her face changed, her eyes widened with terror, and she screamed, falling backward and crawling away from me.

That was the moment it became clear to me. She *had* been attacked; by me, in Mexico. She had escaped back to this moment, and she knew exactly what I was planning to do. My heart raced. The plan I had carefully laid out didn't work; she was still alive, and now she knew everything.

Blood pounded in my ears; I couldn't hear anything through a ringing noise that grew louder and louder. My mind was fixed only on her crawling figure, trying to get away from me, terrified, still screaming silently. I looked away, trying to figure out what to do next, and my eyes noticed the wall, badly plastered where I'd tried to cover up the damage from the knife Jodie had thrown. The knife. It was my only opportunity to end this. Now or never.

I opened the kitchen drawer and took that same brutally sharp knife that had sliced open my finger, and lunged towards her. She screamed, and I roared back at her, an animal noise.

'You listen to me now!' I held the knife a few inches away, pointing directly at her face. 'You listen to me!' I repeated, desperate for her to hear me. I only had one chance to do this right, and I didn't want her to go back before saying what I wanted to say. 'I know everything–'

'No!' She screamed, not listening to me.

'Jodie!' I tried to get her attention. 'I know everything you did!' She had her hands ready to defend herself. I moved closer and shouted again. 'I know that you got your powers back. I know you killed them all!' Finally, she was listening, and her face changed. She wanted to know how I knew. She wanted to find out *how long* I had known.

'What?'

'I know what you did, Jodie.' I said firmly, repeating her name, trying to make her focus. My hands were sweaty, the knife sliding in my grip. 'I know that you murdered Laura!'

She stared at me, breathing heavily.

'I already told you that!'

'You planted her there, asked her to take a photo of the Shard, right where that truck couldn't have missed her. It was no *destiny*.' She clenched her teeth, scared and angry. I held the knife ready.

'The first time, she was.'

'What?'

'The very first time she went to the shop, on her way back, she was hit by a truck and died in the hands of a paramedic.'

'The first time?'

'Yes. I saved her as soon as I heard, but then as time passed I understood I couldn't also save Theo. I tried to make it work, Ethan. Believe me, I almost lost my sanity trying. And then I had to make the awful decision to go back and let destiny take her, to save Theo, *but that time around she didn't die*. Something must have changed, she wasn't hit by the truck. That's why I had to plant her there and arrange it. To replicate the original accident.' She was covering her face with her hands, remembering. 'Jesus Christ, I can't...'

'Yes, but this is–'

'I *admit* I did it. I had no choice! This is something that will always stay with me, and the nightmares might never go away.'

'You murdered your friend!'

'Stop!' She screamed. 'What would you have done?' She was talking fast now, sensing a way out. 'Who would you have let die if you were me? Theo or Laura?' Leaning against the wall, her hands still held in front of her, futilely blocking the knife I still held.

'I would have never chosen–'

'Then it would have been Theo,' she exhaled, her eyes finally wavering from mine. 'That is what happened when I decided to do nothing. Soon after he killed himself, you and Laura split up anyway, and Amy wasn't talking to any of you. When I met Laura that day, she told me she no longer wanted to live. Her family and her friends all despised her for what she'd done, and you both lost everything!'

'Don't lie to me. It was always about you! You did whatever suited you the most!'

'Me?' She slowly started to lift herself, one hand on the wall, the other in front of her. 'Are you seriously saying this?'

'Charlie.' I said quietly. 'Then why did you kill Charlie?'

'Who?'

I gripped my knife and took half a step closer to her, bending my elbow, leaving space between the blade and her. She didn't flinch.

'Don't pretend you don't know who I'm talking about!'

'But I don't!' She breathed in deeply, feeling cornered.

'The doctor from the clinic!' I screamed. 'Dr Charlotte Leigh! The scaffolding accident! During the storm! I know it didn't fall on her by accident.' Her mouth opened ever so slightly. She didn't know what to say, because I knew everything.

'Why would I have done that?'

'Because you saw her in the clinic on the day of the accident, and she knew you were lying to me about your infertility. She was going to tell me, but you got rid of her first.'

'By burying her under the scaffolding? By somehow killing her?' She raised her voice back at me.

'Don't lie to me, Jodie! Not again!'

She screamed back at me. 'Are you delusional? If I didn't want her to tell you anything, I would have just gone back in time and never visited the clinic in the first place. I already knew the results; there was no reason for me to go back again, to kill her. Why would I do that?' She slowly reached for my hands, still holding the knife. 'Why would I go to all the trouble of dragging her into some sort of accident, risking my own life in the process? I could just erase her memory.' She sounded convincing. She was convincing. For the first time, there was a seed of doubt in my mind.

'You wanted to get rid of her because I was having an affair!'

She laughed, lifting her hands away from the knife, now; she laughed as if I'd told her a joke. I took a step back. Shocked and confused.

'Wouldn't be the first time! So what? You think that list of women in my notebook is some sort of a hitlist? The women I've killed ... *for luurrve?*'

She was mocking me, now. Playing with me, like a cat plays with a mouse that's about to die.

'You tell me, Jodie.'

'You give yourself too much credit, *Ethan*.'

'You wanted to keep me in your life; you wanted to eliminate her. It's pretty simple.'

She laughed again. 'I wouldn't kill innocent people just for this relationship. You're special to me, but not so special I'd go around murdering people for you.' Now I stood stock still. 'Do you want to meet those women? I can assure you they're not dead. Stacey, the yoga teacher, is safe and well in her studio - a few blocks from here. I heard she's taking on some extra work as a fitness coach, moving up in the world. Jordan's now dating Theo.'

'But you lured Charlie into the street, where the scaffolding fell on her. I saw your raincoat in the CCTV footage!'

'My raincoat?'

'The woman who fled the scene after the accident, the woman that lured Charlie to her death, she wore a raincoat just like yours!'

'That crap raincoat I got from Primark? That's your evidence? Did you even see my face?'

'No, but–'

'But of course, the raincoat was the same and so it has to be Jodie, because Jodie is an evil witch.'

'This is not...' I was starting to doubt myself.

'The only person whose life I took was Laura.' She spat it out. 'But that was different.'

'Was Jill different too?'

Jodie just stood there, watching me without expression or anger. She turned slightly to gaze at the painting of Jill and Adam, then back to me.

'Jill was sick,' she sighed. 'She was born with an immune disorder; we only found out just after her third birthday. Our sweet fragile innocent baby, she had harmed noone, and she was treated so unfairly by life. I did everything I could to save her. I replaced every bad medical decision with the right one; I became an expert on SCID.' That was what my father died from. 'You quit your job, because you were afraid she might not be there when you came home from work. But no matter what I did, Jill got worse and the decisions got harder with every passing month until my hands were tied, there was nothing I could change that would help, and every path led to her dying. Again, and again, and again.' Her voice trailed off, disappearing into the walls of this empty flat.

'But I saw your sketchbook. She didn't look... sick.'

'I didn't want to remember her like that - sad and in pain. Every day, fighting for her life. I painted her and the life she deserved; not the one she was given.' Jodie wiped her tears. 'When Jill died the final time, I told myself she was in peace now; her suffering was over. But it didn't end yours. I couldn't carry on, Ethan, and neither could you. You always wanted a child, and the child you were given brought you nothing but pain.'

I was watching the painting of Jill as Jodie talked, our beautiful daughter, the knife forgotten in my hand. I turned back to Jodie, defeat etched on her face. The guilt in me grew as I watched, and I felt a shared moment of deep sadness.

'But Jodie, you didn't even cry when you–'

'Ethan, I cried for months - I just never let you see, because for you it wouldn't have made sense. Every time you confronted me about why I was upset I just went back, and smiled, so you could live your life in peace.'

'You deprived me of these experiences. Of my daughter.' I said slowly, resolutely.

'The experience of your daughter being ill, her watching the other kids from the window, her asking us when she could go outside and play? Trying to explain to her why she couldn't go to school, like everybody else? Lying to her, telling her that she will get better, that we would be together forever, that one day she would be able to swim in the sea, to build a sand castle, to climb the stairs without help. Is this the *experience* you wanted?'

'You could be lying about all of this! Maybe Theo never jumped from the roof after Laura left him, maybe you *were* at the scene when Charlie got crushed under that scaffolding, maybe Jill was never sick. You could be lying about everything!'

'Of course, because Jodie is always the bad one, isn't she? The devil's seed, the evil witch,' she spat out. 'I was always to blame, always, no matter how much I tried to be good. To help.'

'Show me the truth, Jodie. Prove to me that Jill was ill.'

'If you don't believe the words from my mouth, then

you'll need to answer these questions yourself.' She didn't want to fight any more.

'You lied to me before, and I have no way of knowing if you're lying to me now.'

'I lied because I couldn't bring myself to tell the man I love that his daughter died in agony.' She wiped the tears with her palm. 'Do you think I'm lying now?'

The million-dollar question. Was Jodie capable of lying about all of this, so convincingly? Was she the machiavellian sociopath I'd imagined, or was she just a troubled girl who was muddling through? Someone who wasn't evil - just a sad, lonely person trying to navigate their life. Trying to be the best version of themselves.

'But Jodie, everything in my life has been decided by you. I didn't have a say in any of this.'

'We live in Bermondsey because you wanted to, Ethan, we live in this flat because you bought it. The car we own, the movies we watch - everything is decided by you, so don't tell me you have no control over your life.'

'Since you came back from Edinburgh, you lied to me about having your powers back, even after I asked you if there was anything else I should know; you lied again about arranging Laura's accident.'

'And you lied too, Ethan. You lied when you didn't tell me how you felt, you cheated on me with that doctor, you took me to Acapulco to...' There was a strange moment where all I could hear was our heavy breathing, mixing in the stale air of the flat.

Maybe I wasn't that much different from Jodie after

all. She was right; I withheld the truth from her, in the beginning, to protect her, and later to harm her. But she never did that to me. She had never hurt me, not intentionally.

'I don't know why having this power made my life such a misery - why my father hit me, why my mother chose him over me, why the girls at school bullied me, why Gary couldn't accept me, why Jill had to die. It's been a while since I accepted that my life would never be perfect. It was damaged, and no one - *no one* was there to make it any better, to fix it. But then you came along, sitting under a tree, with your passion for those silly zombie games. I admired your ability to wake up so early every day. To go running even when you were tired, or hung over. I loved your experimental cooking failures, and the way you suppressed your smile when you won a difficult case. I loved you watching me gardening, or swinging me around like I was the Hollywood princess that got the happy ending. You made me love you, with all of your flaws, and I told myself that if I can make at least one person happy, truly happy with everything that they have, then maybe my life really was worth something. I've cared for you every moment since the day we met. All I wanted was to protect you, and that's why I shielded you from the knowledge of your actions. *I erased our daughter to give you a blissful life!*' All the accumulated pain and anger of thousands of different timelines burst from her in a single cry.

'Jodie I...' I was lost, now.

She looked at me now, really looked, as if trying to read

my mind; trying to understand the man she had married.

'My mother stuck by my father because she loved him so much - hoping one day things would get better, that she would change him, and she lived her whole life in fear. I won't do the same. I'm sorry.' Jodie glanced at me for just a second, and then started to walk carefully around the dining room table, towards the bedroom where our suitcases still lay.

'Where are you going?'

'Away.' She said it without looking at me.

'But I'm not finished!'

'But I am, Ethan.' She turned around, her face angry and flushed. 'You stabbed me in the throat and told me I should burn in hell. I'll never be able to trust you ever again. You lied so well, so convincingly, I had no idea how you felt until the day you attacked me. You almost succeeded.'

'Jodie, this was a huge misunderstanding! I know this now,' I walked over to her, but she backed away.

'Stay away!' she shouted. 'I can erase your memories, but I'll never be able to erase mine.' Tears rolled down my cheeks. She kept moving backwards, increasing the distance between us.

'Jodie!'

'I'm sorry, Ethan,' she sobbed. 'I don't think I can fix it this time.'

EPILOGUE I

Ethan

As I dabbed cologne on my cheeks I couldn't ignore the stare of the man in the mirror, his shiny face frozen in the painting behind me. He hung there on the wall, standing high up on a tall, slender building with his wings spread across the dark London sky. It will always remind me of my fight for freedom.

I'd put on a fresh white shirt and a blue tie for dinner with Charlie's sister. She wanted to say thank you for everything I'd done for their family. After almost 5 months of legal wrangling, going back and forward through the evidence, we had built up a strong case against the company responsible for Charlie's death. Yesterday the judge had ruled that The Crane Logistics Ltd had neglected their safety procedures, resulting in the manslaughter of Ms Charlotte Leigh. Of course, no amount of money would ease Caroline's pain, but we both fought for closure, and to avenge Charlie.

My Wife Jodie

In the beginning, when Jodie had moved out I felt relief. She was gone. I didn't expect my freedom to last, and I was sure that within a few months she'd be back, to try to amend things, or worse, she would turn back time and I would only find out via some cryptic message from my future self.

Without Jodie there to watch over me, my life changed as if someone had cursed me. I would stub my toe on the frame of the bed when I woke up in the morning, or accidentally knock a vase or a mug - missing the catch, and watching it smash on the floor. I would burn meals so badly the pan was almost unsalvageable, adding salt to mask the taste. I couldn't help but think how much Jodie had done for me.

She came, once, to see me at court, and I was startled to see her. She gave me the divorce papers and her wedding ring - *I will love you for ever*, a broken promise, a sign of the end of our relationship - and I expected her to still be mad at me for what I had done in Mexico, but she wasn't. She was just the regular Jodie I had known for years, with a hint of sadness in her eyes.

I began to long for her kindness, her sneaking up on me to say that she had just mopped the floor, and it was slippery. Her constant reminders to stay safe when I drove, or skiied, or walked late at night. I couldn't ski any more, the idea of being injured terrified me.

In the weeks after the divorce, a police detective came to ask questions about my ex-client Amar Patel. Apparently he was somehow associated with Jodie. I didn't know what to tell him, I was completely taken aback. But as the detective kept asking questions I realised just how little I knew about Jodie - who she really was. When I met her, 21 years ago, I thought she was a beautiful, smart, kind girl. Now I know that she was much more than that.

I looked her up, and found that she had finally opened her gallery. Browsing the trendy website I found the paintings that had once hung in this apartment; she had taken them when she left. I bought every single one of them. The man with the wings, the pig in the cage, even that creepy one with a dead leopard in the snow. I asked my colleague to collect them so Jodie wouldn't know it was me. I wanted Jodie to feel better, to think that strangers were interested in her work.

I hung them back in their original places.

Amy remained true to her word and we stayed friends. I guess Jodie never told her about the events in Mexico, in that future timeline that never happened. Amy stayed close to me through the divorce, just as much as she was there supporting Jodie. And then, one day as I was helping Amy look after Emmet, she quietly told me that Jodie was in a relationship with another guy. The news shocked me - I hadn't seen anyone since she left - but I had one advantage: the photo from Jodie's book, of all the women I'd supposedly dated.

First, I went to Stacey's yoga class. I wasn't very interested in the yoga, and after several dates and some reasonably good sex it ended there. She was too superficial. Then after some sleuthing I found that someone called Riley had worked in the accounts department at our company, around 2012. I tracked her down with the help of HR and dated her for a while, but we weren't a good match either.

As time went on and there was no news of Jodie breaking up with this other guy, it hit me. They were serious. She had actually moved on. *That* hurt me a lot, pain, a real physical pain like I had never felt before, right in the middle of the chest where the heart is supposed to be. I invited it in, wondering if Jodie felt this too every single time I cheated on her. Maybe it was only fair that this was my time to experience it. To grow.

It wasn't her job to look after me, to sacrifice her life just to make me happy. It wasn't a fair trade to trade my happiness for her sanity. And it felt right that she finally got her freedom, as much as I got mine. In other circumstances, maybe we could have remained friends. In another timeline, perhaps we could have attended Anneli's birthday parties as godparents, being civil, being grown-ups. Would I change anything now, if I could go back?

I grabbed my woollen winter coat off the rack. Jodie had given it to me 6 years ago, for my birthday. I wrapped it tightly around my waist. It was so well insulated it almost felt as if it had heated pads inside.

Before leaving home I blew out the candle in the bedroom, double checked to be sure that I hadn't left wet laundry in the washing machine and that I had indeed closed the freezer door. Wrapping a scarf around my neck I stepped out into the cold winter wind, hopeful and excited for the future.

EPILOGUE II

Jodie

An intense cold spell had swept through London, and all the streets were like ice rinks.

'Please, be really careful when you're driving.' I touched Denny's shoulder. He nodded. Tomorrow The Guardian would report that four people had died in accidents in the icy conditions, and many more would be injured. It would be a tragedy.

'What time Theo's expecting us tomorrow?'

'At 5pm,' Denny nodded, and I rested my head against the cold window. Denny and Theo had grown very fond of each other. I met with Theo the day after Ethan had left the flat, and he told me how Ethan had confessed to him about Laura. I respected Ethan for doing that, but I wouldn't ever admit to Theo that I'd been responsible for Laura's death. The fact was, it wouldn't change a single thing, and Theo would lose yet another friend, hold another grudge, and receive nothing in return. I loved Theo like a brother and I would do anything to protect him. Now, thank god, he seemed happy. He and Jordan were getting along well. To my surprise, I liked her too. Back in university, I'd thought of her as a homewrecker, but maybe eighteen years of life experience had taught her not to go after men who were in relationships.

She was not Laura, and she'd never be, but I still hoped that one day I'd be able to fix that and see Laura one more time. That one week in the summer of 2016 still blocked me from going back any further in time, but I felt something changing in me. The barrier was shrinking, and if I ever did feel strong enough, I would surely go right back to 1996 straight away, without hesitation. Start fresh. But for now, Denny was making me happy, and I know I made him happy too.

I'd opened my own gallery in Shoreditch. It was small, cosy, and I loved it. The rent cost a small fortune - far more money than I ever made selling my art, but it didn't bother me. Money was never an issue, and Denny and I had moved to a beautiful four bedroom terrace house in Knightsbridge. It was beautiful there.

'Would you like to watch a movie tonight?' Denny asked.

'So, ... Netflix and Chill?' I raised an eyebrow, and he laughed.

'Come *on*. We're way too old for sex,' he whispered to me, smiling.

Denny and I joked a lot about our age. He made me very

comfortable in my own skin, and sometimes I wondered if it would be nice to grow old with him, watching Anneli, Emmet, and Emma grow up together. Emma was Denny's daughter from his first marriage. His wife had died four years prior of liver cancer, and I had written the date in my calendar. When I could go back to my teenage years again, I'd make sure to save her life.

Looking at the photos of Denny with Lucy, it was easy to recognise the special couple they once were, and Denny was clearly still very much in love with her memory. They both were climbers and seekers of adventure. I wasn't jealous, and I wanted Denny to be happy. So for now, we kept each other company.

'Aunt Jodie?' Emma's sleepy voice piped up from the back seat.

'Yes, sweetheart?'

'Can I get some water?'

'Of course.' I passed her the bottle with a sports cap. She gulped almost half of it. She was seven years old and loved playing with Emmet and Anneli, though Anneli would sometimes loudly and undiplomatically announce that she was too old to play games with babies. Anneli enjoyed being the oldest one, bossing everyone around.

My goal was still to save Laura, more than anything else, but every day that passed made the calculation harder. I didn't want to lose Anneli and Emmet the way I already lost Adam - Theo and Laura's first child. It would have been an easier decision if the kids were younger, before their personalities developed. Now, they were all growing up, becoming part of our big family.

But at the same time, the idea of hugging Laura again, seeing Theo's smile as they danced with each other - I would do anything to go back and try it all again. And now I knew that Ethan wasn't the man I was supposed to be with, there was no reason why I shouldn't fix the mess I'd made. When Ethan first kissed Laura during that visit to the gay club, I would step aside and let Theo deal with it. Maybe this was what should have happened, and everything that resulted was my punishment for intervening in other people's lives.

'Here we are.'

'Yes. Here we are,' I repeated with a sigh. The outside of the building still looked the same, even though the snow made everything look much cleaner than it was. 'This is where I lived for almost 12 years,' I pointed to the apartment complex as Denny leaned in to get a better look.

'Nice,' he said, looking around. 'Bermondsey is supposed to be a very nice place to live.' Ethan had always said that. In those words.

'I know - it was.'

'Dad, why are we here?' Emma was growing impatient. Denny looked back at her.

'Ask Aunt Jodie,' he grinned, clearly wondering the same.

I raised my hands. 'Give me a couple of minutes.' I opened the car door, and the cold air hit my face. I stepped outside as the snow crunched under my boots.

This was very unusual for London, and the city wasn't built for really cold weather. Airports and trains struggled to operate, and no one had winter tyres on their vehicles. The roads were murder. I walked around the car and opened the boot. Nestled amongst the shopping bags was a shovel we had bought today, and a hammer I'd packed this morning before leaving home. I grabbed both of them and closed the boot. Step by careful step, I walked the path that I had walked so many times before, though never in snow, old memories tugging at my mind. Once I reached the corner of the building, I threw the hammer down and began to use the shovel to clear the snow from the path.

'Jodie, what's going on?' Denny shouted from the car. I could hear the shrieks of an impatient seven-year-old through the open window.

'Two minutes!' I replied, showing two fingers, not sure if he was able to see them through my mitten. Then I got back to work.

As I scooped the snow to one side, a thin layer of clear ice was revealed, so clear it almost looked like fresh water. Resting the shovel against the wall and crouching to pick up the hammer, I touched the ice; it was smooth, perfect. I raised the hammer and smacked the ice. One, twice, three times. It shattered into hundreds of pieces, and I scraped the shards away.

Taking a deep breath and one final look at the destroyed ice, I picked up the shovel and walked carefully to the car. Both Emma and Denny were staring at me like I had gone mad. I raised the hammer into the sky like a superhero. *Superhero.* I never wanted to be called that. I just wanted someone to thank me for what I did for them. I joined them back in the warm car.

'What on earth was that all about?' Denny tilted his head.

'You told me you weren't going to ask any questions,' I tilted my head back at him, like I was a particularly enigmatic mirror from a fairy tale. I haven't told him about my secret, yet.

'You're funny, Aunt Jodie!' Emma clapped her hands a few times.

'See,' I pointed to Emma. 'She thinks I'm funny.' I smiled at Denny, who shook his head and started punching a new destination into the GPS, then I turned to look back out the window.

A man walked around the corner of the building, wearing a long black coat over jeans and a crisp white shirt. Ethan. He looked thin and withdrawn, shielding himself from the cold. This wasn't how I remembered him; he always had a big smile for me, but not today or any of the other times I'd seen him since the divorce. I blamed myself for a lot of what had happened between us. Maybe if I had been stronger and protected him less, maybe if I had allowed him to feel guilty about cheating, things might have turned out differently. But who knew? There were a lot of maybes, and I still blamed myself for hurting him.

He walked towards the corner of the house, noticed the patch of cleared snow and broken ice, and stepped carefully over it. As he continued on, into the rest of his life, there was a part of me that wanted to leap out of the car, to call his name, hug him desperately. To tell him that everything would be ok, that he wouldn't suffer any more. I had created this reckless person, and it was irresponsible to let go like this, but I can't go back, not now, not ever. He wanted to experience real life, the life everyone else had; making decisions for yourself and facing the consequences. This was his moment.

'Ouch,' Denny exclaimed, his finger in his mouth. 'It's just a paper cut,' he said, annoyed.

Emma reached for the pot of yogurt that Denny had just opened, with the sharp foil lid.

Something inside me twisted as he took his finger from his mouth and revealed a small, red line. It mocked me. People would always get hurt, and there would be no end to it.

'Shall we go?' he asked but I couldn't lift my eyes to meet his. All I could see was that paper cut, bright blood on his finger.

'Yes let's go!' Emma shouted from the back seat.

I closed my eyes, trying to find focus.

'It's just a paper cut,' I whispered to myself. 'Just a papercut.'

'Damn, it hurts a lot.' Denny laughed, and his words were a punch in the gut.

'...just a tiny paper cut.'

'Sorry what?' He was talking to me now. 'Jodie, are you ok?'

I took a deep breath, again, trying to find some calm.

'Shall we?' Denny said.

'Yes,' I turned away from the window and placed my hand on his warm, red cheek. 'Let's go.'

And he drove the three of us home.

"I had to deny knowledge
in order to make room for faith."
—Immanuel Kant

Acknowledgments

I had never thought I would write a novel. But here I am, happy and thankful to so many people who supported me throughout my journey. Lukas, the first to hear the idea, and who challenged me to write; to Patrick, my partner, who told me to stop whining and finish the goddamn book.

My editor Roxx, who with her magic hands made my dyslexia vanish. To Patrick again who spent days with me fighting over Jodie and Ethan's relationship, trying to give this story the treatment we believed it deserved. To Ignas, who diplomatically offered to help with the cover art when he saw my own attempt. To Jenni, a GP, who made sure Charlie was a good doctor. To Lady Cordelia, a bad-ass lawyer, who made Ethan better at his job. To Karolis, Ann, Vitalija, David, Paolo, Luana, Pip and Olivia who helped with feedback and photography, and so much else.

To my brother, my sister, and my loving parents Regina and Bronislovas, who supported me through this project - and encouraged me to be the best I could be. Thank you, and I hope one day this book can be translated into Lithuanian, for you to read.